The Brol
A Cod

To Mr Summers, for championing medical humanities!

Pablo Benitez
Suarez

This is a work of fiction. Names, characters, places, and incidents either are the product of the author's imagination or are used fictitiously. Any resemblance to actual persons, living or dead, events, or locales is entirely coincidental.

Copyright © 2022 by Pablo Suárez

All rights reserved. No part of this book may be reproduced or used in any manner without written permission of the copyright owner except for the use of quotations or references in a book review.

Book design by BespokeBookCovers.com
Maps by Pablo Suárez

Published by Pablo Suárez
www.pablosuarez.co.uk

To Kate, I promised this one was for you.
My promises are kept.

Acknowledgements

When I was a young ball of unrefined excitement (younger, at least), I wrote a little short story for English class. I was ecstatic because, for once, I could relinquish the asphyxiating essay structure and let my imagination fly. My teacher, the same teacher that had been kind enough to put up with me from three years of age, hammering English into my distracted brain, told me that story was no different from any of the books she was reading at the time.

To this day, and coming from her, that is the best praise I have ever received. I am proud to say, I now have a book of my own.

Carmen, without your endless patience and unparalleled teaching skills, the writing of this book (or my medical career in England, for that matter) wouldn't have been possible. Gracias desde lo más profundo de mi corazón.

A heart-felt thank you must also go to the Haus of Dragons, the perfect friends to offer constructive criticism and bolstering praise whenever needed. David, Maza and Daniel, I hope you enjoy this love letter to fantasy.

I would be remiss if I didn't mention my beta-readers, most valiant of them all, who braved the first manuscript of a first novel that required *a lot* of work. Adriana, Abi, Anex and David, know my writing has improved thanks to you.

Lastly and no less importantly, I would like to thank Hans Zimmer and John Williams personally. They have composed the soundtracks of my adolescence and young adulthood, the perfect themes for an overactive imagination always seeking epic, grander worlds. How boring and quiet life would be without you.

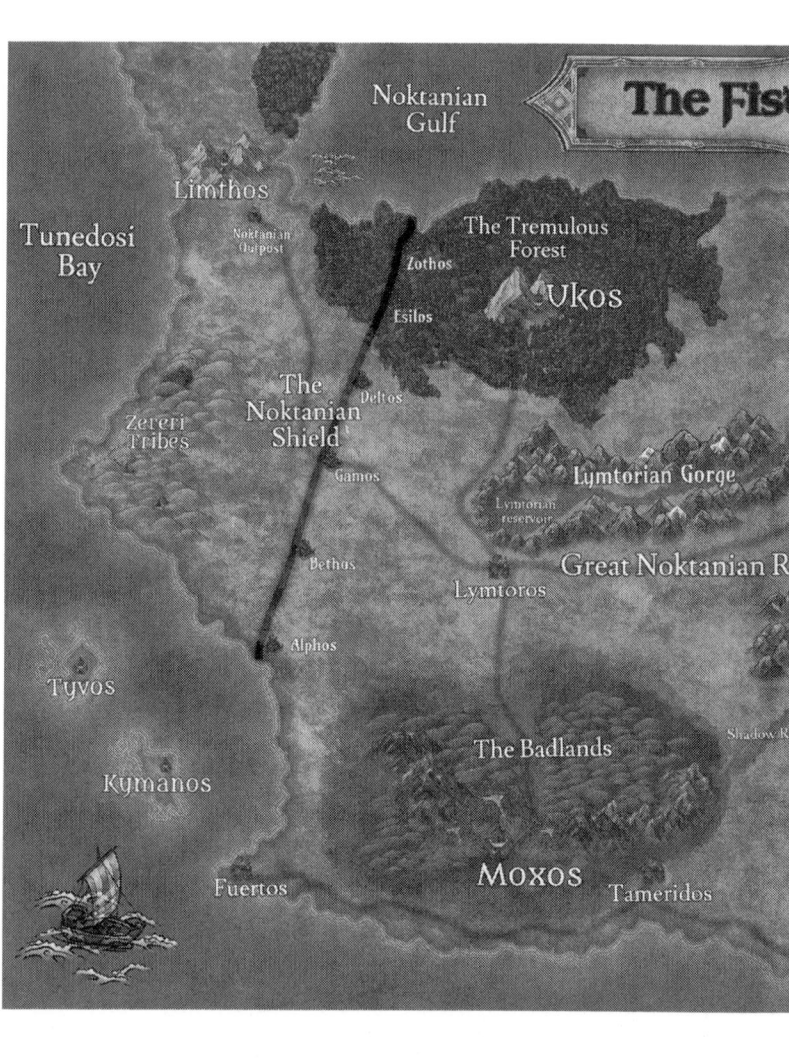

# of Nok

Yorthos

Northern passage
Hulos
River North
The Serpent's Spine
Yotho Pass

Tethimos

The Eye of Nok
Londos
Bamoria
School of Physicians
The University

Noktanos

River Tethim

River Parth

Parthos

Southern Passage
Parthosi Pass

Constituent City-States of the Noktanian League

- Noktanos (capital)
  - Yorthos
  - Tethimos
  - Parthos
  - Mozos
  - Ukos

Noktanian Protectorates
  - Tyvos
  - Kymanos

THE CONTINENT OF HELADOS

TUNDROS

WESTERNLANDS

MESN
TEUTOSI CHAIN
YORN
TEIDOS

THE REMNA

DEATH'S CROSSING
BASHORK'S EYE
ER'UK
PYRINOSI CHAIN
AR'ES
FREE CITY OF QA'THRAR
CRUK'IX
KAHMIRIAN ROAD (RUINS)
UNA
VINIA
MARTHIA
PENINSULAR SEA
LI'BERA
SMALL PENINSULA
GREAT T
IK'TAR, THE BLOODIED CITY
VAST PENINSULA
FIRIA
TYMAVIR
TUL'AHIA RIVER
SAN
U'IMAI
TA'GIRIA

EI'TULAH

PROLOGUE
* * *
Resplendent No More

"**AT THE BEGINNING** of time—"

"No. No, Arten. What way is that to start a story? Give your listeners more credit, do not tell them you are beginning a story when you are beginning a story."

Arten's face was an exquisite mural of bewilderment. The old man had a most infuriating way of speaking. Odd, not in the use of strange words like Mother, but in the order. The order was always odd. Conversations with Old Hal were like being dealt half a deck of cards in a game of Fotia and expected to win. It made his head hurt.

"Master, I am very confused."

"So am I. Perpetually."

"I heard some Pantheon scholars—"

The old man shook his head so vigorously the precarious tower of books on the table wobbled threateningly close to collapse.

"So it was not even an *original* attempt to insult your listeners' intelligence. No, that cannot stand."

"Master, I— "

An unnaturally powerful gust of wind blew through the balcony, another offensive to the book tower's integrity. Arten thought he could sense something different in the air, the way it felt against his skin. Was it hotter than normal?

He didn't think about it for too long, it was summer after all.

His brow furrowed at the thought of that. It *was* summer, why wasn't he playing with his friends?

"Start over," the Master said, introducing his long, spidery fingers in the stack of books. He heaved at least a dozen heavy tomes, producing a dry grunt as he carried them to the shelves covering every wall of the study, shoulders slumped, and spine bent.

"Do you need any help with that, Master?"

"The only help I need is for you start over. *Your* start, not some mindless Pantheon scholar's."

Arten looked through the opening to the balcony, a perfect frame of the many gardens and pools in Oasis.

It was such a lovely day. The sweet breeze was pregnant with the laughter of other children, the playful splashes of water and the sound of harmonious strings, competing for rhythm with the accompanying clapping of hands.

Oh, but he could almost smell the dried dates and taste the juice of grapeberries. What he would give to be down there with his brothers and sisters, enjoying the sun and the crystalline water.

Instead, he was in Master Hal's stuffy study atop one of the six pyramids, sweating through his robes and being asked stupid questions.

"Well?"

"Err… nothing. Nothingness."

"Nothing, you say?" the Master kept his hunched back toward him, stacking the books in the shelves.

"Yes. There was nothing. And then, there was something."

Arten's spirits flew high when his Master turned and he saw the smile of approval.

"That is much better. Well done, Arten."

"Thank you, Master."

"So, what was that *something*?"

"Um, Hel'Adad?"

"Is that so?"

"Yes. The Goddess Creator is Queen of the Pantheon, and—"

"Again with the Pantheon, dear boy. Did you hear this from scholars, too?"

Arten scratched the back of his head, grimacing.

"Um, yes. I did."

Master Hal rested the last book in place, pushing on the spine with his twig of an index finger, and returned to the table.

"They say Hel'Adad, Goddess Creator, birthed Virthos and blessed it with the Kahmirian Empire. Is that true?"

"Yes."

His master stared him down.

"Yes?"

"Which yes, the first or the second?"

"The second."

"And why is that?"

Old Hal also asked *too many* questions. It was like having a conversation with a deaf man. Or a mirror.

Arten blowed his cheeks, looking away.

"Errr, because you said confusion is good?"

"I did not say that. I implied it, but you are on the right track, perspicacious Arten," the old man said, smiling. "What came before our Empire?"

"Nomadic tribes fighting for scarce resources," he recited from memory. All he needed to do to please Master Yu'Kaer in charge of history lessons was memorise the rolls he would give him. Far easier.

"If I wanted a parrot, I would speak with the beastmaster. Let us do a mental exercise, shall we?"

"Is there any chance the answer to that is 'no, thank you'?"

Old Hal tilted his head and gave him a scornful look over his arching, protruding nose.

"Didn't think so."

"Let us say you are the chieftan of one of those tribes, and a curious child with too much cheek for his own good approached you, asking for the something that came after the nothing. What would you say?"

Arten's stare was blank. So was his head.

"You certainly would not say it was Hel'Adad, because you would not even know who that is! If you ventured across the Sylvari jungle and travelled across the Vast Blue, and found an entirely different civilisation, completely removed from Kahmir, would they say that that something was Hel'Adad?"

"Maybe they would not," Arten said dubitably.

"So, what is my point?"

Beats me, old man. Arten bit his tongue. He would *not* say what first came to mind.

"Just because the scholars said so, it does not mean it is the truth?"

Master Hal reclined back on his chair, interlacing his fingers over his lap. There was an expression of self-contentment on his countenance.

"That question alone makes you more intelligent than three quarters of the whole of Kahmir. Certainly more than your Mother's courtiers."

Arten wasn't entirely sure why he was being praised. His confusion was bigger than when they had started, but he would take it.

"Thank you kindly, Master."

"Right. That is enough of that. Let us move on with another subject."

Arten's eyebrows knitted together.

"But Master! I have barely started the story!"

"No matter that. Mind the conversation we have just had, it hides more teaching that whatever else you had to say. Now, onto medicine, the most beautiful of specialties. The art of healing mind and body."

Master Hal shuffled the chair back and stood with difficulty. He walked over to a chalkboard mounted on a tripod and wrote two elegentaly traced words. *Mind* on the left and *body* on the right. He circled the word on the left.

"And what is *mind*?"

Arten repressed a flurry of protestations. All he allowed himself to do was to fidget with his hands beneath the table.

"Mind. Mind is… mind is…" he trailed off, wishing to escape that mental agony. He was near trembling with frustration. He casted his eyes to the gardens again, longing to jump in the pool, chase after Ka'Theria, and Ilio, and Ermi, lie down in the shade of the palms and see who could stare at the sun longer.

He righted himself, elbows poised on the table.

There was something wrong.

He could no longer hear the sound of music, the crisp laughter and din of enjoyment. They had been replaced by eerie silence and a distant sound. *Woosh, woosh, woosh.* It was approaching.

Though he could not label the sensation, a foreboding overcame him. An unfamiliar feeling of utter distress, of fear, of abject terror.

He realised there wasn't any sun.

"What is that?" he said, pushing the chair back. He walked toward the balcony.

"Arten? What are you doing? You will not get out of the lesson that easily."

"No, Master. What is *that*?" Arten pointed vehemently to the outside. His Master's forehead creased.

They exited the study through the opening and observed the city of Kahmir. The sprawling neighbourhoods in every direction. Vast, like a sea of houses, canals, bazaars, palmtrees and temples that extended beyond the horizon. They glanced over Oasis, Heart of the Empire. A walled hexagon with six tall pyramids forming its vertices, covered in bright white limestone and bearing a golden cap at their tip. They would normally reflect the unforgiving Heladian sunlight, earning their name of the Six Stars of Kahmir.

Yet everything was covered by a mantle of unnerving darkness, a massive shadow, shifting. And that *woosh, woosh, woosh* coming closer.

They looked up.

What they saw defied all notion of life, of experience, of what was real and what wasn't. A long pause ensued, necks bent, jaws slack.

A creature, a nightmarish chimera that could only be conjured up during feverish dreams of madness. A serpent, so unimaginably large it was as though an entire mountain range was soaring the skies. Master and pupil couldn't see the end of its reptilian body, scales as extensive as cities, but they were able to see its crocodile head. The sound was created by the slow beating of enormous wings, seas of massive feathers that had completely eclipsed the sun and plunged Kahmir into darkness. Each beat created powerful gusts of wind that tousled and pulled at their robes, strained the flags flying on their poles, curved and shook the palm trees.

"What is that, Master?" Arten repeated softly, his voice breaking. He came closer to the old man, grabbing onto his robes. The shrill screams of despair began.

"I… don't know, Arten. Best get insid—"

The beast had turned its head downwards, emitting a roar loud enough to deafen. To make the pyramid vibrate madly, and crack, and tremble. It opened its maws, like a fissure splitting a continent, revealing a red-black hole. The pleasant heat of summer was replaced by blistering scorch as a torrent of fire birthing from those gaping maws descended from the skies. It obliterated half the city in a matter of seconds.

Their breath hitched as they retreated.

"Go inside, Arten. Go, inside!" his Master pleaded, but the child was too busy looking at the flames and charred ruins, stadia of them, where city had stood several breaths ago. His mind was unable to comprehend the abrupt destruction at that scale.

"But… it…how…" he babbled. Old Hal hooked his hands under astonished Arten's armpits and tugged him inside, still catatonically mumbling incoherences.

"Master Hal'Gamac!"

Two guards entered the study. They were followed by a tall man wrapped in many colourful robes and bearing a triangular hat. High Scholar L'Mor. He wasn't speaking, his eyes moving side to side. He pulled a chair and collapsed, repeating some prayer over and over again.

"…theCreatorhasbetrayedustheCreatorhasbetrayedustheCreatorhasbet rayedustheCreatorhas…"

After him came Empress Iremia Ghart'Vur and her retinue. Her appearance seemed to awaken young Arten from his stupor.

"Mother!" he ran to her embrace.

"Your Highness, take young Arten down to the tunnels. Procure yourself of the fastest horses and exit the city at once. Gallop until the beasts die of exhaustion, and then start running," the old Master said without delay.

She nodded diligently. She was crying.

"You're coming with us," she said.

"No, I'm too old. I would slow you down. My time has come, your Highness."

Hal'Gamac took the Empress' hands in his, speaking tenderly.

"Please. Go, Iremia. Take him and go."

Ash had begun falling from the sky, blowing into the study and making everything black. It was making it increasingly difficult to breathe.

Empress Iremia stiffened her quivering lip and nodded with determination.

"Good."

Master Hal's knees clicked loudly as he squatted. He grasped Arten's face in his callused hands, wiped tears with his thumbs.

"Remember the Tenets, Arten. Remember our lessons. One day, you'll be the best Ruler humanity has ever seen."

The boy was sobbing, clinging to his mother's hand.

"Yes, M-m-m-master. I shall never do harm."

Hal'Gamac smiled one last time, caressing the boy's cheek with paternal love.

The Empress helped the Master stand again. She took him in her arms, an embrace that betold a thousand farewells where words couldn't. Arten started coughing spastically.

"You must go."

Alone, the old man walked to the balcony, a rictus of unbearable pain scarring his expression.

The perfection of human civilisation on Virthos. The craddle of knowledge, of science and land of advancement. Prosperous, beautiful, unifying Kahmir. His home.

The capital city of the Empire was moribund, incinerated beyond salvation. The whole south section was a desolated field of charred blackness, a cemetery of burned buildings and Kahmirians. His nails scrapped the stone, arms shivered.

"Kahmir, oh Kahmir."

He shut his eyes and looked over the balcony with his memory instead. The Pantheonic Parade tinting the streets with colours and dancing. The Festival of Water, when the aqueducts opened at the height of summer and bathed the rejoicing masses. The military parade after the Peninsular Campaigns, celebrating Kahmir victorious, undefeated, glorious.

Kahmir in all its splendor, living on in his memory. *Only* in memory.

A few whispered words lingered on Master Hal'Gamac's lips. His final words, murmured for no one but himself, before an ocean of fire engulfed Oasis.

"Resplendent Kahmir. Resplendent no more."

A solitary tear fell down his cheek.

"Resplendent no more."

CHAPTER 1
* * *
Never Hand a Blade by the Sharp End
Damyra Pynarios. School of Medicine. Guilds Association University.
Fist of Nok.

THE CADAVER LAYING on the table looked fake.

The process of embalmment was followed by the Biothotic fixation of tissues, a procedure refined by the Guild of Physicians over decades. She had seen it many times: lifeless bodies swelled, distorted, then shrank and became waxy-looking, almost like a wooden sculpture.

Life. What a truly astounding thing. After all, what was really the difference between the table upon which the cadaver rested, and herself? Same ingredients, different conformation. A divine recipe.

Damyra was pulled out of her reverie by a flicker in the corner of her vision. An open blade in front of her in the wavering hands of a medical student.

"Have I wronged you so, child?"

The question caused a near histrionic distress on the student, a degree of upset that somewhat escaped her full comprehension and tickled a macabre enjoyment. The shiny edge began oscillating with higher frequency.

"Pardon me?" the girl managed. Damyra wrapped her hand around the girl's and the wavering stilled.

"*Never* hand a blade by the sharp end. Always by the handle. Do you want to cause a laceration to your superior?"

She took the blade from the student without looking and focused on the inanimate body in front of her.

"My apologies, Doctor Pynarios," the shaking student whispered, face erupting in vermillion. She fused with the crowd, disappearing towards the back.

Damyra's attention was with the cadaver. She felt the bony raises on the lower side of the neck, the jugular notch, then traced with her fingers the full length of the sternum and followed the lower ribs right and left. She proceeded to carve a straight line on the centre of the chest with the scalpel and in one precise motion continued down the ribs to either side.

"Today we start with—" A thought popped in her head. "Anyone with a high tolerance for pain?"

She looked around, placing the blade on a nearby tray and grabbing a fresh one. She supressed a smile when the circle of pallid faces seemed to step away in unison.

"You, lad. You look brave and strong."

The broad-shouldered boy opened his mouth, babbling incoherences as she deftly took his right forearm and made a palm-long incision.

"Ah!" the boy gasped, more out of surprise than actual pain. Damyra pressed her first two fingers lightly upon the boy's skin, close to the elbow.

"*Norvos, serim vosu aktos,*" she intoned the familiar incantation, keenly aware of the vibration her vocal cords emitted against the sensitive metal plate on the inside of her Smaragdos. She was not terribly fond of the Guild of Engineers, but they were cunning devices, that much she thought was true. At first, she hadn't been too enthused about having a tight-fitting metal collar around her neck, but once accustomed, the amplifying effects on her channelling were too great to reject.

The Smaragdos pulsated with her voice, and the segment of the nerve that innervated the area was numbed under her touch.

"*Dermos, asvun iontos.*"

The edge of the blade was so sharp it only left a fine red line. After Damyra's incantation it disappeared completely without a trace.

"*Aesthetos, tiron,*" she said as she retired from the boy, who now held his intact right forearm looking at it from every possible angle.

Damyra placed her hand over the cadaver to the tune of gasps and whispers of impressionable first year students, easily one of the most responsive audiences.

"*Aesthetos, tiron,*" she repeated the incantation and waited for a different sensation.

There.

A pulling in her stomach. A sinking feeling, like pushing an unmovable wall.

Nothing changed.

"Why didn't it work the second time?" she asked the room, staring into the students' confused eyes.

"Two cuts, same incantation. What's the difference between this specimen and...?" she gestured toward the boy.

"Lysos," he said, tracing his unscathed flesh with his thumb.

Again, she was met by a multitude of startled expressions.

"Death?" Lysos offered.

"Or lack thereof, that's correct. *Karnos, uk'tovos*," she intoned this time. The Exios drainage was minimal when the incisions she had made on the cadaver joined up instantly.

"Different incantations, different dialects of the Language of Nok," another student said, a plump boy that looked too old and too young at the same time.

"Precisely right, though I would dispose of the unnecessary religious connotations and call it Nokator instead. Biothos is the only dialect that allows us to tap into the Titillation and manipulate living tissue. Unfortunately for you, Biothos is considerably more difficult than other dialects, more Exios-draining, and with more severe consequences if things were to turn awry."

Damyra picked up the blade again and prepared to repeat the same incision.

"For now, no Biothos for you until you fully understand human anatomy."

"Doctor Pynarios?"

The blade hovered above the specimen. Lymos, the morgue caretaker, was standing on the door to the poorly lit room.

"What?" Damyra barked, profoundly irritated.

"My apologies. There is someone looking for you in the annexe."

She held Lymos' eyes, frowning.

"Who the... Well, it doesn't matter. I don't know if you can tell but I'm in the middle of something. Tell them to wait or come back later."

"My apologies again, Doctor Pynarios, but he insists. He said he knows Zar'Aldur and that you would know?"

Alda Zar'Aldur.

A name she hadn't heard uttered in over thirty-five years.

"Right," she said stiffly. "You. What's your name?" she asked to the rotund boy-man on the opposite side of the table.

"Phenyros."

"Phenyros, repeat the incision I did at the start and separate the skin from the fascia, then fascia from muscle. Today we are looking at the external thoracic wall."

She offered the blade by the handle. Phenyros took it tentatively and nodded.

"Good. Chop, chop."

She whirled and headed for the door, circumventing the tables with the other cadavers and jarred organs under the flickering light of sea serpent oil lamps.

"This had better be good, Lymos. Who is this man?"

They stopped by the door of the annexe to confer.

"He goes by the name of Lashos Domenikos. That's all I know."

"Do you recognise the name?"

He shook his head.

"I despise uncertainty," Damyra sighed, opening the door.

The annexe was used as a storage for specimens, old records and textbooks. The orange hue of the lamps reflected on the rows of embalmed kidneys, livers and brains, bouncing back from two round lenses on the eagle-like nose of the man inside.

Domenikos was a wiry man, slightly darker skin pointing to Peninsular heritage. He was leaning on a desk to her right, leather case and a neatly arranged paper pile with thin leather cover laid out by his side.

A fucking lawyer.

"Grim. This is grim."

Domenikos covered his mouth and nostrils with a delicately woven silk handkerchief.

"I would normally recommend against coming down to the morgue to those lacking the required gastrointestinal fortitude."

"Is there anywhere else more... *pleasant* where we can speak?" He looked queasy.

"I thoroughly disagree. I believe this room is quite pleasant. How do you know the name of Alda Zar'Aldur?"

"May I sit, at least?" he asked with an unctuous smile, sickening her to the core. He started pulling a chair back, legs screeching across the floor.

"You may not. I ask you once again. How do you know Zar'Aldur?"

Domenikos' smile did not waver a second. Standing, he picked up the pile of papers, two flaps of leather bound together by golden-coloured thread and offered it to her.

"At open peril of eliciting your renowned irascibility, I am afraid I do not know the relevance of this name, Doctor Pynarios. I was told it would facilitate our encounter, and so I used it. It should tell you the importance of this meeting."

Damyra's lips curved unbidden with disgust.

"You have quite the nerve, little man."

Domenikos laughed.

"That I have been told before. I serve a group of very important people that require assistance of a professional. Someone with the right... background and skills."

"Few reach my expertise, I will you give you that, but I know plenty of talented doctors in the School of Physicians that fit that description. Now, I would appreciate if you vacated the premises before I turn your skin inside out, you oily little shit."

She turned to go.

"I lied!" Domenikos yelled. Door half-ajar, Damyra stared down at him.

"I lied. About not knowing more. I do know one more thing about the name Zar'Aldur. The people that hired me knows her exact location."

Damyra closed the door. She snatched the papers from the man's hands.

The pages were rough to the touch, she recognised it as being made by a newly developed technique the Guild of Engineers was calling the print. Blocky letters, lines too perfect, too consistently geometrical to be handwritten. It was unnerving.

Akitos'i'Legos.

The words were written in Nokmollos, the legal dialect of Nokator. *Binding Agreement.* A contract.

"What is this about?"

"I am terribly afraid I am not at liberty to say. If you sign that you agree to meet my employers and carry out the deed. This is specified in article twelve-fifteen of the Agreement you are holding."

"What deed?"

She flipped through the pages. Her knowledge of Nokmollos was woefully insufficient for the legalese.

"I am not at liberty to say."

He entwined his fingers in front of him, displaying that wide, nauseating smile.

Damyra stared at him for an unnaturally long time, all the while his eyes darted from the papers to her face, to the embalmed organs floating in the many jars. She thought she could see sweat beading on his forehead, his bony laryngeal prominence bouncing up and down as he swallowed nervously.

He tries to hide it, but he's scared.

"You must think I am dull-minded if you harbour any thoughts of me signing this wretched thing."

"I do understand it is a most quaint request" he said, visibly relieved she had broken the tense silence, "yet I am but a humble lawyer. My employers are dealing with information of utmost sensitivity and if it were to be known by the populace, it would have dire consequences both for them and the Great City of Noktanos. They believe a Non-disclosure Clause is not enough, conducive to the nebulous nature of this here Agreement."

"You contradict yourself. You say they require someone with refined skills, but I surely am regarded as intellectually challenged. You come to my place of work, throw in my face a name of my past, entrap me into meeting you and try to persuade me of signing a Binding Agreement of which I am not able to know a single damned thing."

Domenikos nodded pronouncedly.

"I understand your predicament." Unsurprisingly, fake empathy was part of his arsenal.

"What happens if, for some reason, I suffer a brain infarct, descend into madness, and sign this contract?"

Domenikos wiped the sweat from his brow, grabbed his case, and squared up to exit the room.

"If you sign the Agreement, you are to bring it to the Anathema Theatre in two days at midnight. In the town of—"

"I know the place," she interrupted him, feeling momentarily faint.

They can't know. How would they know?

"My employers have spent a great deal of time cautiously deliberating who the best person for the job is, Doctor Pynarios. I suggest you sign the Agreement. Believe me when I say, you want to be on my employers' good side. They might have... *other ways* to get what they desire."

Domenikos motioned hastily to the door, eyes pointedly avoiding the jarred organs. Damyra banged it open and moved aside, looking at him with infinite disdain as he scurried away.

Damyra found herself strangely nostalgic of the city of Noktanos as she overlooked the calm meadows of the eastern border of the Fist of Nok.

The sky was painted with beautiful tonalities of orange, blue and violet this side of the Serpent's Spine. An evening so clear she was able to see where the waters of the river Tethim, tinted golden by the setting sun, joined the Heladian ocean. She could even distinguish some twirls of smoke from the city of Tethimos, a sprawling metropolis far away in the delta.

Yet, for the first time in years, she stood on the balcony of the most opulent of the Residences, overlooking the twilit Heladian skies, and she was not content. She found herself strangely overwhelmed by a sense of urgency, clashing constantly against the boundaries of her mind.

Alda. The Agreement. The Anathema.

Perhaps the nostalgia was a primal instinct to flee. To run home. *Real* home.

She went back in, irritated by the tormentous whirlwind of thoughts, and started brewing some Ei'Tulahi tea. She felt a shred of solace in the familiarity of the nocturnal ritual, spooning the dried leaves on the latticed recipient, sniffing the container before screwing back the lid, pouring the boiling water in a ceramic mug.

She stirred the contents, mesmerised by the gyrating infusion, reflecting on the stirrings within her. Thought to be long dead.

Curious, how impulses work. Utterly disconnected to facts. I have spent more time in the Residences than in Noktanos, and yet when I long for home, there is only one place in my mind.

She held the mug between her hands, close to her chest, and though it was uncomfortably hot against her skin, it helped the insidious ache in her joints. Exhaling a weary sigh, she shuffled to the dining table and settled down, eyes on the sky. The day had reached its demise, relegating the warm amber light of the sunset to the toned-down penumbra of the approaching night. Vysios would arrive from the city soon.

A knock came on the door.

She jumped, a twinge of pain travelling down her stiff spine.

"Damn this bastard pain," she cursed, rubbing her lower back. She was uncertain how long she had sat still. Only pitch-black came through the glass door, and her tea was cold.

"Coming."

She intoned an incantation as she wobbled to the door, the many candles on walls and furniture coming alight.

"Hello, Damyra," Vysios said when she opened the door. Her husband placed a chaste, loveless kiss on her lips and entered the residence, dropping his bags with a thud.

"The roads were a nightmare," he muttered lifelessly, heading for the cupboard. He seized a bottle of Portosi wine and two glasses.

"I'm not having any," she sighed, sitting back down on the table.

Vysios furrowed his brow and sat across Damyra. He stifled a yawn and poured wine in his glass.

"Last thing I need is inebriation."

The stoic man scanned her sullen expression, eyes grey and pondering. Eyes trained to obtain answers. They eventually laid on the contract on the table.

"What is that?"

Damyra smirked and shook her head.

"Am I under official interrogation, Inquisitor Pynarios?"

He remained unfazed. He was waiting for an answer.

"I was approached in the morgue today," she began reluctantly, eyeing the papers. "By a man called Lashos Domenikos. Do you know the name?"

Vysios leaned back on the chair.

"Tangentially. He's a young lawyer rumoured to be embroiled with some shady characters. That's all I know."

He glanced at Damyra over the edge of his glass, emptying it down his gullet. She grabbed the contract, tracing the creases of the leather with her thumb.

"He gave me this contract."

"What is it about?"

"I don't know."

"You don't know? How is that possible?"

"He didn't say. He just gave it to me and recommended I sign it. Said I don't want to be on his employers' bad side."

Vysios shook his head slowly. He puffed some strands of his bright, colourless hair out of his face and stared at her with piercing clear eyes. Grey circles that burned through her, devoid of colour. Of expression or understanding.

"There is something you are not telling me, Damyra. How can a stranger waltz into the morgue and confer with you? Just like th—" he trailed off, flashing a sinister smile that sent chills down her spine.

"This is about her, isn't it?"

"Domenikos knows about her, but it's not like that, Vysios. He knows, and his employers know. What else do they know?"

He gritted his teeth audibly and stood, wrapping his fingers around the neck of the bottle.

"I agreed not to dig into your past. That was part of the deal that was struck."

He staggered to the hearth, drinking from the bottle. He stared into the dying embers.

"I thought I had made myself abundantly clear about *her*."

Hatred seeped out of that last word.

Damyra looked straight ahead, a rictus of disgust fracturing her face.

"That's not the issue here."

He continued to drink with his back to her.

"Dangerous people might have information about the Voice, the rallies, the collections, the attacks and the… other things. You said it yourself, Domenikos might be involved with the Factions. It puts us in a precarious position."

"It puts *you* in a precarious position."

Damyra grimaced.

"You are a high official of the Coalition of the Codex. How kindly do you think the Table of Elders will look upon you colluding with someone with my history if it gets out?"

"Ha!"

A single, sonorous syllable that gave her pause. A humourless laughter.

"Do you really think the Elders don't know? They know *everything*, Damyra. I'm sure they have their reasons to overlook it, whatever it is."

He placed the now empty bottle on the worktop, barely resting on the edge. The second he turned, it plummeted and crashed against the floor.

Shards of glass sprayed everywhere, the jarring sound magnified in the eerie silence. They both looked at the scattered mess for an unnaturally long time before Vysios shuffled away toward the adjacent room, boots kicking the bigger pieces of glass across the floor tiles.

"I'm going to bed."

"You are *what*?" Damyra's voice cracked as shrilly as the glasses clinking.

"I'm going to bed."

She scoffed, grabbed the contract and tossed it in front of her with a bit too much force. It skidded and fell from the table.

"I need to know what they know, Vysios! This could have terrible consequences."

Her husband shrugged his shoulders.

"Do as you please, but you must be daft if you are even thinking about signing an agreement to something you don't know."

He disappeared into the bedroom, leaving Damyra to stare at the document. Ruffled pages open on a carpet of broken glass.

CHAPTER 2
***
Life is a Straight Line
Nymor Strethos. The Slopes. Rich Quarter. The Great City of Noktanos.

LAZY RAYS OF sun found their way past the oscillating blinds, painting geometrical shapes on the two bare bodies. Nymor stretched his aching muscles and sat up on the bed, back against the headboard.

"Hmmm," moaned Kymos next to him, rolling and placing his hand on Nym's inner thigh.

"Not now."

Nym batted the hand away, but Kymos didn't quite give up with the advances. That excited Nym. By the time Kymos wrapped his hand around his manhood he was fully erect.

"Ahh…" Nym sighed, lying back on the cool headboard, and letting Kymos work his hand up and down.

"I thought you said 'not now'. I don't know what to think, I like men with convictions," Kymos teased as he repositioned himself, sitting across Nym's legs. He began lowering his head, slowly moving his mouth toward him.

"No!"

Nym pushed him back. "I'm serious. I have to go."

Kymos slumped, cheeks tinted red. He sighed audibly, bothered, and fixed his eyes somewhere in front of him. Nym moved from the bed and started picking up his clothes, strewn across the floor.

"We can't keep doing this," Kymos sputtered as Nym did up the laces of his airy shirt.
"Doing what? Fucking?"
Kymos looked away.
"Yes, *fucking*. It's... not right. Besides, my father wants me to do my Cyrosox."

Nym opened his mouth, ready to fire away a clever rebuttal without thinking. When he looked into Kymos' eyes, charged with incipient tears, he realised it wasn't religious guilt or the Cyrosox, the Citizen's Duty. Kymos was falling in love with him.

His heart jolted in his chest.

Sex is your most valuable weapon only when it isn't your worst enemy.

Mastress Zhemyra's voice resonated in his head. She had been awfully fond of that assertion, yet on the occasions Nym asked how one keeps sex from being your worst enemy, she never offered an answer. It had come down to him, and only him, to learn quickly from his mistakes. Granted, seventeen years of life are not many, but there were few amassing the same number of experiences, lovers, and misadventures, as Nymor Strethos. No, Mastress Zhemyra had never told him, but he knew the answer was never to succumb to emotions.

And so, thus far, he had managed to make sex his most valuable weapon.

He ignored the sinking feeling and sat down on the edge of the bed, churning thoughts. In all fairness, his pursuing of Kymos was terribly ill-advised, given the circumstances. It could potentially complicate things for him and couldn't help with the guilt Kymos felt about that sort of carnal exchanges. Such could be the extent of his fervour for the teachings on purity of soul the Church of Nok priests had been recently raving about.

"You are right. We can't keep doing this."

Kymos' eyes were still lost in nothingness, a solitary tear rolling down his cheek. Nym wiped it with his thumb, moved his hand to his chin and lifted his head.

Hazelnut eyes refocused on Nym's, and his heart gave another jolt.

"Go," Kymos whispered hoarsely. Nym nodded ponderously. He grabbed his rucksack and climbed on the windowsill, squatting.

"This was wrong, and I'm sorry for that, but Kymos I—"
"Just go, Nym."
His lips drew a taught line on his face.
"Think of what *you* want to do, rather than what's expected," he said as goodbye, exiting through the window and scaling down the ivy covering the whole side of the ostentatious manor.

Sex is incredibly fun. Until it stops being so.

Then again, ruptures tended to be more of the unsavoury and hysterical persuasion. He would not complain when an easy break came his way. That was the last thought spared for Kymos.

When his feet touched the cobbled street, he looked up, realising the angle of the sun was too high, his stout shadow mocking him against the wall. He was running *very* late.

"Shit."

Doctor Tysides Romos would not be amused.

Fortunately for him, the clinic wasn't too far away. He secured the rucksack on his back and picked up the pace through the streets of the Rich Quarter, the neighbourhood built around the base of the Forbidden Citadel.

The typical commotion of early morning long ended, the mid-morning lull was another stark reminder of how late it was. Still, Nym glanced up at the Citadel as his battered boots pounded the cobbles, echoing in the distance of the empty streets.

Built Nok knows when, the large hilltop was walled off, hiding all castles and fortresses of the old nobility. Only one stood proudly above the tall walls.

Dytalis, with its dizzyingly tall towers, intricate arches and buttresses. Old seat of power in the Fist of Nok long before it had received that name. Nym had travelled across all corners of Helados and failed to remember a more breath-taking sight. Constructed entirely with glistening Moxosi obsidian, earning the name of the Dark Fortress, Eternal Shadow.

Yet no shadow did he see, as the sun had just surpassed the zenith of the tallest tower, bearing directly down.

It must be past half-bell.

How different his life would be if he lived inside those walls.

"I could really use a horse-drawn carriage right about now."

He began running, darting right and left through the ever-sloping streets and attracting more than one suspicious look from armour-clad watchmen patrolling the Quarter.

He recognised a side street ahead leading to Astis Way, a big diagonal avenue that divided the Rich Quarter in two: the Base closer to the Forbidden Citadel, and the Slopes. He wasn't far from Romos' clinic.

"You there! Stop!"

He came to a grinding halt. He shut his eyes and sighed.

Please, not now.

Two men approached him. Armed with lances and round bronze shields, they wore boiled leather armour, coloured blue, and white steel caps. The Quarter Watch, commissioned by the wealthy families and prominent statesmen.

"State your business in the Quarter."

"I'm employed," Nym said despondently, reaching for his trouser pocket. The watchmen raised their shields and thrusted their lances at the ready in his direction. Nym put his hands up immediately.

"Fuck."

The escalation in aggression wasn't lost on the vendors that stood in front of the businesses aligning the street. They went inside and shut the doors as a man with grey steel-plate, black chains crisscrossed on his chest piece, stepped from the jewellery shop he was guarding. He positioned himself between Astis Way and Nym, hand on the hilt of his sword.

A Silencer, skilled warriors of the Order of Nyxos that underwent gruelling Nokator training. They were only second to the Nokturia in their combat abilities using the Titillation.

"I just want to show you my documentation. It's in my pocket. There is no need for violence."

Nym emphasised every word with the least aggressive tone he could muster. After a tense pause, one of the watchmen nodded.

Nym reached into his pocket with careful, slow moves and handed over a small leatherbound case.

He always carried the letter written and signed by Doctor Romos and countersigned by Senator Dastios, representative of the Rich Quarter. A Writ of Employment that allowed the population of the Slums to work in the city in compliance with the curfew rules. Nym's father had made sure he had free mobility within Noktanos.

The watchman clicked his tongue.

"A low citizen working in the Rich Quarter, and for none other than Doctor Romos. I don't buy it."

Nym joined his hands in a pleading gesture.

"Please, I am his understudy. I am more than happy for you to accompany me. He will confirm it. I am running late you see, that is the reason for my unduly haste, so we mu…"

"No. This is probably fraudulent documentation. You could be an agent spying for the Revolution for all we know. You're coming with us."

Nym clenched his fists.

"Do you really think a revolutionary spy would be running around in daylight, you utter donkey?"

I don't have time for this.

"*Eysos, domon vosu Exios.*"

The air around Nym became denser, tangible. He thrusted his hands to either side as he pronounced the next incantation.

"*Alros!*"

A potent current of wind birthed from under him and blew powerfully outwards. A miniature tornado with Nym in its epicentre that crashed against the Silencer and the watchmen, blowing them away.

Nym caught his documents in the air and whirled to run away, taking advantage of the confusion. The Silencer, however, had quickly recovered. He unsheathed his sword as Nym came closer.

"*Prysos, domon vosu Exios,*" he intoned. A hazy orange halo coated his steelplate armour and sword.

"*Dotros!*" Nym counter-summoned. A gust of wind propelled him from behind.

"*Arrantos!*" the Silencer shouted, swinging his sword in earnest. From the blade an arc of flames roared forth just before Nym fell to his knees, sliding under the fire, so close he felt unbearable heat washing momentarily over him. It was only momentary. The added push of the wind gave him monstrous inertia, he was soon past the Silencer and dashing away across Astis Way.

The mad sprint, fuelled by his last incantation didn't stop until he had crossed the wide diagonal avenue and he was in front of the clinic on the other side.

"*Eysos, haltos,*" he whispered, using his shoulder to lean against the walls that surrounded the clinic after the prolonged use of Exios.

What a way to start the day.

Romos had built his practice following traditional Noktanosi architecture, refusing the cold brutish monoliths of the new wave known as Gigos. Wedged in-between two big cubes of unnatural grey stone, a big cylinder of white curved walls and blue domed ceiling surrounded by smaller ones.

Nym took a couple of seconds to recompose until the bells of the House of Nok on Astis Way tolled eleven times.

"Shit, and shit again."

He knocked on the gate.

A slot slid open and Yevia eyed him up and down.

"You are late, boy. Doctor Romos won't be impressed."

"I know, Yevia. I know. I was… otherwise engaged."

The guard slid the slot shut and opened the gate.

"Your 'engagements' will have you kicked out of the practice, Nym."

Oh, you have no idea.

"How's the boss' mood today, anyway?"

"Difficult to say."

"That's often worse than overt anger."

"Good luck," Yevia said, a smile tugging at her lips.

Nym rushed across the front terrace, a gorgeous garden with benches, olive trees and a central pond that made for the city's best waiting area.

He stormed into the reception, startling Lena.

"Nok Almighty, Nym!"

"Sorry about that, Lena." He leaned into the high counter of the reception desk, showering her with his most charming smile.

"Even though I'm late, I always have time for you."
"I know you do," she shifted toward him, twirling a strand of red hair. "You do realise it's past the eleventh bell."
"I do… Yes, as a matter of fact, I *do* need to go," he broke the debonair act and shot a nervous look up at the gallery.
"He's in room three with a patient. Carry the grace of Nok with you."
"That bad, huh."
He climbed the steps in twos, then threes.
The top floor of the clinic was a circular corridor with an overlooking balcony in the middle. He stopped a fraction of a second to throw Lena a kiss from the heights and lunged to the right door.
"I'm with a patient!" a stern voice came from inside when he knocked.
"It's me, Doctor Romos."
"Come in!"
Nym breathed in deeply, adopting his most practiced expression of consternation. He opened the door.
Romos sat on his stool with fitted wheels. When Nym entered, he pushed his generous weight backwards using his heels. He pushed and pulled across the room to the other side of the desk with remarkable agility. It had always struck Nym as quite the oddity, how such a fat man could be so lithe.
"Mighty glorious of you to come," Romos stared over the semilunar lenses hanging on the end of his bulbous nose. "Have you got any valid reasons this time or are you resorting to your classic repertoire of thinly veiled excuses?"
Well, I can't possibly tell you I was in bed with your son.
Nym opened his mouth, only to shut it straight away. He had nothing.
"Right. I believe I got my answer. Cyrosi Demirios, this here is my time-challenged understudy. Do you mind if I do some teaching?"
"By all means," the Cyrosi said, regarding Nym with care.
"Cyrosi Demirios is with-child and lately has been feeling lightheaded, having blurry vision intermittently. Occasionally she feels palpitations in her chest. Thoughts?"
Nym clenched his suddenly very sweaty palms and narrowed his eyes into slits.
Medicine is about enquiry. Start from the beginning. Anamnesis.
"Has it happened before?" he asked Romos. Instead of answering, the Physician stood from the stool and kicked it toward him, gesturing to the patient.
Nym swallowed nervously. Romos had never before let him take the lead with a patient.
Well, this feels punitive.

He sat down on the stool, and stapled his fingers over his lap, only to immediately change position. He found that he had forgotten how one sits.

"Have you ever felt like this before, Cyrosi Demirios?"

"Not really, no. This is my first pregnancy."

As the patient elaborated on her case, Nym paid close attention. Romos was fond of saying that skilled doctors needed but a handful of questions to diagnose.

Cyrosi Demirios was a very well-spoken High Citizen, probably educated in the University. In her early twenties by his estimation, of Noktanosi descent. Light complexion, Nym wouldn't have been able to guess she was with-child had she not said so. Likely in the fourth month of her pregnancy.

"So?" Romos demanded.

"From her set of symptoms and history, I don't believe this is Sphymos disease. It is more likely Baby Curse."

"Baby Curse?" Cyrosi Demirios clutched her incipient belly.

"Non-sense folk name. Nymor, there is a reason we use medical terminology. We need to avoid causing unnecessary distress."

"My apologies, Cyrosi Demirios. I meant to say Eklos syndrome."

"What is that? Is my baby going to be alright?"

Romos shook his head, throwing Nym a reprobatory glance as he approached Demirios, kneeling next to her chair.

"Let me reassure you. Medicine has a come a long way in the past ten years. Things like Baby Curse or Bashork's Touch are of the past. Nymor, what do you do next?" Romos didn't deign look at him. He simply returned to his seat behind the desk.

"I... I..."

"Don't further marr your consultation with indecision."

Nym took a big breath, stilling his nerves.

"I would check her blood pressure."

Romos nodded, pointing to the Horvos device.

"What is *blood pressure*?"

Romos looked at Nym again.

"After your blood is pumped by your heart, it hits the walls of your arteries. Normally, the compliance of the arteries is enough to withstand that pressure. However, on occasion and due to different factors, that pressure becomes excessive and can damage tissues."

Cyrosi Demirios nodded, hands still on her belly.

"This contraption is called a Horvos device," Nym continued, now deep in the flow of things.

He reached for his rucksack and extracted his Smaragdos, cinched it on his neck and grabbed both his small leatherbound Biothotic Codex and his normal Codex.

The Broken Oath

"It is completely innocuous. All I need to do is adjust this cuff on your arm, then it will fill with air and I will be able to tell how high or low the blood pressure is."

She gave a half-hearted affirmative grunt and Nym fitted the cuff around her arm. He advised her to relax and opened his Nokator Codex.

The inflatable cuff, made of sheep's guts, was connected to two pale brown tubes crafted from fibres of the Kythosi plant. One led to a glass circle containing a needle and quicksilver, the other to a rectangular receptacle.

Nym ran a mental list of everything he needed and grabbed the stethoscope on the table, an instrument also envisioned by Horvos that was gaining a lot of popularity in the medical field. It consisted of a single tube of Kytoshi fibre connected to a pair of earpieces on one end and a metal semi-sphere on the other. This last piece built with a membrane of the same very material used in Smaragdos to amplify sound. In the hands of a skilled doctor, it conferred the ability to listen to the lungs working and heart pumping.

He opened the Codex and searched for the correct incantation.

"Exios, alton Persos Grados, dokon Eysos oytos."

A faint hiss followed, air slowly swooshing into the rectangle and up the tubes, inflating the cuff gradually.

"You will feel it tightening around your arm, maybe pins and needles in your fingers, but it will only be momentarily until I release the air."

Cyrosi Demirios stared at him and the growing cuff, slightly ashen-faced.

Better be quick.

He placed the flat surface of the stethoscope on the inner aspect of her forearm, immediately below the cuff near the elbow. He listened for her blood pulsing as the cuff expanded.

The *lup lup lup* disappeared.

"Exios, seruintin vosu aktanos."

The hiss halted and he expertly slid down a tiny hatch on the side of the rectangular box, trapping the air in the system. He then rotated a small knob on the other side of it, slowly releasing small amounts of air as he listened carefully.

There, a pulse.

Nym looked at the measuring needle. First Horvos sound at 195 milimetres of quicksilver, sound patent until the needle hit 110 milimetres and disappeared.

"All done."

Cyrosi Demirios looked thoroughly relieved.

"195 over 110 milimetres of quicksilver, Doctor Romos."

"Right. How do we proceed?"

"Errr... Given the pregnancy I wouldn't go for Elder plant extract. Vylar elixir?"

Romos' mouth flashed a brief smile of approval.

"What dose?"

"I would recommend the quarter-litre flask. Three drops, three times a day and we follow up in a week."

Tysides Romos showed a proud smile now. He approached Nym and patted him on the shoulder.

"Well done."

Nym basked in the warmth of the doctor's appraisal as he opened a drawer full of elixirs and potions.

"Exactly what the lad said. Three drops before each meal of the day and we'll see you in a week's time. Does that sound reasonable?"

"It does, doctor. Will my baby be alright?"

"There are no fixed certainties in medicine, Cyrosi Damirios, but I can assure you we are doing everything we can.'

"Thank you, Doctor."

She grabbed the flask, nodded lightly toward Nym and left.

"Nymor, Nymor…"

Romos plopped onto his stool.

"It pains me, it does. Seeing all the potential you harbour, unmet by equitable motivation."

Nym looked down.

"I apologise again, Doctor Romos."

"It is not me you have to apologise to, Nymor. I became a physician a long time ago. I have a successful practice, loyal customers, important friends in important places. I have lived a fulfilling life. It is *yourself* who needs an apology."

Nym stared at his teacher, eyebrows bunching up together.

"Let me ask you something. What do you want?"

Nym continued to stare blankly.

"When your father cashed in a favour a year ago, begging me to teach you to be a physician, was that what you wanted?"

It was a simple question. One that had walked around the edges of his mid for quite some time. It should be followed by a simple answer, yet Nym found himself at a loss for words for the second time that day.

"Nymor, the old Kahmirian addage that says 'life is a circle, and our…'"

A loud knocking came on the door, interrupting the physician.

"Doctor Romos! Doctor Romos!"

"Do come in, Lena. What's the matter?"

The receptionist stormed in, tumbling down to the floor. Her breathing was rapid, eyes bulging and rolling franctically. There was blood splattered all over her clothes.

They stood.

The Broken Oath 25

"The Dionos boy. Xenos. He was pla… playing with his brothers on top of the stairs. He slipped and fell. I couldn't feel his pulse. I didn't know… what…" she explained in between the quick respirations.

"Nymor, get your Biothotic Codex and head to the surgery room," Romos ordered, jumping over Lena and disappearing down the corridor.

Nym embraced the surge of adrenaline, the hammering of his heart in his neck. He moved fast, grabbing hold of his Biothotic Codex and the stethoscope. He pushed the wheeled stool toward Lena and helped her sit, offering a clean towel.

"Lena, will you be alright?"

She nodded slowly, her eyes avoiding the stains of blood.

That would have to do. He was needed elsewhere.

By the time Romos burst into the surgery room with bloodied Xeno Dionos in his arms, Nym had already prepared the knee-high table and a tray with sterilised scalpels, suture material, gauzes and Romos' case of elixirs and vials.

Trailing behind them was distinguished Guildmaster Xhemiros Dionos, leader of the Guild of Lawyers and one of Romos' most distinguished clients.

"My son, my son," he kept muttering under his breath, face contorted in pain and worry.

Dionos pushed past Nym, motioning to follow Doctor Romos into the room.

Nym remembered one of Romos' lessons. *Medicine does not care about titles or stations. Bodies are bodies all the same.*

He stepped in front of Cyrosi Xhemirios Dionos.

"Cyrosi Dionos, I must ask you to stay out of the room."

"Step aside, child," Dionos tried to shove past Nym again, yet he didn't budge. He puffed out his chest and stood his ground.

"Listen, here *you*…" Dionos bunched up the collar of his shirt in his fist and brought Nym's face close to him. Nym squared up, unafraid, drunk with the excitement of confronting one of the most powerful citizens in the Noktanian League, shielded by the authority of the medical professional.

"Out, Xhemirios!" shouted Romos as he was placed Xeno on the table. Guildmaster Dionos deflated instantly, trading imposing solemnity for paternal preoccupation.

"Please take care of my boy."

Nym held his hand up and after a tense pause, Dionos took several steps back as Nym shut the door.

Now, how about that?

"Nymor, Xeno fell from a height of approximately 3 metres, broke his right femur and slashed the posterior aspect of his right thigh with the Ei'Tulahi encasing of the balustrade. Judging by the amount of blood loss, I believe he nicked the profunda femoris artery. We must regain haemodynamic control immediately. Please, prepare a blood infusion," Romos said with a calm and commanding tone. His hands moved with dizzying speed as he spoke, tying a tourniquet up Xeno's thigh with a strip of leather and pressing down layers of gauze against the ample slash.

Nym moved to action.

He grabbed a vial from Romos' case and pressed it against Xeno's limp leg, catching some of the red rivulets. With a finger-width of blood in the glass container, he dashed to the working top on the right wall.

He checked again his Smaragdos was secured to his neck and reached for the high cupboard, extracting two bottles of Athospos. He downed them with trepidation.

Sanguine Transfiguration was a difficult incantation, he had tried it a few times in his practicing sessions. He had failed every single time.

The effect of Athospos kicked in quickly. He felt instantly invigorated, sharply focused, euphoric.

"How many bags do you need?"

"Three to start with," Romos grunted. He had his own leg on top of Xeno's to stop the bleeding and was using the stethoscope to listen to his heart.

To start with!? Alright, breathe. Don't think. Do.

Nym placed five wooden chests on the worktop, packed with compacted lichen and moss. He then grabbed three leather pouches from one of the drawers and connected the first one to the blood vail using a Kythosi tube.

Don't think. Do.

He flipped the pages of his Biothotic Codex, franctically looking for the necessary incantation. When he found it, he read it over and over in his head, slowly articulating the words without creating any sound.

Don't... think... I'm so fucked.

He took a big breath and closed his eyes, touching the box closest to him with one hand and the vial with the other.

"*Bioxos, leron eaosuri thosi Bios, t—*" he stumbled, tongue tripping over the exact pronunciation of the verb. He bent forwards, accusing a massive pull of energy from his insides. A painful drainage that would deplete all his reserves if he didn't finish the incantation. He plunged on.

"*—t'creon myron Biontos!*"

Exios flowed out of him, rushing, leaving him empty. Another potent tug, different, as though he was running on a slippery surface, getting nowhere. He understood the sensation and moved his left hand to the second chest. Only then, he opened his eyes and looked at the vial.

The blood was stirring, fizzying. All of a sudden, the vial filled completely with the red fluid, the tube convulsing on its own as blood flowed up filling the bag. Nym waited until the pouch was completely full to intone the terminating incantation.

"Bioxos, seruin vosu aktos."

His hands felt leadened as he checked inside the chests. The first one contained a black-grey putrid pulp of dead matter, the second one still retained some vivid green.

He had performed his first succesful Sanguine Transfiguration Incantation.

Only living things can create life. Biothos only allows you to transform it.

He drunk two more bottles of Athospos and repeated the process with the other two pouches.

Upon uttering the final incantation, he began feeling strange. Swirling dots in his vision, deafening crackles in his ears. Tongue heavy and palms sweaty.

I'm having a vasovagal. I'm going to faint.

He fought hard to stay conscious, rapidly squatting with his head between his legs and closing his eyes.

"Nymor. Are you alright, lad?"

He heard Doctor Romos' voice very far away, muffled and distorted. He opened his eyes. The feeling went away as quickly as it came.

"You have exerted yourself, lad."

"I am well, Doctor."

Nym searched the drawers and grabbed a pot with honey. He poured water from a metal container into a cup and mixed it with the amber substance. After three avid gulps of the solution he felt instantly better.

"Good lad. You know what to do when fatigue kicks in, but you must know your limits. Now, come help me. I suspect his heart is fibrillating. We need to shock him before we infuse him."

Despite the circumstances, Nym felt a jolt of excitement. Tysides Romos was probably the only physician with the expertise and equipment to try the novel procedure outside of the University Hospital.

"I need all my focus in the incantation, or I could kill him," Romos said, producing a Nokator Codex from his case, leafing through it.

"Get the equipment from that drawer over there. Two metal plates welded to two rods, metal wires and a ring. And don't forget to put on the gloves."

Nym followed the orders, fitting the thick woollen gloves on and putting the equipment on the tray.

"Hand me the ring."

Romos stepped onto two blocks of wood several feet away from the table.

"Make sure the wires are not touching anything and hold the rods from the other side of the table. One plate goes on Xeno's sternum, the other one on the lateral aspect of his left thorax, on the midaxillary line."

Nym's excitement was fading into fright. They were preparing to deliberately shock a human being.

"Are you ready? Nothing in contact with the wires?"

Nym double-checked the wires hanging in the air, Xeno on the table, all instruments back on the tray. He nodded to Romos.

"Clear."

"Clear," Romos repeated. He cinched his Smaragdos in place and re-read the Codex in front of him, hands clutching the ring.

"Exios, hosn Elektros kidon sinon-dor trovos thosi Kaukhos."

The air around Romos' hands warped, blue and yellow sparks clicking on the surface of the ring, increasing in intensity. The sparks flowed through the metal, making Nym's hairs on arms and head stand erect as the current reached the rods and then the plates, like a domesticated lightning. Xeno's body convulsed savagely.

"Exios, seruintin vosu aktanon!" Romos shouted and the current stopped. Nym retired the plates as the physician moved quickly toward Xeno. He placed his naked hand on the boy's neck to check for a pulse when a visible yellow spark travelled between the two, emitting a soft clicking noise.

"Bashork's Hall!" he cursed. He tried again, nodding.

"I've got a pulse. Nym, get the pouches."

Nym dropped the rods with a loud clang and dashed to the counter while Romos expertly introduced a girthy Kytoshi cannula in one of Xeno's veins. Nym brought a pole on wheels from a corner, hanged the pouches from it and connected the tube to the cannula.

Another wave of fatigue hit Nym out of the blue. He turned around, knees buckling. Luckily, he was able to grab a stool from under the table before ending up sprawled on the floor.

He expelled a long, weary sigh and pushed himself to Romos' side, head hanging low.

The doctor shot him a glance and chuckled. He was busy examining the tourniquet and the state of the open wound with forceps and blunt needle drivers.

"You've done brilliantly, Nymor," he said, peering down a set of loupes installed on his glasses.

"I have this from here. I just need to tidy the wound. Go home and rest."

Nym was too tired to speak, but he shook his head. Reconstructive surgery was too fascinating to miss.

"Alright, I might need some assistance here, but don't exert yourself again."

Nym pulled the tray closer to have a good reach of the instruments.

"Here, put pressure on this," Romos indicated the bunch of clumped gauzes. Nym had just about enough energy to drop his body weight on it.

"There was something I wanted to tell you before we were interrupted by poor Xeno's misfortune," Romos said distractedly, eyes fixated on the pulp of white and red that was the boy's leg.

"Though I'm getting fat and old, my memory never fails. I remember I was saying not to trust the old Kahmirian notion of life as a circle. 'Our deeds preceed and proceed our deeds', so the saying goes. That's terribly wrong, Nymor. We can never go back. We don't get second chances. Life is a straight line. We can only look back and never return."

"Huh."

What are you on about, old man?

"I had a very interesting conversation with a friend of mine the other day. He was saying how difficult it is to find competent trainees from the School of Medicine. I happened to mention I have a very talented student under my tutelage in desperate need of hospital teaching. This friend of mine is situated high enough to, we could say, *bend* the rules and grant you an interview.

"It is time to decide what to do, Nymor. If you really want to be a physician, this is your one chance. If you accept and go to the interview, you can share your time between my practice and the University Hospital. If you don't, then don't bother coming back here."

Nym was bereft of words for the third and final time that day.

CHAPTER 3
* * *
A Question of Knowledge
Damyra Pynarios. The Grand Chamber of the Rectorate. Guild's Association University.

SHE HAD BEEN itching to leave the round chamber from the moment the meeting had started, almost three bells ago.

Located inside the base of the Rectorate building, the sober room of enormous proportions was bordered by ostentatious columns at regular intervals. In its centre, a round table with all the School Heads sat in big, throne-like chairs. In front of the entrance and overlooking the table, three platforms of differing height. The lowest had a scribe who jotted down the minutes, a bored Chair was in the middle. University Rector Pelpharios Arthos sat on the highest tier.

The Grand Chamber of the Rectorate. The helm of the Guilds Association University, where the Intercollegiate Council met to take important decisions.

What a load of bullshit.

The reality of University politics was far from such a romantic idea. Interminable bickering from avaricious people, vying for more power without the faintest consideration for education.

The Broken Oath

Over the years, she had come to regret her own blind race for power. Indeed, she had been rewarded with the sought-after title of Head of the School of Medicine, but also with endless meetings, constant pandering, only a few anatomy sessions she had refused to give up, and virtually no time to practice medicine. In the end, she had retired from praxis altogether.

She missed it dearly.

"Chair Perenthias, any other matters in the agenda?" Rector Arthos droned from his pedestal. He was leaning back and to the right over the arm of his chair with a visible deficit of interest.

"No, that would be all the ordinary matters, Rector. If there are no other matters, we shall motion to adjourn."

"Rector Arthos, may I raise a motion?"

Everyone in attendance looked at Magister Braxos Oremos, Head of the School of Metallurgy. Rector Arthos sighed and sagged further back in his seat.

"You may."

"I am mindful of the inconvenience this causes the Chamber, but I am bound by the University Charter to bring up any extraordinary matters that follow Protocol. Professor Kalavis asks once again to be granted aud—"

"Ha, ha!" Magister Surk'Imla, Head of the School of Natural Sciences cackled openly.

"Not this again, Oremos," pleaded Rector Arthos.

"Again, Rector," Magister Oremos puffed his cheeks. "There isn't much I can do. Kalavis is following the rules and I must oblige."

"This is preposterous," Enkir Eupides Mesopos, Head of the School of Law removed his glasses and pinched the bridge of his nose.

Damyra exhaled.

"Send him in," the Rector addressed an aide, a young student with the plain beige robes of Humanities who scuttled behind the pedestals toward the doors. "The sooner we listen to his foolishness, the quicker we can adjourn."

Professor Kalavis was a dishevelled man, stout and barrel-chested. He was in charge of the Forges, and usually showed up in the Chamber straight from his workshop. Sweaty and covered in grime. For a change, he wore a ceremonial toga, tightly wound around his muscled torso, showing arms the size of trunks. A thick ledger was pinned down under one of them, making his monstrous bicep stand out even more.

He walked with defiant expression and sat where the aide had placed a chair.

"Professor Kalavis, you are bringing forth the only extraordinary matter of the day. You may address the Chamber," Chair Perenthias succinctly gave him permission to speak. Kalavis put the ledger on his legs, two meaty hands on it, and looked up.

"I have on my lap a Declaration of Independence."

He paused for suspense, but he had started his speech the same way over a dozen times. It was no longer the shocking opening statement he intended. The Heads of School waited for him to continue with void expressions.

"After decades of increasing growth, the Guilds Association was continually flooded with people from all over the Fist of Nok and beyond, seeking to learn under Master Guilders. Twenty-five years ago, a decision was made to divert them away from Noktanos. The Association needed to funnel and sieve the masses, and that is why the University was created."

"Non-sense pseudohistory!" Magister Tremos Impalos, Head of the School of Humanities interjected. Kalavis ignored him.

"Not a single Guildmaster was truly expecting to create *the* leading centre for education in the whole of Virthos. For twenty-five years we have diverted away from many of the initial axioms promulgated by the Association, creating our own identity. And yet, the Association acts as an authoritarian octopus, extending its greedy tentacles to every aspect of Unversity matters.

"Our curricula must be ratified by the Association, and in their childish games to vie for power in the Senate, they accept a Heresy Policy from the Coalition. Secularisation, indoctrination, restrictions, and those are but a few examples. None of that shall stand! I defend a free-thinking institution that is not shackled to stale ideals of organisations or governments. Where doctrine is thrown out and knowledge becomes paramount! We must break away from the old notion, break away from a University that isn't but an expensive and lengthy ceremony to access the ranks of the Guilds, and pursuit knowledge for knowledge's sake!"

"For the hundredth time, Kalavis," Arthos interrupted. "Spare us of your faux zeal. You sound like a first-year philosophy student who's read one too many books. How naïve are you? We are the *Guilds Association* University. We were *founded* by the Guilds Association, and most of our funding comes from the Association's Treasury. We are not a nation, but an institution adjuct to the sovereign Noktanian League."

"That is precisely the problem, Rector Arthos. We can talk logistics if you so wish. We produce in the Forges the entirety of the armament of the Senatorial Legions. Who sees the profit? Not the University. We also have the bureaucratic infrastructure to operate independently."

"I don't know about you, but I am not in the mood to invite the Legions over for a casual occupation."

"I am not saying it would be an easy or quick process, Magister Surk'Imla, but one necessary, nonetheless. I am prepared to speak in front of the Senate—"

"Oh, you are *prepared*. Isn't that grand. Kalavis. I have lost count of how many times we have voted against your foolishness. Your stubbornness astounds me."

"It's called having ideals, Enkir Mesopos. You should look it up."

"Kalavis, refrain from juvenile exchanges," Chair Perenthias interloped. The Professor conceded, raising a hand.

"I understand where you are coming from, though. That is why today I am trying something different. I am not demanding a vote of the Intercollegiate Council, because all of you are obviously appointed by the grace of the almighty Guilds Association. Under the Representation Articles of the University Charter, I am formally requesting a Campus-wide referendum. Every faculty member and enrolled student has a saying in this matter."

What?

Rector Arthos leaned forward.

"Can he do that?"

Enkir Mesopos removed his glasses again.

"I believe so, yes."

The Heads stared expectantly at Chair Perenthias, who heaved a hefty tome in front of her. For a minute, the only sound in the Chamber was the rustle of old pages.

"Indeed. The Representation Articles abide it."

"Fine. Larnos, put it in the agenda for the next Chamber meeting. Any other *requests*, Kalavis?" Rector Arthos looked down, his left foot on the set of stairs that climbed down the pedestal.

Professor Kalavis seemed surprised. He shook his head, stunned.

"Excellent. Ymena?"

Chair Perenthias closed the tome and ceremoniously slapped her hand on its leather cover.

"Meeting adjourned."

Rector Arthos didn't wait for the official proclamation. Before Ymena Perenthias had finished the sentence, he had already climbed down his chair and was the first one out the door.

Damyra was a close second.

The rasp of quill on paper was the only sound in the small room as Damyra approached the desk. It was a calming, familiar sound, associated with fond memories of studying for exams and debating what conditions would be tested.

It was a young student scribbling something on a ledger that occupied the whole surface of the desk. Columns and columns of strangled, hieroglyphical writing. He wore the beige robes of Humanities, and even though he couldn't be past twenty, a pair of thick lenses rested upon his nose.

"Good afternoon Cyrosi, may I take your name?"

"Doctor Damyra Pynarios."

The student nodded with a solemnity that defied his youth.

"Will you be retiring any books today, Doctor Pynarios?"

"No. I just need access to the Vault."

The student nodded ponderously again.

"Certainly. May I ask for—"

Damyra produced a small wooden replica of a Codex, blue and white, before he was finished. Most every faculty member had one such token, but only a few had one with a golden triangle embossed at the top, granting entrance to the Vault.

"Thank you, Doctor. I gather you will not need directions," he smiled, exchanging the token for a hefty copper key.

"That shan't be necessary, no."

He motioned her to the centre of the room and she obliged with a slight limp, positioning herself on an intricately patterned platform. Its edges were carved so that they resembled massive chains, the sort that anchored ships to the docks.

The student actioned some lever under the desk and a circular veranda sprung up around Damyra right before the platform began descending with a screech of metallic gears.

Vysios was convinced that the Coalition of the Codex knows everything, but she refused to believe that. If a question of knowledge was what separated her and the whereabouts of Alda, there was only one place that she could visit for answers. If the information wasn't there, then she would have tangible proof that absolutely *no one* knew.

If it was… Well, that was another wholly different matter entirely.

During the construction of the University Campus, the Guild of Builders had carved a gigantic cylindric space deep underground, just below the Rectorate. Big loadbearing pillars arose, converging at the top and right at the centre of its apex, a hole through which Damyra's platform appeared.

Between the pillars, oval depressions displayed big, mounted lamps within a network of magnifying lenses that yielded a light so powerful it blinded when looked at directly.

The platform slid down on spiralling poles, slowly rotating as it descended toward several concentric rings, sublevels that stacked on top of each other. By the time it reached the topmost sublevel, she had done a full circle and the platform aligned itself with a set of steps. She stepped down and walked away with purpose as the platform ascended, avoiding the throngs of grey-robed clerks that pushed trays and carried books, ledgers, scrolls and loose papers alike.

She could navigate the tall labyrinth of shelves with her eyes closed. She had spent the greater part of ten years down there. Endless hours memorising the most obscure syndromes to beat her competition and become the youngest Head of Surgery in history.

She reached the series of lifts at the edges of the lowest sublevel and picked one without students crowding the doors. Once inside the lift, she introduced the copper key in a lock embedded on the left wall and turned it. A section of the wall protruded with a click, revealing a hidden compartment and a red lever. She pulled it and the lift began descending jerkily.

How bad could it possibly be? How difficult can it be to mask any involvement with the Factions if it meant knowing where Alda is?

The lift halted with a jolt, snapping her out of her reverie. The doors retracted to show a dimly lit corridor, torches instead of oil lamps mounted on pre-Kahmirian sconces. Weak light that in combination with a patina of humidity on the damp stones created a phantasmagorical vision.

She felt slightly queasy as she advanced, supporting part of her weight on the wet walls of the corridor.

She eventually entered a big chamber, a hundred metres across, with a domed ceiling so high it was lost to her eyes. The only source of light in the cavernous place was a large brazier in its centre, proud flames that licked the delicate filigrees of the structure. Cut in its wavering light, a silhouette of stone slabs arranged in a throne covered in furs. Before it, a dark pit with steps.

There was a man lounging on the petrous throne, reading a book. Black armour with seamless junctures, chains crossing the chestpiece. The Foundation Charter stated that at least one member of the Order of Nyxos was to always to vet entrance of the Vault. For centuries, long before the University Library was built above it, a special branch of the Order called the Dylos Conclave appointed someone to oversee the most precious documents on the continent.

That was no simple Nyxos knight, no common mercenary Silencer, hired for money. This was Lamenthos, Guardian of the Vault, for as long as anyone alive could remember.

Damyra's footsteps echoed in the vast space as she approached.

"Damyra Phalmerios, long has passed since your last visit," the statuesque man lowered the book to speak. There were tears in his cheeks. He did nothing to wipe them.

"It's Pynarios, Guardian. A long time indeed, I have been married since."

He regarded her with old eyes that contrasted an otherwise youthful appearance. Tears kept rolling down his cheeks, no other signs of sadness in his face.

"So you have."

"I seek entrance to the Vault."

Another lingering look.

"It is granted," he announced, waving to the pit. He reclined back and returned to his reading.

Damyra climbed down the pit precariously, wincing with every uneven step and avoiding the troubling thought of having a million cubic tonnes of soil above her head.

At the bottom of the pit there was an old gate with iron bands running along its length, surface nicked arbitrarily with the uncaring passing of time. Small, pitted shadows exacerbated by the shifting light of a single torch.

She used the same copper key to enter the Vault.

The old gate opened to a semi-spherical chamber of naked stone, harsh lines of compact granite showing the pressure of the depths. She crossed the threshold, taken aback by the hot, asphyxiating sensation. She could almost feel the moisture escaping her body and dissipating in the dry room.

Circular rows of shelves, arranged in concentric circumferences, only interrupted by a slender entryway in front of her. She walked into the corridor formed by numerous old tomes, cracked leather covers and brittle scrolls, and spiralled until she reached the very centre of the helical arrangement. On the far side of the circle of books, a sturdy desk dominated the space.

Lighting a fire inside the Vault was punishable by death, and likely you'd be persecuted by every ghost of the Dylos Conclave after that. Fortunately, no such thing was necessary. The domed ceiling had veins of a translucent material that let through a hazy orange-red light, creating a mesmerising effect.

Though the veins bifurcated multiple times, the pulsating light concentrated on the cusp of the chamber, directly above a circle of an unknown metal in the stone floor. Its diameter was roughly the width of a person, glinting strangely with unreadable symbols on its external edge.

"Don't you just burn to know what's down there?"

Damyra emitted a surprised squeal, retreating to the shelves.

From a pool of shadows emerged a man, broad-shouldered, unkempt beard, his face a canvas of disorderly scars. He wore a travelling cloak, boiled leather armour and muddy boots.

The University Roamer, tasked with finding every book worth having, every incantation in existence to add to the Guilder's Codex. A job no one envied.

"Dasterios."

"Doctor Pynarios, we go way back. Lyo, please."

"Lyo. You scared the fuck out of me."

The Roamer's laugh was a hoarse crack, marred by years of smoking Tobos root.

"I apologise, Doctor. I am not used to having company down here."

Lyomar Dasterios moved with purpose, owning the room. Filling it. He had a wide, flat nose that had been broken one too many times. A bushy, filthy beard split in five places by lines of knotted scars. Crooked, yellowed teeth and low rumbling voice.

Granted, he wasn't handsome by any interpretation of the word, but he was likely the most attractive man she had come across in her life.

Damyra exhaled and waved a hand toward the metallic circle.

"Just a plate. There's nothing down there but another hundred tonnes of bedrock."

Dasterios shook his head ponderously.

"Oh no. That's not just a plate."

"How do you know?"

He shrugged.

"I know these things."

He walked over to the desk, licking his teeth, and sat on the edge of it.

"What brings you down to my solitary realm, Doctor Pynarios?" he rattled, digging into one of the pockets of his cloak. He extracted a small sack with dried leaves and a wooden pipe.

"I know my way around, Lyo. No need for a tour."

"I'm sure you do. I was simply curious."

He started filling the pipe with a silver spoon.

"I suppose curiosity is a good quality for a Roamer," she said, turning toward the shelves. Her fingers traced the ancient spines as she read the titles with her head slightly tilted. *Lord Irethios' Journal*, *Tales of the Vanishing*, *Secrets of Kahmir*, *Complete Compendium of Virthan Terms*, *History and Mythos*.

Dasterios finished packing the leaves into the pipe and put it in his mouth, unlit. He headed toward the shelves.

"I'll tell you one thing about curiosity, Doctor Pynarios. It's got me nearly killed more than once."

Her lips drew a flat line, grimacing at the all-too-coincidental impertinence. When she looked up to say something, Lyontos Dasterios had already left.

Her fingers landed on the book she was seeking. She grabbed the only copy of *Full Account of the Nok's Voice Trials* in existence and carried it to the desk.

She sat down, drew a long breath, and began reading her past.

The first half of the document comprised knowledge of public domain, historical accounts of the socio-political scene of the League and the events that precipitated the creation of Nok's Voice, the most popular independent party in the history of the Noktanian League. She didn't care about that.

She flipped pages, past the origin, the Senatorial representation, the upheaval. She paused at its outlawing.

If it's not here, it's nowhere.

Only six people knew about it. It had never been written down. Of those five people, four had killed themselves before being apprehended and tortured by the Coalition Inquisition. One had vanished without trace. One remained.

Damyra read furiously, skimming paragraphs, barely registering words.

...through the demagogic prowess of Alda Zar'Aldur, Nok's Voice gained considerable traction with the Populus...

...its disbandment proposed by Senator Blongatos after several suspicious attempts on the lives of...

... rumours around the disappearance of several prominent Zereri tribesmen, prisoners of war held by the Senatorial Armies. Though their bodies were never retrieved...

...never proven, an independent joint probe by the Senatorial Intelligence Corps and the Coalition Inquisition yielded no results...

...after no substantial evidence, Damyra Phalmeria was absolved of all charges and no further investigation was pursued...

She reached the end of the documents. She gave it another reading. Then yet another, more carefully, absorbing every single word.

It wasn't there.

She reclined back, the old chair emitting an ugly creak.

Nobody knows.

She allowed herself to breath in deeply. Her eyes fixed on the orange light of the veins, pondering.

She frowned.

"Huh."

She had been waiting for a wave of... of... something. Relief? Determination? Confirmation?

She stared at the cramped handwriting, feeling empty.

CHAPTER 4
***
More

Nymor Strethos. The Slums. Engos Territory. The Great City of Noktanos.

HIS CODECES, A few beaten-up ledgers, a couple of shirts, a small leather case with thread and fabric, a rolled-up blanket, a spare pair of battered boots and his Smaragdos. The entirety of his life possessions only occupied a ragged rucksack.

He rubbed his face vigorously and sat on the edge of the rough folded blankets that constituted his humble cod. He had spent the night staring at the moons and starry sky through the cracks of the nailed-together planks, a poor pantomime of a roof.

He would miss all that luxury.

Good while it lasted.

He smiled sadly and grabbed his rucksack with slow, calculated movements. Careful not to make any sound as he stepped outside of his doorless room furtively, casting a quick glance at his father's room across the hearth. There, shadows shifted with the elusive light of the two moons, populating the space. It was difficult to tell if there was a bulge in the cod on the far end, so he decided to play it safe, removing his boots and walking barefoot.

He stopped by the entrance, one hand on the corroded wooden beads of the curtain. He felt a sudden, unshakable urge to do something meaningful. To say farewell.

You survived for twelve years without him. You don't need him.

He set his jaw, painstakingly drew the curtain one thread at a time, and egressed into the Noktanian night.

Daesho's gruesome stories of people falling to their demise, tumbling into the mass of sharp rods and splintered chunks flitted in his mind as he walked along the planks of the swaying scaffolding. He scoffed as he sat on the edge, lowering himself onto the row below with ease, dangling momentarily over the abyss. To Nym, jumping around in the Slums was far from the most perilous activity he had done in his life.

He followed the scaffolding, holding onto the metal railings that didn't look too brittled by rust, and entered the system of manmade tunnels inside the hill.

Torches were mounted on the right wall, painting the passages with sad yellows, oranges and reds. His mind raced with the many possibilities ahead, liberated by the decision he had taken. He was unsure where he was going, though anywhere would be better than the asphyxiating city he had only recently learned to tolerate.

Maybe I'll visit Miramor, check up on the old crew. Or maybe I'll go to Portos. Nok, but I miss the wineries.

He dashed left and right until he reached steps that spiraled deep down into the belly of the Engos Faction headquarters. He descended them two at a time, then three.

Soon, he reached the bottom. From there, it was but several more tunnels to the nearest entry to the Grand Hall, and though his feet were lithe with the imminent prospect of Roaming, he halted right before the door, taken aback by muffled sounds of a multitudinous crowd.

He shut his eyes tightly.

He had completely forgot about the rally.

The entirety of the Engos faction would be congregated on the other side of that door, listening to Boss Kyrdos Engos deliver one of his increasingly regular speeches. Throngs of zealous supporters separated him and the canteen.

Nym contemplated turning on his feet and leaving immediately, but experience told him the worst thing you can do when setting off for a journey with unknown destination is to forget food.

He repositioned his rucksack on his front across his chest and pushed the door open.

He was instantly met with protestations from the bodies pressed up against the edges of the Hall.

"What are you doing?" a man shouted.

"What in Bashork's Hall do you think I'm doing? I'm trying to get in," Nym grunted, finally squeezing in.

He was convinced the man would have been happy to discharge a hearty fist on his face under different circumstances, but he was rather busy being shoved back against the door by the tide of spectators.

Nym was quick to keep his back to the wall, extending arms to the sides. The rucksack on his chest repelled the constant barrage of torsos as he shuffled with short, lateral steps along the edge of the big oval that was the Grand Hall.

People from all over the Slums occupied every available space. The open area on the left, the stands and even the arena below floor level. All of them were enraptured by a tall figure on a balcony high above. Slender frame, incipient beard and surety in his eyes, Boss Engos was a master rhetorician.

"They will tell you the Noktanian League is the most equitable nation in Helados. Well, just this morning a worried dad came to me with a very sick child. A pale, wispy little thing that hadn't eaten in weeks. Food was not going to cut it, so we took her to the Slumwall where the City Watch refused to grant us exit because it was past curfew! That little girl died not two hours ago in her father's arms! Meanwhile, our beloved Senators, which, may I remind you, do *not* represent any of us in the Slums, eat like avaricious pigs! They dine and wine and whore away without a care for the world. They are happy to build a big wall, lock us in and forget about it. Where is the equity!? Where, I ask you!?"

The crowd erupted, screaming and waiving fists in the air. Nym's head banged the wall with one of the pulsations of anger, like waves in a storm.

"How much more must we endure?! Dead are the times of the Old Nobility. Of peasantry. They say every Noktanosi citizen enjoys the same rights."

"Bullshit!" someone yelled, eliciting multiple murmurs of accord.

Engos conceeded with a bow of his head.

"Yes, brother. Bullshit of the highest order. What difference does it make? Call it Lord, or Cyrosi. They repress. They oppress. They indoctrinate the rest of the Noktanian population to make us obey. What do you say to that?"

Chants of *revolution, revolution* filled the hall. Engos waited until the crowd settled again, urging them to calm down with grandiose waves of his hands. Nym kept shuffling along, closer to the other side of the oval.

"Well, brothers and sisters. I am appalled to communicate to you all that, as of this morning, the Senate has passed a bill to revoke low-citizenship status to all Slum inhabitants. Alas, the ultimate insult! To stripe us of what little we have!"

Once more, the crowd swelled with outrage. His left-hand fingers were grazing the frame of the door, but the fluctuation of the multitude pressed hard on Nym. He tiptoed, back flush with the wall and bag providing enough room for him to breathe. He waited for another lull in Engos' speech to attempt a desperate squeeze through the exit, heaving and elbowing indiscriminately.

"So I ask you. I ask you once again, brothers and sisters! When the time comes, will you heed the call? Will you rise against tyranny? Will you follow me into a *better tomorrow*?!"

Just as the explosion of blind furor spread across the hall, Nym shut the door behind him.

"Nok's Grace…" he exhaled, relieved to be rid of bodies mounting up against him. The whole population of the Engos territory must have been pressed in there.

Muffled shouts of revolution travelled far in the austere chamber, a low-ceilinged area with multiple rows of communal tables. The smell of smoke, stew and sweat had seeped into the old wood and crevices on the walls and become chronic.

It wouldn't be long before the masses would dissolve and rush in there, so he headed straight for pantry on the opposite side without further delay.

"Nym?"

He froze with his hand on the pantry doors, partially bending the wood that humidity and time had turned malleable.

"I thought I'd seen you. What are you doing here, son?"

Nym turned to face his father.

"I… was feeling peckish."

Tanor's lips curved into a knowing smile.

"Of course, one does wear travelling clothes and full rucksacks when they feel peckish. How else would one casually have a nocturnal snack?"

Nym looked down, shutting his eyes and rubbing them. Tanor's eyes narrowed into slits.

"I have snuck out of places uncountable times. I know what it looks like. What's the matter, Nym?"

"I am leaving, father."

Tanor rubbed the mangled remnants his right ear, pensive. He sat on the closest table and motioned Nym to do the same.

Nym sighed, staying put.

"I have decided."

"So you have. I think I deserve an explanation at the very least."

You deserve nothing. You abandoned me.

Nym fought the thought, biting hard and turning his head. He tossed his rucksack on the table and sat across his father.

The Broken Oath

Tanor retained his gentle smile and stapled strong fingers, weathered by harsh labour. They faced each other intently. Nobody broke the silence.

Tanor rested his head on the entwined hands, eyes focused on Nym, waiting patiently.

Nym rubbed his head.

"Do you remember," he started reflexively, his own voice startling him, "when we were in the Pyrinosi chain that one time? That one Pyrinoc, what was her name, Dah'Mur or Dar'Mahur?"

"Dara'Madur," Tanor grumbled, nodding.

"That's the one. Nok, I almost shat myself when she kicked down the door of that shed."

"I almost did too."

"She did that thing with her metal cape. Sliced the leg of the bed and made me roll around naked on the ground. There was this nail lying around that really hurt, I think I still have the scar..." Nym trailed off, eyes lost in the wavering flames of a torch in the distance.

"She just threw us out in the middle of the night. I have never felt so cold in my entire life."

Tanor nodded again, caressing the scars of his former right ear. He had lost it to the unforgiving claws of frostbite that very night.

"Remember being down that gorge, heading for Tamasyos' cabin? When we had to decide whether to press on at the bottom and risk being buried by an avalanche or go up the safest route and die of hypothermia?"

"Yes. I remember that very well."

"That's... what I feel... like..." Nym was choking, vision blurring from incipient tears.

No crying, boy. Crying is bad for business.

"Out with it, Nymor. Whatever it is, it will always be worse in your head."

Nym rubbed his head again, then his shoulders.

"Doctor Romos gave me an ultimatum. He arranged for me to have an interview with a doctor in the University Hospital. If I don't go, then I am not to show my face again in his clinic. And I am *not* going."

"You'd rather go back to Roaming," Tanor said, more a statement than a question.

"It is the only thing I know."

"It is the only think you've *known*, until now. I have Roamed all my life, forced by circumstance and opportunity, or lack thereof. There is a reason why I spoke with Tysides—"

"Exactly!" Nym snapped. "*You* spoke with Tysides. *I* didn't. *You* have decided I am to be a Physician."

Tanor's expression softened. He uncrossed his fingers, walked around the table and sat next to Nym. He pulled him closer, hand in the back of his son's neck and they fused in a warm paternal embrace. Nym hated himself for breaking down, unable to keep the tears restrained to his eyes as they rolled down his cheeks.

"Did you know I was a year or so younger than you are now when your mother had you?"

Nym came away from his father chest, sniffling and shaking his head.

"I have never told you how I came to be a Roamer, have I?"

"You haven't. You are from Tys and ended up as a Roamer, that's all I know," Nym said, wiping his tears.

"I was born in Tys, that much is true," Tanor began, returnig to his place across the table. "I don't remember my parents. All I know is that they struck a terrible deal with a City Patron and were forced to sell their youngest child to slavers in order to save his siblings."

Nym came away from the table, furrowing his brow.

"I thought slavery was abolished a half-century ago."

"It was. In the Noktanian League. The Tunedosi city-states followed only very recently."

"How old were you?"

"Hard to say. Couldn't have been more than three."

Nym looked at his father in a brand-new light.

"My first solid memories are of Cruk'Ix, the Crossroads City. My slavers must have sold me to a labour company. Heartless bastards that push children to near-death building roads, repairing buildings, mining... Whatever suited the employers.

"One day, a Tymavir merchant obsessed with the ruins of Old Kahmir bought me off. He was convinced his family were descendants of the Ghart'Avuria Dynasty and needed expendable bodies to carry his stuff across the desert. In this group there was a Roamer, Darma was his name."

Tanor's attention was on the table, eyes unfocused as his mind travelled the feeble paths of memory.

"A strange fellow, he was. Always camping away from the rest. He did take a liking for me, he did. He would explain what it was like to be a Roamer. To see the world, to have the entirety of Helados as your home. I was enraptured by his stories, swearing that was what I wanted to do with my life. In the end, he paid for my Freedom Writ and gave me my first Codex.

"I Roamed for years, Nym. I Roamed without a care for the world, scavenging for food and no roof to sleep under. Trading, brushing shoulders with truly repulsive fellows and shagging anything that moved. And look where it's got me," Tanor looked at Nym, sad smile across his face. "Abandoning a son I didn't know I had. Forever trying to earn his forgiveness. Nok only knows how many others are there…"

That felt supremely odd to Nym, thinking about the possibility of having family other than Tanor. Somewhere in Helados.

"I was in your situation, Nym," Tanor continued. "Rejecting choice, strolling down the path of least resistance, presented with choices that were never made. I wish I had someone to tell me I was *more*. That I could be *more*."

Nym grasped his head from the sides, extending his fingers and pressing down.

It was through his abandonment, after all, how he had been taken advantage and suffered at the hands of men and women. He wondered how Tanor would feel if he knew.

No. That is mine. Mine to bear, mine to keep. Only mine.

"You say I can be more. Tysides says I can be more. Only I know I am *not*. I am not a Cyrosi, I am a nameless bastard that lives in the Slums and thinks they are a palace. They are just words."

"Doubt is poisonous, son. Forget about station and let me ask you something. Do you like what you do with Romos? When you help people, heal them, learn the ways of Biothos?"

Nym surrendered, nodding.

"We spend most of our time doing what we think people expect of us. What fits the conventions of society, the mould, what is most accepted. We rarely chose to do what we *want*. Nym, forget about the world and just *do*."

That last word carried finality. A challenge, even. A future he could fulfil.

A bastard orphan. A pleasure boy. A Roamer. A Guild-certified Physician. Sure makes for a great story.

Previously immiscible pieces of himself that perhaps, just perhaps, could meet without clashing. Nym looked up, overwhelmed by emotion.

"I'm not sure I can do it."

"You certainly cannot if you don't at least try."

Nym wiped tears again. A different sort of tears.

"I… I would have to go back and forth to the Hospital, and it takes half a day to walk Guild's Way and… and… where am I staying? It's just not possible."

Tanor gestured his son to stop just when the doors to the canteen opened and a sea of people began spilling inside.

"You leave that to me. Come on, let's pay someone a little visit."

Faction Boss Kyrdos Engos conducted his meetings in a room several floors above the canteen, a cross-section of a cylinder with an impressive glass wall opposite the door overlooking the underground arena in the Grand Hall. There was a narrow exit next to it that led to the balcony from which Engos delivered his rabblerousing speeches.

Nym had expected something radically different.

The only furniture was a *U* carved directly out of stone that surrounded a crackling firepit. Discoloured and thready cushions and blankets covered it. To their left, a squat table with an assortment of documents and a chest of drawers that had seen better days.

That was it. Nym had expected the opulence that invariably comes with power, just as he had experienced in every single place he had visited across Helados. Yet the only difference between a regular Slum dwelling and that room was the size.

That, and the fact that the Five Faction Bosses that ruled in the Slums were sat together around the fire. Harsh faces of harsher people you did not *ever* want to come across.

"I am so sorry Boss Engos, I was not aware you were in a meeting. I will come later," Tanor bowed his head and retreated sheepishly, pushing Nym out.

"Non-sense!" Engos stood like a spring, resting one hand on the shoulder of a man of impressive bulk that was far from amused at the physical contact.

"We were just saying how very long it has been since the Bosses had a harmonious sit-down, weren't we? I will let my good friends to get re-acquainted while we speak, I'm sure they don't mind."

The other four Bosses looked at each other without uttering a word but Engos was already walking around the stone *U* and gesturing a stunned Tanor and Nym toward the corridor.

"Nymor, pleasure to see you again," Engos said, shutting the door behind him. His height impeded him to stand fully erect in the corridor, though even with his head slightly tilted he exuded confidence. Leadership. Nym doubted there were few others that could manage looking this calm while locking away all Faction Bosses in a room.

"Tanor, have you had a thought about what we discussed?"

Nym furrowed his eyebrows.

"I have, Boss."

"Kyrdos, please. Well?"

"I accept. On one condition."

Kyrdos Engos smiled with candour.

"I wouldn't expect any less from you Tanor!"

Nym's head darted right and left as the two men spoke, forcing his brain to follow a conversation where he was missing half the information.

"My son has been granted an interview to study under a prominent doctor, but the University Hospital is in the mainland."

Boss Engos waved his right hand in the air.

"Say no more. You can meet me later and we will discuss the details of the deal further. Nymor, your father sees great potential in you, and I know for a fact your father's intuition is to be trusted! You have the Faction's full support. Whatever you may need, you come directly to me."

Nym looked at Tanor with befuddled expression.
What deal are they talking about?
His father seemed to be spurring him to say something with his eyes.
"I…" Nym began tentatively. Another nod from Tanor. "I suppose we could start with a horse."

CHAPTER 5
* * *
Revenge
Damyra Phalmeria. The Base. Rich Quarter. The Great City of Noktanos. Forty-eight years ago.

"THEY ARE DEAD, Damyra. *Dead.* Do you not understand that?"

She was sat by the big window, where many hours had been spent bearing interminable lessons from the eclectic tirade of tutors her parents had appointed. Parrah, Portosi, Noktanian or Tunedosi, regardless of their origins and bodies of knowledge, Damyra would always soak up what they had to offer in mere weeks, then spend endless dull afternoons training her patience. That window to the outside had been her only reprieve. Buried in cushions and blankets, Damyra had comfortably observed the comings and goings of the Noktanian elite, memorising patterns by simple observation.

She saw the burly men outside carrying her effects and shifted with unease on the now cold stone bench, striped of its expensive furnishings. So crass, they were. Mindlessly tossing her chairs, crates, wardrobes, tables, books, and bookshelves.

"Yes, Uncle. I understand that very well," she responded, flat voice echoing in the completely naked room.

"Then why must you complicate things so, child?"

Her Uncle was chiding her from the entrance arch of the Phalmeria estate, bulbous face interred on some ledgers. He was a repugnant man. The closest personification of a worm in Damyra's eyes. Sickly pale skin, withered, a crown of wispy grey hair at the base of his bald head.

"You're meeting with the Pynarios family and that is the end of it," he said, tapping onto the papers with his finger. "We need them, Nok knows my sister had no mind for finances, and your Father was always too distracted, the poor fool. Atrocious, simply atrocious."

Damyra had long stopped caring for his Uncle's remarks, developing a keen sense to making her ears impermeable to his poisonous, contempt-laden voice. A few more objects, guarded by the Phalmeria family for centuries were hauled into the carriages parked outside, like rotten fruit at the end of a market day, to be disposed of. Rather, to be sold to the highest bidder by order of Uncle Peraklios.

She didn't despair. No, that was over now. She had already done all the despairing. And the crying. She had cried and cried for days on end. She had shouted too, screamed until her throat was raw. None of that had changed the fact that her parents were still very much dead indeed.

No more of that.

One of the men entered the room, meekly addressing her Uncle.

"That's the last of it, m'Lord," he said, bowing his head servilely.

"Good. Much obliged," Uncle Peraklios said, waving him out as he continued writing on the papers.

Damyra noticed the low citizen hanging by the archway, not fully retreating.

"You have just taken everything I own, you brute. What more could you want? Are you seriously expecting money? How should I pay, then? With my body? Is that what you want, you filth?" she said with emotionless voice. Words and tone incongruous, her face to the window.

"N... no, of course! Pardon me, m'Lady, erm... Cyrosi, pardon me," the Pharosi said, bowing his head half a dozen times more before leaving.

Her Uncle was oblivious to the exchange. "Alos is a portentous match, if I say so myself," he carried on. "There's always his brother Vysios. A bit odd for my taste, unlucky lad has the White Touch, but he would do just fine."

"Are you done?" she snapped, standing from the bench, planting her feet firmly on the marble floors.

Uncle Peraklios rose his eyes from the ledger, staring her down from the other side of the room. Damyra was aware caving his dumb face in would not return his parents from the dead, but it couldn't possibly hurt.

"What?"

"Are you done talking?" she said again.

He continued to stare at her, frowning as though she was speaking some strange, exotic language. Absolutely *no one* spoke like that to Peraklios, head of House Ivanos. The more pleasure it caused her.

The astounded silence more than sufficed as acknowledgement. She left, running out of the estate with no destination in mind, nothing more than her house toga and her sandals on her.

Her aimless sprint saw her leaving the Base, legging it across Astis Way and past the Slopes. She started breathing heavily, thoroughly winded by the time she reached the Western Avenue, traversing this portion of Noktanos. She slowed down, but her feet took her forth, joining the masses flowing toward the heart of the city. She simply wanted to be away from Uncle Peraklios, from his treatment and the removal of her *everything*. Most of all, she wanted to be away from having no saying in anything happening to her.

Central Square was a swirling vortex of people, a maelstrom of bodies fed by the ceaseless influx from the four cardinal avenues, the imposing Senate Building its calm centre, separated from the swarm by guarded steps. Damyra was forced to relinquish control to the multitudinous movement, just as one wouldn't try to control the currents of the sea.

She walked the whole circumference of the Square, repulsed by the instant barrage to her senses. Shouts from vendors in Neokahmirian, Tunedosi and languages she didn't recognise, sour odours and sweaty shoves. She shored up naturally with the rest of the crowd by the left-side of the Western Avenue, where those flowing human tides were slowing down. When she came to a halt, she craned her neck this way and that to get a better view of what laid ahead.

Finally, the big, smelly man in front of her moved to the right and she was able to see a ramshackle platform. It had clearly been erected in a rush, in fact calling it a platform was exuding optimism. It was but a series of planks held together with brittle chains, a mixture of rubble and sandbags, and even a broad-shouldered man pushing upwards, as foundations.

A girl, not much older than herself was perched atop, speaking to the growing rabble and gesticulating vivaciously toward the Senate.

"... responsible, are they not? How many of you have lost friends in the Limthosi Wars? How many?" she pressed on, keen eyes tracked on the swelling crowd. Damyra had never seen so many grown men and women that enraptured.

There was a raising wave of ayes and grunts, even some slapping sounds as several men banged their fists on their chests, a salute she had seen in the Legions during the ceremonies her father used to drag her to.

"Fought the pale bastards myself, I did!" shouted the man that had been blocking her view a moment ago. The girl squatted, eliciting a pained grunt from the man beneath the planks as they creaked and shifted. She encouraged him with an enthusiastic wave of her hands.

"What's your name, brother?"

Damyra was struck by her manner of speech. She spoke loudly and clearly, mellodious, compellingly.

"Darhos."

"Speak up, Darhos, speak of your experiences in the front."

"I've been a commissioned soldier my whole life, grew up in the Legions. Came back a hexad or so ago, I did. After the bloodiest battle of the lot, nearly cracked the bastards' exterior defenses before Centurion Wesios called retreat."

"Did you lose any friends during that battle?"

The man Darhos had his fists closed tightly.

"Don't know a single man that didn't."

"And why did you come back, Darhos. Why did the Legions abandon the cause?"

"Some deal or other, they said."

The girl stood, pointing with zeal to the centre of the Square.

"I'll tell you what happened. *They* happened!" she shouted, a shrill scream that suspended the veritable act and showed her real age. "What do you think, Darhos? Do you think we should have pulled back? Left our fallen brothers die for nothing?"

Damyra could hear the man grinding his teeth.

"NEVER!"

"The cowards that call themself *Senators*. They are nothing but a bunch of liars! They say they represent us! Represent us..." she said, her voice cracking. She seized the opportunity and lowered her tone conspiratorily, eyeing the crowd.

"I'll tell you what, so fond the Electorate is of their polls, we'll do a little polling of our own here. You there," she pointed to a tall man by Damyra's left. "Was the Senate representing you when they spent your taxes, all your taxes, thousands upon thousands of drakmas, and spilled wantonly the blood of good Noktanosi citizens securing the Tunedosi Protectorate? Only to call back the Navy and let the Krossosi pillage the islands?!"

"NO!"

Damyra sensed the masses pressing from behind angrily. She took several steps forward and turned. She noticed how the vortex of bodies was behaving differently, changing its flowing pattern. People had stopped coming from the Southern Avenue, more and more stopping to hear the girl's rousing speech.

Perhaps I should return.

"And you over there, with the cart. Do you feel safe travelling to Moxos or Ukos? Are you happy with the constant harrassment of the Zereri savages?"

Damyra stopped. She turned back.

"NO!"

"No," Damyra repeated herself, a furious whisper.

"Would you rather build a big wall and hide behind it, just like Senator Blongatos proposes? Or would you rather stand up and fight?"

"YES! FIGHT!"

"And you, brave Darhos, were they representing you when they made Centurion Wesios retreat when victory was assured? Letting your friends perish for *nothing*?"

"NO!"

"So, you see, I ask you again. Do they represent us?!"

A resounding NO that seemed to come from every throat in the Square.

"They don't! Of course they don't—"

The zealous girl stopped mid-sentence, eyes glancing at the distance.

There by the gaping mouth of the Southern Avenue the masses had parted to let through an organised line of Senatorial forces. Red and bronze armour, hefty ceremonial shields called scothos and golden caps. Damyra recognised the elite soldiers, the Praetorion, tasked with guarding the most important members of the Noktanian government. They were formed up in a perfect double-lined square around some men with expensive togas, complexly wrapped over their torso and leaving the right arm in the air.

Damyra could see at least fifty Praetorion, locked shields moving the populace like a hoe carving soil.

"Oh, and there you have them. There you have them!" the girl continued from her precarious heights. "Senator Blongatos. Senator Marakavios, Senator Kernos, and Senator Amanthios. So terrified, so scared shitless of those they presumably represent they need the Praetorion to protect them! I say if they truly represented us, they would be unafraid! Proudly walking among us!"

The man under the plank lowered it, yanked at the girl's leg.

"That's quite enough! Leave it be for now, speech over," she heard the man saying.

No need, as it turned out. The girl wouldn't have been able to continue eitherway. The girl had ignited a spark in the unhappy masses, a spark that had burnt into a full inferno. Damyra was rocketed to the sides, first lightly, then increasing to a frightening intensity.

Raging chants intermingled in her shock-addled mind as more and more people grew brave enough to confront the Praetorion, throwing whatever was at hand to the formation.

"…want to fight! Cowards!"

"…died, all of them did and…"

"…slay them, I will. With my own hands if…"

She struggled to stay on her feet, elbowing, punching and grabbing with no discretion.

Half of the Praetorion changed formation. The Senators were rushed up the staircase and into the Senate Building whilst the rest of the forces rearranged themselves into a sharp V that advanced rapidly in the crowd.

Heading straight for the girl on the platform.

They covered the distance with astounding speed, leaving little time for reaction.

Suddenly, several of the scothos parted and a torrent of fire burst forth as they advanced.

"*Eysos, domon vosu Exios. Arrantos!*" the girl shouted, thrusting her hands forwards. Damyra's jaw hun. She was in command of the winds, a monstrous current shooting from her and dissipating the pillar of flames.

"How did she…" she whispered.

She saw the girl thrashing about on the ground, platform collapsed on top of the man that had been bearing most of its weight.

"Leo. Leo, get up! Get up!" she was calling desperately, undeterred formation barrelling through to her.

Damyra looked to her right, where a horse was yoked to a cart. The animal was battling against its binding, unable to move because of a wooden wedge lodged under the cartwheel.

She moved without thinking. She bent down, extracted the wedge and the horse and cart shot forth, plunging uncontrollably into the spiked formation. The animal was impaled by the many spikes, cart breaking into a thousand pieces, yet they had carried enough momentum, and surprise, to dissamble the formation.

They were now looking at her.

"Oh."

In a show of inhuman coordination, something only attained by hours and hours of training, all spears left their holding hands in unison. A deathly volley hurtled toward Damyra.

Even as she threw herself on the ground, she realised how futile that was.

She was buffeted from the side as another gust of wind blew hard on the projectiles, deviating their trajectory far to the right.

Damyra dared retire her arms from her head.

"Come on! Let's go!" the girl was beckoning shocked Damyra. She scrambled to her feet and ran full tilt toward her and the Western Avenue as the soldiers dropped their heavy scothos and unseathed their xyphos.

They gave chase.

Damyra ran with abandon, pushed by a survival instinct she wasn't aware she had. Something she probably would rejoice at if it weren't for the circumstances. It was exhilarating.

"We can't go back through the Rich Quarter! the Forbidden! We'll be trapped between them and the Quarter Watch!" the girl screamed as they run madly through the Avenue, dodging passersby as best they could.

"Follow me!"

The man took a sharp turn to the left, entering a secondary street. Damyra looked back before turning and regretted it. The Praetorion were tailing closely behind. One of them had uttered an incantation.

The cobblestones broke away and a boulder flew in her direction, narrowly missing and crashing against the façades of nearby buildings, sending an avalanche of stones down.

"Quick!" the girl said, grabbing her toga, pulling her savagely in a neck-breaking change of direction down some dark alleyway.

They did just that several times, following no apparent pattern, led by the man who was proving to have an astounding cardiopulmonary capacity for physical exertion.

Her lungs were on fire.

Right before she felt as though she couldn't possibly carry on without fainting, the man skidded to a halt. He squatted, inserting his fingers under a loose slab of stone at the back of a house, grunting. He pulled on something and the cobblestones parted, revealing a hidden tunnel. There was an eroded rope tied to a metal hook, frayed and mossy. Despite the uninviting stench coming from it, the man squeezed his bulk in, both hands about the rope and disappeared into the ground.

"In! Now! Or the Equios will get us!" the girl implored, hands on Damyra's shoulder.

She looked at the hole, dark and fetid.

Despite herself, in that moment, she saw sense in those words. They might have outrun the heavily armoured Praetorion, but they wouldn't the cavalry. Besides, she trusted this girl for some reason. She had done ever since she saw her atop the platform in the Central Square.

Damyra grabbed the rope.

Another triggered mechanism had slid the stone into place as all three waited in the darkness. The only light came from a thin slit a dozen feet above, between the contraption and the cobblestones.

Tense minutes passed as they heard incoherent shouts outside. Eventually, her eyes adapted to the darkness. She saw they had descended into some tunnelage adjacent to the sewers, hence the nauseating efluvium. Minutes kept passing, heart rate stabilising, tingling of her fingers subsiding.

The bulky man grabbed her toga and pulled up, towing her whole weight without much difficult.

"Who are you? Who do you working for?" he barked, pinning her against the damp wall of the tunnel. "Are you with the Corps?"

He punctuated each question with a thudding shove against the wet surface. Dust, cobwebs and Nok knows what other muck showered her, making breathing difficult.

"It's alright, Leo. She's obviously not with the Corps, she's just a child for Nok's sake!"

Leo dropped her to the ground. Gathering all her cold indifference, Damyra coughed up and dusted herself off, acting as though they had only bumped in the street.

"No matter. I suppose by its mere biological definition, yes, I am a child, though you are not very far away from infancy yourself," she said to the girl.

"Ha! Doesn't sound like a child to me, and damn her if she's wrong," Leo cackled, stepping behind the girl. He kept laughing as he fumbled with something on the ground.

"What's your name, valiant non-child?"

Brief flashes illuminated the tight space as Leo worked flint and stone to light a torch.

"Damyra."

She nodded.

"Why did you get involved, Damyra?"

"I..." she vacillated. *Why* had she done it?

"Does it matter? We've got to get to Londos before they call a curfew," Leo said.

"What you said in the square... It must have got to me, somehow," Damyra found she was indeed surprised by her reaction. "My parents were killed by Zereri raiders half a year ago."

The girl expression turned solemn. She squatted next to Damyra and placed her hand softly on her shoulder, a gesture Damyra would have found unacceptable, repulsive even, coming from anyone else. Hers, however, made Damyra's strength falter.

"I understand. What happened?"

Damyra took some moments to gain a composure she was losing.

"Father was a diplomat. Him and Mother were on their way to Lymtoros. The riders..." she trailed off, voice wavering. "Nobody survived," Damyra said flatly.

"I'm very sorry to hear that, Damyra. That's something you should not carry on your own. How do you feel now?"

Damyra stared at the ground.

"I feel nothing."

The girl clicked her tongue, grasping her shoulder tighter.

"See, that's no good, valiant Damyra. There can be no change without feeling, without *passion*. What is it you want?"

She didn't have to think too hard for that one.

"Revenge."

The girl smiled, standing back up and offering her a hand.

"Then stand up. I think we might be able to help with that."

Damyra took her hand.

"I'm Alda. Welcome to Nok's Voice."

CHAPTER 6
* * *
Xhalenfros
Nymor Strethos. Town of Bamoria. Fist of Nok.

THE HOUSE OF Nok in the coastal town of Bamoria struck the ninth bell when Nym handed over the reins of the exhausted horse to a jittery stableboy.

"Thank you, Master, thank-you-thank-you," the boy said, words garbling together as he bowed down multiple times. Nym flipped a dorok, a half-drakma, in his direction. The boy grabbed it quickly in midair and disappeared round the back of the inn.

"That'll be ten drakmas," the innkeeper said from the front entrance, patting his protruding belly. Nym looked at him from below, clicking his tongue and moving his head side to side.

"You must think me dull-minded if you expect me to pay ten drakmas, innkeeper. If I pay more than five, I'll throw myself in The Eye of Nok."

"I'll have seven," the innkeeper said casually, as though he was doing him a favour. He was digging into his gums with a stick and the vacuum sound he was making with his tongue, trying to fish some remnant of his meal, made Nym's stomach to twist.

"I'll give you six *and* won't report you to the Town Watch for blatant robbery."

The innkeeper rolled his eyes and extended his hand.

The Broken Oath

Bamoria was a small town, barely more than a dozen inns, a market, and a House of Nok around a rudimentary dirt square. The only reason for its existence was that the University Hospital was within walking distance.

The town bustled with travellers on their way to the University from the Noktanian capital, farmers from nearby towns trying to sell their stock and Roamers shouting out their Trade. Nym walked into the flowing mass, the cacophony of labouring society like music to his ears.

He secured his rucksack on his back and joined the torrent of people leaving the town to the east of Bamoria. They followed along a big road, a connecting thoroughfare to the Hospital and further ahead to the Spine mountains and to a tunnel traversing the chain.

Nym had heard of the University Hospital before, a one-of-a-kind medical facility. Everyone in the Noktanian League had. Yet nothing could have prepared him for the moment when he first saw it.

He summited a short bulge of the terrain and contemplated the view.

Rolling hills against a backdrop of the Serpent Spine, a sprawling complex of Gigos buildings. Cubes and prisms of black and grey fused in a monumental rise of sharp lines.

Before long, he was standing in front of a monstrous staircase leading up to the big prism that made for the main building. His pause for admiration didn't last long though, as he was forcibly pushed aside by a distraught woman.

"Ah, Nok, please, please, help her!"

She ran after a pair of burly men carrying a stretcher, an inert body bobbing on top of it. They dashed to the left section of the complex, where he assumed the Emergency Department was located.

Four sets of doors preceded an ample hall where patients from all over the Noktanian League queued endlessly and sat on rows upon rows of seats. He ambulated, lost, until he naturally shored to a circular desk.

"May I help you?"

A man in white uniform smiled at him from behind the desk.

"I have an appointment with Senior Physician Danos."

"Most certainly. Doctor Danos' office is on the seventh floor, you need to take those stairs," the man pointed to an arch separating the main entrance hall, the other sections and the stairs.

"Once you are there, look at the signage for Senior Physician Offices."

The man sported an unnatural smile, eerie in its out-of-place extravagance. Nym spent a second thinking about having to smile like that all day long as part of his job and shivered.

"I hope you have a wonderful day!" he chirped as Nym walked away.

"I hope so too."

The Hospital was truly a marvel of engineering, its elegance and functionality centred around how simple it was. The prism had an empty space in its central axis running from the reception area to the ceiling, where a massive glass dome had been erected. It meant the Heladian sun provided more than enough illumination all throughout the many floors, which had corridors with balconies overlooking the central space. Luckily, he soon found a door with the right sign.

He entered the big anteroom, ample chairs and tables in a waiting area and a reception desk with yet another white-uniformed man perusing stacks of ledgers.

"You must be Nymor Strethos," he said, face as radiant as the Eye of Nok on a summer's day.

Where do they get all this people from?

"Please have a sit. Doctor Danos will be with you in a short while."

Nym sat down near a rectangular window, craning his neck around. The glass pane was fully transparent, allowing for views of Bamoria, the Guild's Way and Noktanos far in the distance.

"It is a spectacular view, isn't it?" a voice from several chairs over startled him.

Nym was so submerged in his thoughts he didn't notice he wasn't alone. Two clear green eyes, clearer in contrast with her obsidian-black skin, peered at him from across the anteroom. He simply nodded.

"You never really see these kinds of views where I am from."

"Ei'Tulah?" Nym guessed. The majority of Sunkissed in the south of Helados were from the Peninsulas.

The girl offered a knowing smile.

"No, from Tymavir."

"Ahh, close enough," he joked. The girl just stared at him.

"Wars have been fought for that *close enough*, you know?"

Nym was taken aback.

"I do know. I have been to Tymavir. Beautiful city in its own right," he said, changing the subject. He should know better than to joke about Peninsular identity with a Tymavirian. "What brings you to the heart of the Noktanian League?"

"Studies. I am pursuing a career in me—"

The door to the office opened.

A man in his early forties stepped into the waiting area. He was in surprisingly good shape, lithe and broad-shouldered. He wore a tight-fitting Guild-issued scrubs for medical professionals.

"Amyra Surk'Imla and Nymor Strethos."

They looked at each other, confused.

"Doctor Danos, I think there must be some sort of confusion. I was under the impression I was going to be interviewed for the position…" Amyra trailed off, hoping her befuddled expression would drive the point.

The Broken Oath

"Your impression is correct. You are being interviewed to study under me. So is Nymor here. Come along, we don't have all day. I have patients to see."

Amyra stared at Nym. He could almost sense the nature of her curiosity changing from meeting a stranger to assessing an opponent.

You didn't think this was going to be easy, did you?

Nym had a strong feeling that the office was a perfect physical simile of Doctor Danos. Two sober chairs in front of a slender desk, a view of Noktanos in the back, a gurney and half-empty shelves to the right.

Functional. Cold. Clinical and effective.

They sat in front of Danos' desk.

The Physician wasted no time. He walked over to the big glass wall, hands crossed on the small of his back and looked away.

"Why is the Hospital *here*?"

Amyra answered instantly.

"The University Hospital is the best medical facility on planet Virthos. We are here to provide the best medical care to our patients."

A clearly rehearsed answer. No reaction came from Danos, who kept staring at Noktanos in the distance.

That's not what he means, is it?'

"I believe The School of Physicians needed a hospital close to both Noktanos and the School main complex, as well as being easily accessible by all cities of the Noktanian League," Nym said.

Danos faced turned to face them. He nodded several times without uttering a word and sat down on the desk.

"Someone has catastrophic blood loss. What do you do?"

"Trigger code blue and rush the patient to an operating theatre. You need an anaesthetist, two surgeons and a standard squad of nurses." Again, Amyra answered with rapid-fire speed.

Danos nodded again and stared at Nym, head slightly bent to the side.

Is he... expecting something different?

"Erm... Patients don't tend to just *catastrophically bleed* when they are in hospital. It would be because of an accident. If the haemorrhage is caused by an object, leave it in place and attempt to tourniquet proximal to it. Before you do anything about the repairing, you need to gain vascular control. I would prepare some bags of blood."

Amyra turned in his seat, a frown of confusion on her face.

"We are not allowed to do Sanguine Transfigurations."

"You... We aren't? Well, I would if I didn't want my patient to die."

Amyra carried on staring down at him, eyebrows bunched together. Nym was more interested in the smirk tugging at Danos' lips.

"A woman in her early twenties presents to your clinic. She can't sleep."

"How long has the insomnia lasted?" Amyra lunged forward on her seat.

"She has had trouble falling asleep for the better part of her entire life, but now it has deteriorated. She suffers severe insomnia."
"Was she born in the Noktanian League?"
What does that have to do with anything?
Danos, however, raised an eyebrow.
"She happens to be from the northernmost point of Helados, born in a close-knit community in Kausanos."
Amyra smiled.
"She has Asomnos syndrome, also known as familial insomnia. Pelioros Asomnos described the disease when travelling the north of Helados. It is caused by inbreeding in the island of Kausanos."
Oh. That.
Nym had never heard of such thing before, but he had to say something. He couldn't just stay silent.
"I have been told the mark of a good Physician is to admit one's own limitations. I am afraid I did not know about Asomnos syndrome, so I would trust my colleague's opinion on this matter."
Danos turned back to Amyra.
"What would your advice be for this young woman?"
"It is important to do expectation management and break the bad news. It is an incurable disease that will likely lead to her demise. I would use Professor Baros' protocol for breaking bad news. On top of that, I would offer some sedative potions like Myrphid extract or Molosbark, making sure I explain it is purely palliative, not curative."
Nym started sweating. Amyra was clearly an enrolled medical student at clinical stage in the School of Medicine of the Guild University. She had access to the best professors and resources in Helados. Nym had his Biothos Codex, Tysides' sparse attention and a handful of outdated books in his clinic.
He shifted on the suddenly very uncomfortable, hostile chair.
"A child has continuous seizures, twenty to thirty every hour."
"Any other symptoms?" Nym asked.
"No."
"History of symptoms?" Amyra said with an inquisitive index finger over her lips.
"She was fine until she was six years of age. After her Coming day, she started suffering the seizures and deteriorating ever since."
Why is this familiar?
Amyra carried on with her questioning.
"Any family history of seizures?"
"No."
"Any other neurological conditions?"
"No."
"Anything critical that happened around her Coming day? Something that precipitated the attacks?"

"On her Coming day she did the same thing as she always did. After breaking fast she would play in the fields behind her family's stead before her tutoring. After that, her extended family would come for a celebration."

"Has she visited any Physicians before with regards to this problem?"

"She has obtained opinions from the best Physicians and Professors in the Noktanian League, yours truly included."

"So, this is a real case?" Amyra asked wide-eyed, both hands on the chair's armrest.

Danos laced his fingers.

"All of them are."

"What is her current management plan?"

"Nothing we have tried has worked."

Nym wasn't fully listening. His mind had been jerked back to one of his travels, when his father had taken him to trade in a Tunedosi island. There was this boy, his mother told Tanor and young Nym about the Shakes, how they came suddenly, and nothing could be done except for some desperate treatment from a healer. Nym remembered sitting on the wooden deck, feet splashing on the warm shallow waters. The boy was inside the cabin, bedridden and unable to form any words, forever chained to dull-mindedness.

But why was he dull-minded?

He perked up with excitement.

"I don't know exactly what is causing the seizures," Nym jumped in, "but I do know the most effective way of stopping them is excising half of the child's brain."

Amyra shook her head with vigour.

"Hemispherectomy as a treatment has been continually regarded as a savage procedure and the most prominent surgeons recommend against it."

"With an unknown cause and no known management, if you want to stop the deteriorating symptoms, which will undoubtedly lead to an untenable state of body and mind, this is the only route."

"Well, I strongly disagree," Amyra repeated. "According to Professor Horkos, we shall never recur to treatments that are worse than the malady. Hemispherectomy is *barbaric* and would cripple the patient beyond recognition. It is also in contravention of the First Pillar of the Hal'Gamac Oath. *Pir'Madur Nun'Sa Horiva.*"

Nym rolled his eyes.

"Really? You *had* to say it in Old Kahmirian?"

Senior Physician Levantios Danos stood.

"That shall suffice."

He turned and walked to the window, his back to them once again.

Nym and Amyra looked at each other.

"Well?" Danos said after a few moments, eyes far away in the distance. "What are you two still doing here? I want you to have a good night sleep before I see you tomorrow at seventh bell. *Sharp.*"

"B... both of us?"

"I am not keen on repeating myself, Amyra Surk'Imla. Yes, both of you."

Amyra's shoulders sagged, tension fading away. She even smiled to Nym.

What... was that*?!*

They shuffled from the chairs and headed for the door.

Before they left, Danos turned his head toward them slightly.

"And bring me at least three differential diagnoses for the seizure patient."

There wasn't going to be any such thing as a 'good night sleep' for Nym.

The day had brought unexpected successes, and the lack of expectation doubled the feeling of victory. Something like that surely called for a hearty celebration. He would let morning Nym deal with the consequences. Morning Nym would hate present Nym, but he was a big boy, he would get over it.

After the interview, Amyra had given him one of her cryptic looks and a succinct farewell. He had strolled out of the University Hospital, thinking the smiles from the men in white were far less obnoxious, and collected his horse from the inn in Bamoria.

All of a sudden, Engos' few remaining drakmas for the day in his possession felt awfully heavy. With pride in his chest swelling, euphoria all sense felling, he mindlessly directed his mount south.

After all, it was but a short ride from Bamoria, across the tunnel and onto the Guild's Association University.

His Roaming had taken him to many different places all over Helados, he had seen marvels of architecture that defied human intelligence.

For a second time, he was terribly underprepared to take in the views of the Guild University.

Back in its conception, each School had been given carte blanche for the creation of their main buildings as part of a contest. A panel of judges from each Guild decided which School would get a starting budget considerably higher than the others as prize. The endless possibilities that Nokator offered, and the ingenuity of the Builders resulted in constructions equal parts outlandish and breathtaking.

He guided his horse to the University Entrance, a wide arch that bottlenecked everyone, through it he could see the Schools in all their splendor.

To either side of a main central avenue, an enormous tree with sprawling branches the size of a mountain, the School of Natural Sciences. A flowing sea of metal traversed by a long spear, the School of Metallurgy. An enormous, solitary slab of stone, the School of Law. Everywhere his eyes landed, there was something incredible that required his attention.

Those constant distractions almost caused the banning of his entrance.

"I *said*, stop there!"

Nym blinked, twisting on the saddle to the right. Two University Watch guards, donning their usual black leather padding with chains crossed over their chests were pushing their way through the crowd of robed students and visitors.

"...hear me saying bloody stop!? Horses are not allowed in the premises!"

"Dismount, you halfwit!"

Nym was too excited to pay any attention to their manners. He apologised and dismounted, handing over the reins to the guard that had stepped in front of the horse. He was an ugly pile of muscles and sinew.

"Do I look like a stableboy, halfwit?"

"You look like someone that wants this horse out of your beautiful Entrance. The quicker you tell me where to stable my trusted stallion, the faster I'll be out of your way."

The guard stared down at him. All he got from Nym was an unwavering innocent smile.

"Take it outside the arch and around. There are stables there."

After his horse was stabled, he made sure not to cross paths with the guards again and joined the masses flowing into the avenue.

As he advanced, flanked by the strange buildings, he overhead several students with blue robes talking about a place called the Red River Tavern in the School of Law. It just so struck him like a good a place like any other to conduct his ill-advised celebrations.

He followed the group from afar to the School of Law, the complex closest to the Entrance. The Main Avenue gave off smaller paths to grand staircases and ample squares in front of the main buildings.

Nym contemplated the gigantic monolithic slab from below. No windows or balconies. Endless, solid stone. He whistled in admiration.

The Red River tavern was behind it, clearly a place where professors and law students met regularly. He straggled for a couple of minutes and approached the maroon door. As expected, the ambience was electric, buzzing with activity. He caught disjointed fragments of ten dozen conversations as he approached the bar.

"...the best, though not as good as..." "...come? That's a shame, I really wanted to see her..." "...family was not happy, at all..." "...that barrel and roll it over here, Kothos!"

Nym was imbued by it, a smile painted on his face he could not repress.

He strolled with a spring on his step toward the bar, where a bearded man busied himself with customers' orders. Pints were filled with precision, cups and mugs exchanging hands, beer and liquor in tall glasses and jugs flowing to no avail.

"What will it be?" he asked with husky voice when he reached Nym.

"What is the finest wine on your shelves?"

The tender raised an eyebrow and looked at Nym, up and down.

"The sort served only to Portosi City Patrons in their palaces."

Nym's smile wavered.

"Perhaps your second-finest would suit best."

"I'd say third. Or fourth."

Nym looked down at his worn-out attire. Shirt laces threading at the end, trousers and boots dusty from the travelling. He blushed slightly and nodded.

"Krossosi wine it is, then," the man grumbled.

Nym frowned. He didn't even know the Krossosi made wine.

His ears perked up at a high-pitched sound to his right. His eyes rested on a face with a mischievous smile, eyes the colour of the sun conspicuously darting from the glass in her hands to Nym's increasingly red face.

"Joyous, is it?" Nym said. "Rejoicing at others' misfortunes?"

The girl looked to the sides, as though she didn't know why Nym was addressing her. When it was clear she was not to fool Nym, her lips turned into a smile that would convert the Elder Council to pre-Kahmirism.

"Infinitely better than rejoicing at my own."

"Isn't that a Limthosi postulate? What was it, Xahma or other?"

"*Xhalenfros,*" she said.

"Well, I don't know about you, but I have always thought the Limthosi are a tad strange." Nym had his hand on the side of his mouth, feigning secrecy.

"I agree with you lad," the bearded tender startled him. "But don't tell Kothos I said that." He pointed to the redhaired man wrestling with a barrel. He thrusted a slender cup with a red-black liquid in Nym's hand and left to attend the ever-growing clientele.

Nym took a sip and grimaced, sticking his tongue and emitting a guttural *ugh*.

The girl's hearty laughter that ensued was Nokator poetry to Nym's ears.

"Xhalenfros," he raised the cup toward her.

"Xhalenfros," she repeated, amused.

Nym ventured another swig and regretted it instantly. He shook his head.

"That's a definite no." He held the glass with the murky fluid in front of his face.

"Did you know the Krossosi make wine?" he asked the girl, mustering enough courage to walk over and sit next to her. Her body language remained the same, not that Nym was paying too much attention. He was enraptured by her golden eyes.

"As a matter of fact, I did. My father is a physician and he uses it to sterilise surgical equipment. Works wonders."

"Isn't that great," Nym pushed the glass as far as he could. The bartender shouted from the other side of the bar.

"You still paying for that, boy!"

Nym put both his hands up in the air. He fished a drakma and placed it on the bar.

"So, your father is a Physician? Hopefully I'll be one myself soon enough."

"Is that so?"

Nym couldn't get enough of her. Noktanian bronze skin, curvaceous figure, beautiful waves of auburn hair. She was wearing the blue robes of a law student and had a hefty tome by her side. And her eyes. They had a maddening effect on him.

"That's the reason why I'm celebrating. You are looking at Senior Physician Levantios Danos' newest understudy!"

"So that's what you are doing. Celebrating, is it? Alone and with a glass of Krossosi wine?" she looked at him, propping her head with her hand. The gesture instilled a painful longing feeling in his chest. He placed his right hand over his heart and moaned.

"Ompf! But you hurt me so. In any case, I am not alone, am I? Apart from the jabs at my crumbling dignity, you are quite pleasant company."

Her lips drew a flat line.

"As much as that flatters me, I came here to brush up on Kahmirian law ahead of my exam, and it is getting rowdy." She downed the rest of her drink and closed her book. Nym's heart sunk to his stomach. He huffed out on his hand and sniffed.

"Krossosi wine can't leave that bad a breath, can it?"

"You'd be surprised," she said as she left. Before disappearing into the crowd, she touched Nym's shoulder slightly and a tingling wave descended over his body.

He stared into the fluctuating bodies for a time, reluctantly coming to the sad realisation that he hadn't asked for a name, and he would likely never see her again.

CHAPTER 7
***
The Four Pillars
Damyra Pynarios. Guilds Association Headquarters. The Great City of Noktanos. Twenty-nine years ago.

"HAAA... DAMN, PHEW! Today is finally the day, huh? Haaa... ha... How are you feeling?"

Damyra pushed herself to the edge of the bed, leaving Phanon to do his piggish heavy breathing. He had a remarkable talent to bring the brief relief she obtained from the sex to a catastrophic, sour ending. Normally he would grace her with some blissful few minutes without interaction, but today there was no such blessing. She grabbed her toga and wrapped it around her naked body as she walked over to the big window. She sensed the uncomfortable itching to disappear, leave the fat man to his unappealing huffing. He sounded like an old dog after a light jog.

"It's only a ceremony. Guildmaster Imathios is a man of tradition. He likes honouring things, pointless as that is," she said, standing by the window and observing the flow of people far below. Phanon's recent appointment as Enthos, seniormost representative of the Guild of Lawyers certainly came with its perks. She had enjoyed watching the engines of industrious Noktanos working at its very centre.

The Broken Oath

She looked at the Senate Building from the high-rising Guilds Association Headquarters. From that perspective only the massive dome was visible, like one of those big round shields, scothos, used by the Preatorion for special occasions. A big pole with the biggest flag ever sewn, flapping majestically in the winds. A field of blood-red, in its centre two golden columns flanking an open Codex, golden chains connecting the columns and crossing over the book, the big acronym SPQN underneath. Initials that should be flying all over Helados, initials that betold of endless prosperity, unbridled advancement. Initials to let people know what the best civilisation on Virthos was.

Senate of the People, Quorum of Noktania.

She shook her head, twisting her lips scornfully.

"How terribly ironic that from the both of us, you shall be the one sitting down there, in one of the Quartercycles."

Though the heavy breathing was slowly subsiding, Phanon grunted, huffed, and puffed as he righted himself up.

"I've told you, Damyra. The League is becoming more and more reluctant to extremes. People want stability. Peace breeds prosperity. Had you toned down your rhetoric, Nok's Voice would have been a major senatorial power instead of being pushed to the fringes. Ultimately you were manipulated by Blongatos, Marakavios and the rest of his lackeys in the Static Bloc."

She bit her lower lip almost hard enough to draw blood.

"We *weren't* manipulated."

She repressed a squirm at the memory of Nok's Voice's fate. The things they had ended up doing, long buried within her never to be visited again.

"Our vision... changed. Got polluted."

"Polluted, you say. A party grows, Damyra, and when it grows, dissent is bound to happen."

He emitted a strangled grunt when he bent down to grab his toga. He wrapped it around his hips and collapsed on one of the chairs by his desk.

"Who polluted it, anyway? Irt'Amor?"

She screwed her eyes shut.

"Nokdamned Parrah and their foolish ideas. We should ban them from entering the Noktanian League, keep that obnoxious, weak pacifism locked in the Peninsulas."

Phanon rubbed his protuberant forehead with his knuckles, a habit of his that infuriated her somehow.

"That's *exactly* what I mean, Damyra. They don't even like being called Parrah anymore. It's got derogatory connotations."

Damyra decided to ignore him. Her gaze followed the Northern Avenue as it reached the city walls and it became the Great Noktanian Road, extending in all directions. Westwardly, it would continue south of the Lymtorosi Gorge and Lymtoros itself until it ended abruptly in Gamos, one of the newly erected fortresses standing guard in the Noktanian Shield.

Cut short. Abandoned beyond ever since the treaty with Limthos.

"So much wasted potential. I truly don't understand how the constituencies favoured Blongatos over Pamyros. Now we'll wither away in this chunk of land when we could rule the entirety of Helados."

"Some argue the Fist of Nok is big enough."

"Some are blind, mindless sheep."

"Blongatos won the Supreme Consulate because he understands how politics work in the League. He had full support of his native Tethimos. He's still clamoured as Unifier in Yorthos after he fought the independentists. He improved conditions in the Moxosi mines. He has long been playing the game, understands well how it's played. And he played it well, Damyra."

She faced him.

"I didn't have you for a *fucking* Flaccid."

Tamyros stopped packing his pipe with Tobos powder, clenched his jaw.

"Curious how you haven't contemplated something painfully obvious to me. Have you ever wondered whether it was your attitude what really poluted Nok's Voice? Maybe that was what drove Alda to exile after all."

Contemptuous silence would have to do as response to that. She was too stunned to speak.

Phanon let a sigh go through his nostrils, as though there was a pressure release, a hiss. He continued packing the pipe, lighted it and took a long drag before speaking again.

"I agree with you. I agree Nok's Gift is too grand a miracle to keep it contained here, our system of government far superior to any other. But yours is *not* the way."

"And yours is?"

"It takes longer, but at least I *am* sitting in the Senate, Damyra. What more proof do you require?"

She felt the burden of fury, burning true in the pit of her stomach. She hated that, like she hated every other emotion. They made you weak. She indulged in wrath far too often in the presence of Phanon Tamyros. She sat on the far side of the bed, across from him.

"We should have backed Pamyros' race instead of starting our own. Our seats were so fragile, Alda was never going to win those elections."

"Yes. That was foolish. I did try to warn you."

Damyra set eyes on him.

"Are you feeling particularly petty today? Our demise also rests on you, Phanon. You joined us just the same as everyone else. It was you that abandoned us the second you sniffed trouble! Always machinating. Plots within plots within plots. Surely you sensed your future career peril and fled like a coward."

"Fled?! You pushed me away! I was trying to make you, Alda, and the others understand the best way to keep our hold on those seats was to keep our heads down and avoid the path of self-destruction you were heading down to!"

"You could have tried harder."

"That's unfair."

"You were weak."

"Well, excuse me. Not everyone can be the stolid mountain that is Damyra Phalmeria."

Her lips drew a thin line, she swallowed the sour pit building up in her mouth.

"It's Pynarios, actually."

Phanon blinked. He took several long drags.

"So it's finalised," he said after a pause.

"Yes. Yes, it is. Which brings me to something I needed to tell you."

Phanon stood and wobbled to the window surrounded by a cloud of the thick smoke.

"I am perfectly attuned to the situation Damyra. I may be weak, but I am no fool. You don't need to tell me anything."

Damyra nodded slowly.

"Good."

"You know where the door is," he proclaimed with finality.

"I certainly do."

The journey out of the city, the island of Katadia and onto the other side of the Serpent's Spine took the better part of the day. Guildmaster Imathios' own ship had ferried them to the town of Bamoria, an anaemic group of squat buildings around a House of Nok, erected on an inconsequential crossroads. There they had paid for seven sturdy mules, one for each of the Guild apprentices and their master, to take them across the low pass over to the other side of the Spine.

The sun now hung low on the far horizon, slowly crawling behind a wall of streaky clouds hovering above the Vast Blue ocean. It covered the barren expanse, spreading uninterrupted in every direction from the base of the mountains, with a mantle of warm orange light. Empty stadia of nothing but grasslands, as far as the eye could see. Shifting erratically dictated by the capricious weaving of the winds.

"When the survivors of the Fall of Kahmir first set foot on the Fist of Nok, then only known as the Astian Peninsula, they settled here. They thought best to put mountains between them and the belligerent Astian, Arenar and Murtanir Kingdoms," Guildmaster Imathos droned from the head of the group, some of his words warped away by the eastern winds, blowing in a steady gale toward the Spine. They had left the mules in a deserted outpost a while back, tradition obligating the rest of the way be taken on foot.

Tradition be damned.

She straggled at the back of the group, letting Emya, Pethos and the other three flatten the thickly packed grass ahead of her.

Six apprentices. Damyra, Emya, Pethos, Marhos, Colos and Ashos. Two women, four men, out of seven-hundred and ninety-four applicants that had tried to pass the gruelling selection process set by the Guild of Physicians. They wore the ceremonial white togas of Physicians and newly issued Biothotic Codeces. Leather-bound covers tinted bright blue with the emblem of the Guild of Physicians, a hydra felled by a mighty sword, singed into its surface. Guildmaster Imathios was carrying an old wooden case.

"Remnants of that first civilisation are all but extinct after the Settlement Wars, but records remain. Records of how, in a very short amount of time, those that had endured the Exodus managed to create a prosperous community, the core of which was the use of Nokator to tap into the Titillation."

The group crowned the slope of a gentle hill, overlooking a series of shallow valleys ahead. Sheltered against the winds, the grass stood eerily still at the bottom, as tall as themselves.

At the lowest part of the closest valley, a flat area raised above the grass. A couple dozen strides across, like the hump of a whale peeking above the waves of that sea of grass. A hump made of rough, black-grey stone.

It was delineated by six tall poles. Thick, roughly forged rods driven deep into the stone. They were positioned equidistant from each other, forming a perfect hexagon and in the centre of the hexagon, four ruined pillars leaning in precarious angles.

"There is ample evidence of profoundly ill Lords and Ladies, even Kings and Queens from the warring Kingdoms, venturing over the Serpent's Spine to seek help from their Physicians. They were far superior to the obscure treatments of their charlatans and crude shamans. Physicians on this side followed the perennial teachings of Great Master Hal'Gamac, as we do in the present. They too, swore an Oath to his Tenets. And they did it exactly *there*," Guildmaster Imathios pointed with a decaying arm, standing in silence with brooding countenance. Since everyone had their backs to her, Damyra allowed herself the luxury of rolling her eyes at the attempt to instill gravitas into the occasion.

Get on with it, old man.

Eventually, Guildmaster Imathios decided enough time had passed and he began descending the gentle slope.

As they approached the raised platform, Damyra distinguished a stone pedestal inside the square made by the derelict columns, a wooden crate lined with rusted metal framing in front of it. She also saw numerous chains strewn about on the ground. Dozens of individual strands that joined together, creating a complex lattice of chains made of progressively bigger links, eventually becoming as big and heavy as a horse as they neared the rods.

Imathios stepped over to the pedestal.

Damyra and her peers knew what to do. Every apprentice sworn into the Guild of Physician did. They dreamt of that moment since they first started their studies.

The six spread out behind another slightly raised section, a circular slab several inches high, as Guildmaster Imathios undid the clasps of the case to extract a Codex.

A grubby, old little thing. The leather was dirty, brown-black after years of manipulation by uncountable hands. Smaller than the copy in her hands, tattered edges and thick pages that looked like soil strata. Imathios handled it with utmost care, rested it on the pedestal.

The Biothos Codex. The first one ever compiled and written by Master Udmar Al'Karir before the conception of the Guild of Physicians, long before the League of Nok, or even the Guilds Association, were a thought.

Imathios spread his arms like an Elder addressing the fervourous masses at the height of Nok's Revelling, as though he was speaking to thousands upon thousands, and not just six.

"Welcome, every one of you who embarked upon the glorious path of Caring. Welcome. I congratulate you, for you have withstood a most arduous training. You have resisted the emotional strain and poignancy of illness, have faced Death with valour, and helped repel it. I congratulate, and salute you, for you have rightly earned the honour of being called Doctor."

Much to her chagrin, Damyra was overcome by the moment. She was unable to stop the involuntary physiological reaction of her heart thumping in her chest, every hair on her skin standing erect, her mouth drying up like the Remnants.

Imathios rose his hands again.

One by one, from right to left, they advanced toward the crate. They opened it and donned sets of heavy chains, crisscrossed on their chest.

A pressing weight on her shoulders. It had a grounding, sobering effect.

"Today begins the rest of your prosperous lives as Doctors. Aiding and caring those who need so. Staving off Death when it can be, helping the poor souls of men and women confront it when it can't. These chains represent the hefty burden that comes with it. Unavoidable. Undeniable. *Necessary*, for you shall never forget we cannot change the fated doings of Nok and His Hand on the Physos that surrounds us, but try to alter it, humbly, as best we can."

He lowered his head.

"Damyra Pynarios. Emya Suaros. Pethos Carbaros. Marhos Ult'Amir. Colos Aenos," Imathios waited several breaths after uttering each of their names. "Tether yourselves to the Rods."

Damyra chose two of the closest chains, hooking them to the ones across her chest.

The added weight pressed further down on her.

Guildmaster Imathios brought down his hands and grasped the edges of the pedestal.

"*Fhoro Bothyos!*" he intoned, old jowls trembling.

Damyra recognised the incantation. It was used at the start of every Codex Games match, a physical manifestation of channelling augmenting the amount of Exios available. A small luminous orb appeared atop the circular slab, birthed from thin air and growing in size. It pulsated, rotated, as though made by condensed swirling mist. Guildmaster Imathios' orb was silvery grey, strands of dusty brown flashing across its hazy surface. The sphere grew until it became as big as a head, the air around it warping, blurrying.

"Ready yourselves, apprentices. It is time."

She was looking forward to finally shutting down that small voice inside her head once and for all. A last nail on the heavy coffin she was using to inter the terribly impertinent whinge of memory. She had no time for something as superfluous as guilt, or doubt.

It *was* time.

"*Ponthon*," all six intoned in unison.

During her studies, Damyra had come across an interesting affliction common among Incantators competing in the Games. Something remarkably similar to substance addiction. A compulsion, a yearning to start a Game and pronounce that incantation, the only place where it was permitted by laws of the Senate and the teachings of the Coalition of the Codex.

She understood why.

No Nokturian incantation, no Biothotic channelling could approximate that sensation.

Sparks flew off from the orb, the chains growing taut, rippling of their own accord. A metallic symphony inundated the valley as the network of metal links jolted rapidly, sung, bridging together the six rods that were now vibrating.

She felt the stone quaking under her feet. Following an impulse, she slid her feet out of her sandals. She rejoiced in feeling the vibration crawling up the soles of her bare feet, toes crawling, heels dug firmly on. She felt *connected*.

The apprentices were successfully Engaged.

"Now, apprentices. Now! Recite the Four Pillars of the Hal'Gamac Oath!"

They opened their Biothotic Codeces, reading from the very first page. Four assertions written in carefully calligraphed letters, in their original Old Kahmirian.

"*Pir'Madur Nun'Sa Horiva.*"

The chains rattled madly, pulling her and the others to their knees. Exios pooled within her, tugged her innards inwardly, stopping her lungs working, slowing her heart, before releasing.

She gasped for air. She was suddenly tired, utterly exhausted in fact. She had to rest her Codex on the ground. The other apprentices were also kneeling or on their backs.

First, you shall never do harm.

The First Pillar had been sworn. They couldn't stop.

"*Seri'Madur Sempur Bo'No Yser.*"

The ground shook, chains pulled in opposite directions.

Second, you shall always endeavour to do good.

The Second Pillar was sworn.

"*Toro'Madur Prokos Sempur Nun Elo'Kero Ayure Wakie.*"

Emya next to her emitted a guttural scream. They had been told time and time again the Swearing of the Oath was an onerous process. All those warnings fell terribly flat.

Third, your praxis shall always end at the denial of those who do not wish to be helped.

The Third Pillar was sworn.

She had never felt as drained as in that moment, chains threatening to rip her in half, ground continuing to quake under her.

Just one more to go.

"*Kuarri'Madur Prokos Sempur Ysto uar Sempur Virio Ok'Teo.*"

The Titillation was manifest in every cell of her body, it had to be. She convulsed savagely, arms and legs flailing about, eyes rolling back. Pain, pain, and more pain, and yet it was so very sweet. She was one with the Titillation.

Is this how I die? If so, let it be. Let it be one thousand times.

Alas, the tension dissipated. The chains stopped rattling, the vibration of the rods died down and stilled as though they had never moved at all. The orb shrunk until it disappeared with a distant *tssss*.

Fourth, your praxis shall always be Just, shall always protect All.

The Fourth and last Pillar had been sworn.

"Though your journey began long ago," Guildmaster Imathios' voice sounded different, weaker and tremulous. "You have now submitted to the Titillation and sworn an Oath you shall respect for the rest of your life. You might think you are at the end of a journey. Could not be furthest from the truth! The journey has not but commenced. Rise! Rise now as fellow Doctors!"

———————

Damyra stood, fatigued, with quite the decision in front her.

To take the lift and give her legs some well-deserved rest, getting to the last floor of the Faculty Residences rapidly and efficiently.

Or climb up several flights of stairs with a knee that had begun faltering as she had stepped down from the carriage. It would be more painful, take longer.

The ride back from Campus had proven to be strangely clarifying. Perhaps what she had needed all along was to tire herself, to reduce the peripheral considerations.

The opportunity was standing right in front of her, yes. The always tantalising potential of knowing.

It would mean crowbarring open an old box full of mental poison and jeopardise her position. Was there a need for that? Might just be enough to tip the scales and send Domenikos and his mysterious employers packing to the darkest confines of Bashork's Hall.

She sighed loudly.

Vysios was bound to return to Noktanos later in the hexad. He was waiting up in the residence, and he would invariably ask questions. He would count her conclusion as a victory of his own. His tacit gloating, his smug expression and his endless pontificating were not something she was in a terrible hurry to experience. Though the day had dragged long after the Intercollegiate Council and her visit to the Vault, she didn't have a particularly strong desire to make it back home.

She headed for the stairs.

The astounding advances in medicine, of which she was a prominent artifex, meant a prolonged life expectancy in the Noktanian League. Physicians were now scrambling to study the normal fluctuations of health that occured with advanced age, an eventuality never before seen in History.

Yet, one thing was research. Other very different was to feel it in her bones.

"Fuck osteoarthritis, fuck senility and fuck joints," she grumbled as she climbed the steps, accompanying her efforts with a healthy assortment of florid obscenities.

Breathing labourously, she opened the front door to an empty common area.

She furrowed her brow.

"Vysios?" she called without answer. After a quick inspection of the other rooms, it became evident.

"He's returned to the city, hasn't he...?"

She didn't bother looking for a note. She knew there wouldn't be one. She bit down hard, pain shooting back along her jaw and up her temples.

She threw her case on the table and opened it, tossing the *Akitos 'i' Legos* on the varnished surface. She took a new fountain pen, a recent design from the Guild of Engineers gifted to her by her successor as Head of Surgery and clenched it in a white-knuckled fist.

She signed the dotted line on the last page forcefully, so hard she etched her name in the wood underneath.

CHAPTER 8
***
Irrefutable Authority
Damyra Pynarios. Town of Londos. Outskirts of Noktanos. Katadia.

THE ANATHEMA. ONE, if not *the* most prestigious theatre in the Noktanian League. How fascinating the winding paths of life are, she had been invited uncountable times but never been inside. Not since before it was a theatre. A long time ago.
 Today, the Anathema. House of entertainment and diversion for the rich and illustrious, where the best troupes fought hard to perform. Before that, headquarters of a prominent law firm that later moved into the city. Before that still, an abandoned temple of an abandoned religion, discovered by Nok's Voice nearly half a century ago. Perfect for their purposes.
 She breathed in deeply. Important people in high places convened regularly in the Anathema. That's why she was meeting Domenikos there, the evidence was clear. A coincidence.
 "Fifty years," she whispered to herself, shaking her head in disbelief.
 The flickering light of her torch showed how the derelict exterior had changed. Only the thick walls close to the ground had been kept as foundations, pre-Kahmirian architecture was squat and unremarkable. It was now a massive white cylinder with a blue cupola as a roof, classic Noktanian.

The lid of her mental box slipped up a little, letting out a powerful surge. She found herself unable to move, not by the arthritic stiffness that had persecuted her joints relentlessly for years, but by the memory of rallies, the proud patriotism, the infectious shouts of the restless crowd. She couldn't help but smile.

Alda.

She walked toward it slowly, cringing every time her right foot touched the ground. The horse ride from Noktanos had exacerbated her pain terribly, cane moving from commodity to absolute requirement.

Tap, tap, clack, she advanced in the night.

"*Exios, abyrin thosi Tos.*"

The door in front opening with a creak. She always advised her students against using Nokator frivolously, but her hands were full.

A pungent smell of varnish and sea serpent grease hit her nose, eyes adjusting to the orange hue of the theatre's interior.

"*Exios, tenyrin thosi Tos.*"

The door creaked shut behind her.

"Doctor Pynarios, I would put that naked flame out. Theatres have incendiary tendencies."

Domenikos' voice came from the stage down below, echoing multiple times in the big chamber.

"*Exios, penthon thosi Pyrotos.*"

The fire fizzled out completely and Damyra tossed the torch aside. All around the spherical space, big serpent oil lamps painted the descending rows of seats, stairs and stage orange-yellow.

"I must say, I am buoyantly jubilant to see you here, Doctor Pynarios."

"How very ironic, as my coming feels undoubtedly like *sinking,*" she said, *tap-tap-clacking* downstairs toward the stage.

"I trust you've brought the signed *Akitos 'i' Legos*?" Domenikos asked the second Damyra stepped on the stage. She produced the crumpled ledger and threw it on the floor.

Without a crack in his nauseatingly content expression, the lawyer picked it up and bounced up like a spring.

"Marvellous. Please, do follow me as I take you to my employers. And now, *yours.*"

He walked over to the set of curtains and disappeared into the backstage. She took a minute to look to the stands from the stage, casting her mind back.

The ceiling had been lower down, and partly collapsed. The main space, a chamber of old wood and stone. After all, it had been a temple for Pavaras, Goddess of Stability. Such place of worship needed to be austere, cold, solid. Her statue had been in the middle, eroded by the hands of time and the elements. It had been standing that first time, a lifetime ago, when Alda first took her into the temple. Not long after that they demolished it and erected an elevated platform to address their growing following, much the stage she was on whilst the countless side chambers.

She pulled the curtains and followed Domenikos.

The light of the lamp on the lawyer's hand swayed to and fro as they descended steps into what had been the temple's cavernous catacombs, their shadows contorting in macabre dances. Open doors to empty rooms, shadows of the past mingling with the present.

For years we've suffered stagnation as a policy! We are suffocating in this tiny chunk of land with Nok's Might at our reach while the whole world laughs!

Alda spoke her mind with conviction, a driving motor for change. Alda's vision was to break with the decades of passive foreign policy and expand, engulf, conquer. Show the world what the Noktanian League was capable of. Damyra was too, but she had slowly realised another vision rivalled with her political aspirations.

They serpented the narrow corridors until they reached a spiralling staircase that was directly underneath the centre of the big cylinder above, exactly where the old statue had once proudly stood. Damyra knew they led to a deeper system of caves recesses they had rarely frequented.

They are too damp, too secluded, Damyra. You want to keep us buried in the dark while we should be triumphantly marching in the light.

She grimaced. Those irregular steps would not be kind to her weathered joints.

"I don't know if you are familiar with the origins of the Anathema," Domenikos started from below as she wobbled down the stairs, every step more painful than the previous one.

Do you or do you not know, you snivelling little shit?

"I'm not, as it turns out."

"Long before its inaugural act, before the Exodus and the Fall of Kahmir, it was a temple to Pavaras, Goddess of Stability."

Damyra used both the wall and her stick for support, engaging her upper body strength to ease the descent on her legs.

"I wouldn't be surprised if you haven't heard of it, she is from a pre-Kahmirian religion."

"I am quite familiar with Pavaras, Goddess of Stability. She in fact *isn't* pre-Kahmirian. She belonged in the Kahmirian Pantheon, just under the name of Pa'Var. You are excused for your ignorance though, it is a common misconception."

"How gracious. I will make sure to brush up on my History. You are a woman of vast knowledge."

She accepted the little victory in the midst of all that pain.

"I am."

When they reached the landing, Domenikos turned to one of the multiple corridors and took Damyra to a small chamber.

Centuries, potentially millennia, were imprinted on the walls of the spherical receptacle. Dark moss grew in the cracks between the battered stones, quarried and sculpted by hand in a time immemorial. A pungent smell of stagnation and putrefaction lingered in the air.

"This was some sort of shrine," Domenikos pointed to the further section of the chamber, where the curved wall had an indented recess. "But you probably knew that already."

The floor had been smoothed and polished, likely by the kneeling of believers.

"It isn't terribly difficult to deduce."

He walked toward it and placed his hand over the rough surface of the bricks.

"Exios, pirton Pordos'otor."

A grinding noise of stone on stone ensued, a straight line appearing in the centre of the shrine. Slowly, the line turned into a gap that grew wider until there was enough room to fit a person.

Damyra furrowed her brow.

"Domenikos, what is this place?"

"Well, let us say this is not the first temple I use to conduct my business. They normally have access to the vast network of underground tunnels in Katadia. The assiduity with which the Anathema is packed with utterly important Cyrosi is nothing but a convenient coincidence."

Huh. That would have been great to know back in the day.

"I would offer for you to go first, Doctor Pynarios, but I am carrying the light."

"By all means."

The uninviting darkness of the concealed passageway led to a space small enough to be illuminated by the weak lamp.

"I must once again apologise for the appalling circumstances. Our method of transportation is far from glamourous."

Damyra looked over Domenikos' shoulder.

A rudimentary wagon, the sort used in the Moxosi mines.

Domenikos hung the serpent oil lamp in a pole toward the front on the wagon and jumped inside.

"How rude of me, would you like some help?"

Damyra *tap- tap-clacked* toward the metal cart.

"Keep your apologies, Domenikos."

She noticed a considerable slant to the left, the rails were on a downwards slope. Minding the gap, she placed both hands on the edge and propped herself up and down onto one of the makeshift seats made of putrid wood.

The stunt made blinding pain blossom from her hip and knees. She let the fire spread inside her and didn't utter a sound.

Domenikos used both hands, putting his whole body weight to release the brake. A high-pitched screech preceded a brusque jerk forward, followed by a loud crescendo of *tch-tch-tch* as they gained speed hurtling down the tunnel.

The noise and teeth-clattering vibration left no room for clever quips, and whilst she appreciated the absence of Domenikos' irritating voice, the pain was unbearable.

Damyra was not in the right frame of mind or place to perform a nerve-blocking incantation on herself, but she always carried a vile of Myrphid extract with her. She rarely used it given its strongly addictive properties, but the up-and-down, side-to-side swaying of the rackety vehicle demanded extreme measures.

With tears welling in her eyes, she took the small vial and downed its contents. The administration route wasn't ideal, as oral formulations of Myrphid extract took several minutes to exert their effect, but again, she couldn't very well start an intravenous line under the current circumstances.

Patience and a trained tolerance for pain kept her going until the drug kicked in. She emitted a sigh of relief, even allowed herself to recline back, opening her eyes to take in the surroundings. The wagon had kept going forever downwards, slowly, and surely gaining three or four times the speed of a sprinting horse, aided by gravity.

Domenikos had his hand on a brake lever, occasionally depressing it. Adding sparks and screech to the terrible orchestra of reverberations. The light was so weak they couldn't even see the walls of the tunnels, rolling darkness all around them. She could only assume they were still in the tunnel by the smell of trapped air and the deafening cacophony.

Suddenly something changed.

The sounds expanded, became lower and sparser. The air smelled richer. The darkness felt deeper, more ominous.

"Domenikos, where are you taking me!?" she shouted, her voice echoing endlessly.

"I am afraid I am not at liberty to say that, Doctor Pynarios. Let me reassure you, my employers have taken all the necessary measures to ensure this meeting remains in complete secrecy!"

The sedative effects of the myrphid flower and her unhinged sense of curiosity helped to contain her rage and frustration. She was in too deep to back down now.

The Broken Oath

After an uncertain amount of time, the constant slope of the rails righted, and the wagon lost some of the speed. Eventually, the overwhelming *openess* of the caverns gave way to another tunnel. Before long, Domenikos applied the brake and the wagon screeched to a halt.

With pain subsided, she was able to stand and step out with agility, barely needing any support from her stick. Domenikos grabbed the lamp from the wagon and showed her the way from the small chamber into a bigger one. The place was similar to the dungeon-like basement of The Anathema, with one glaring difference. The stone bricks were shiny black obsidian.

On the opposite side of the chamber, a wooden platform embedded in the wall, trapped inside a metal cage. Domenikos retracted some of the latticed bars and stepped in the lift.

Once Damyra was in, Domenikos shut the gate and pulled on a lever.

Her thoughts raced in her mind, painfully aware of the strange turn of events. Two days ago, she was teaching an anatomy class, as she had done for the past five years. Now, she was somewhere in the Noktanian underground, with a signed Binding Agreement to something she didn't know, about to meet some mysterious employers.

The lift halted.

"We have arrived," Lashos announced, pulling the lever.

Damyra looked around, confused. The lift had stopped without any indication of an exit. They were trapped within three walls of naked black stone and one of solid wood.

The lawyer started knocking on that last one, listening for a change in sound. When he found it, he pressed on it and a trapdoor flapped open. He introduced his hand, pulled some sort of trigger and the wall started to move following a click.

"After you, Doctor Pynarios," he gestured, retreating to the corner of the elevating platform.

The wooden wall had fully retracted, allowing her to have a good look at the room it revealed.

Circular shelves, rows upon rows of books, several urns and busts. Directly ahead, a glass balcony door offering a breathtaking view of Noktanos cut against the darkened silhouettes of two men outside.

A big desk near the balcony occupied a big portion of the room's floorplan. Ostentatious, the biggest she had ever seen, full of neatly stacked papers and ledgers.

Something on top of the glass door caught her eyes. Two crossed swords over a big rhombus with adjacent triangles and a glistening black fist on the forefront. House Astia's coat of arms.

Damyra had been taken to Dytalis, The Dark Fortress. The Eternal Shadow.

A man opened the glass door and stepped into the room. Razor-shaven head, brown beard littered with patches of red hair and set of stern blue eyes that burnt a hole through Damyra.

"Doctor Pynarios, I extend my sincerest gratitude. I hope the trip here wasn't too taxing," said Lord Uthos, head of House Astia.

"Hard to say what was more taxing, the trip or the company."

Lord Astia nodded, his expression unchanged, waving Domenikos into the room.

"Lashos, please retire to inspect the Agreement and bring the other one. Make sure everything is in order and prepare a set of specific instructions for Doctor Pynarios."

"The other one? More contracts? Don't you think I should first know what I agreed to, *Lord Uthos*?"

"I see we both know each other, so there is no need for extensive introductions. Doctor Pynarios, I am a cautious man. I couldn't afford your negative response, but I also know the legal complications of signing a contract without knowing what it is for. You merely agreed to sign this *other* contract."

Lashos Domenikos returned with more papers from a door to the right. Another Akitos 'i' Legos, only thicker. He bowed pronouncedly and gave the ledger to Damyra before he left again.

"I believe you know Senator Lophos Pamyros," Uthos said, gesturing to the man stepping from the balcony. Pamyros was wearing his white senatorial robes, looking like a statue straight from the Central Square.

Damyra was stunned.

"Know him? Of course I know Senator Pamyros," she managed.

"It must be a poignant reunion, I understand. I was barely born back then, but I have read the accounts. You two almost sat beside each other in the Quartercycle," Uthos pulled an ancient-looking chair and sat down at the desk. He rummaged the stacks of papers and opened a notebook.

Damyra frowned.

"*Almost*. For what it's worth, I think it should be you leading the League, Senator Pamyros."

"Your kind words move me, Doctor Pynarios," Pamyros said with his baritone voice, flashing a debonair smile. He was old, yes, but still retained the qualities of his former tall, handsome, clever self."

"Senator Pamyros, Lord Astia. With all due respect, I feel entitled to some explanation. I only singed the contract because Domenikos assured me you know the location of Zar'Aldur."

Uthos raised his hand. He shook his head, slowly, then pointed to a chair by the desk.

"I'd prefer to stand."

"I must insist," Uthos said with irrefutable authority.

Damyra sat down.

"I understand your current line of work revolves around our understanding of death?" the noble-born scanned the papers in front of him.

"I don't understand the releva—"

"Please, answer, Doctor Pynarios."

"Yes," she sighed. "That is correct. More specifically I am investigating how dialectical differences affect Exios-expenditure, primarily between Biothos and other dialects of Nokator. I am particularly interested in figuring out why is it that the manipulation of life is so much more difficult than that of inanimate objects."

"You must then be well versed in the different ways life can *end*."

She furrowed her brow.

"One could say that my Lord. Yet, I am a Guild-certified Physician. Rather than facilitating life's extinction, I tend to *preserve* it."

Lord Astia's lips morphed into an acrid smile. He flipped over some pages, index finger tracing the words.

"Both your parents died by the hands of Zereri riders during official ambassadorial business, you went on to publicly denounce Senator Blongatos' policies of peace with the Zereri and you joined a political group called 'Nok's Voice' that gained quite a considerable amount of traction before its disbandment. Is that correct?"

Everyone knows that. There was nothing in the Vault. Nothing he can use.

"Those facts are true in isolation, my Lord, yet grouped as they have been, I wonder of the impl—"

"A transcription of a rally where yourself and some of the founding members, Zar'Aldur included, advocated for the total extermination of the Zereri savages, launching a maritime campaign on the Tunedosi archipelago and annihilating the Limthosi chokehold."

Damyra shifted in her chair. The effects of the Myrphid flower extract were wearing off.

"Yes, those were things we defended. So?"

"Do you defend them now?" Pamyros interjected.

Damyra sagged in her chair. Lord Uthos' blue eyes bore down on her.

"As I said, Blongatos' election as Supreme Consul is the most harmful thing that has happened to the League since the First Secession War, but I see no point discussing that now. My Lord, with all due respect. I have not come to have a political debate. Again, the only reason why I am here is because of Zar'Aldur. Do you know where she is?"

Uthos stared at her, a long pause before he answered.

"I'm rather pleased to hear your opinion aligns with ours, Doctor Pynarios. Yes, we do know her location, but I will not tell you just yet."

Damyra bit down hard.

"The rise to popularity of Nok's Voice is a fascinating chapter of our political history," Lord Uthos continued. "People forget these kinds of things quickly, but it is one of my earnest interests. I must say, I am rather pleased to be meeting one such prominent figure in the party's success."

"I retired from politics long ago, Lord Uthos."

"Yes. You are now a prestigious Doctor, a Guild-certified Physician."

Uthos interlaced his fingers over the ledger.

"You see, that makes you the perfect person to carry out a very important deed."

She looked down at the document on her lap.

Right. The contract.

"Lord Uthos, what exactly is it I have agreed to?"

Uthos Astia stared deep into her eyes. Pamyros standing next to him, right hand on the Lord's shoulder. She took in both figures cut against the moonlit view of Noktanos, shivers crawling down her spine. She knew the answer before it came out of Lord Astia's mouth.

"The assassination of Supreme Consul Kahmaos Blongatos."

For a moment, her surroundings entered a state of stagnation. The air hung dead, heart in her immobile chest beating like a hammer against anvil. Her mouth was agape for a long time before she exploded into a distorted, inhuman laughter. Pamyros stepped back.

"You want… Blongatos… you… And me, of all people! Ha, ha! Ha!"

Loud, shrill guffaws that made both the Lord and Senator blink with each resounding beat.

"Doctor Pynarios, I am most serious. I fail to see the humour," Lord Uthos Astia said, a hint of disgust disfiguring his face.

Damyra wiped the tears that had formed in her eyes and waited out a few more stertors of the hacking hysteric laughter.

"Ha! Oh, Nok. The humour, and how magnificent it is, my dear Lord Uthos, is that you could have simply asked."

CHAPTER 9
***
Meeting a Friend
Nymor Strethos. University Hospital. Bamoria. The Fist of Nok.

NYM STARED DOWN, flabbergasted at the vision of the pulsating brain exposed in the air.

Zemya. That was the child's name.

After his thirst for celebration had made an abrupt disappearance the night before, he had decided to ride back to Bamoria. Instead of paying the stingy innkeeper for a bed, he left the horse in the Hospital's stables and spent the whole night researching in the library of the complex.

Hours of perusing academic papers and textbooks thick as a castle wall, aided by the invaluable stimulation of Pylmos root infusion yielded some results. He had narrowed the potential diagnosis to three.

Looking rough and sporting a glorious headache, he had trundled to Danos office. A rougher-looking Amyra had been already presenting her case.

"You are late" Amyra had said, arms on her hips like a jar.

"I believe you are just early."

The House of Nok in the hospital hadn't run the seventh bell, he had been sure of that.

"I apologise for the interruption, do carry on."

When Amyra was finished, he had exposed his most solid theory. Likely the girl had been bitten by a tick when playing in the fields and contracted Lymos disease.

When he had finished, Danos had stood.

"You both made great points. Nymor, would you be able to tell me Professor Horvos' most famous quote?"

Nymor had blown out his cheeks before answering.

"Diagnosis should never eclipse Medicine's true purpose, for Knowing becomes vane. Something to that effect."

Amyra's eyebrows had morphed into a condescending *V*.

"'The search for a diagnosis shall never eclipse the true purpose of Medicine, for Knowing easily diverts from noble cause and strays into the poisonous realm of vanity,'" she had recited from memory without stumbling.

"And what is that purpose he is referring to, Nymor?"

"Helping. Treating." That he had known.

"Precisely. So, whilst the diagnosis can help, there is no point when it stops doing so. Nymor, you'll be pleased to know the Hospital Board of Physicians has approved the patient's hemispherectomy as per my recommendation."

So, there he was. He had slept one fewer night in his life for a pointless diagnosis and a position besides Danos Levantios as he operated on Zemya's once-in-a-lifetime procedure. Two dozen curious eyes sat in the rows of the operating theatre, documenting, and marvelling.

"What is the most important rule of Bithotic manipulation of tissues?" Danos asked, speaking loudly so he could be heard in the highest rows. He had several loupes on his nose, scalpel on one hand and forceps on the other.

"Biothos is the most demanding dialect of Nokator. You have to be smart and use it wisely."

"That's good Nymor, though you need to project your voice, or our spectators will miss your clever answers!"

He repeated his answer for the audience.

"Medicine is a combination of very clever engineering and wise use of Biothos. For example, when managing an external wound, it is better to suture and apply antiseptic, aid the body's own healing abilities, rather that wastefully use Biothos to re-join the skin. However, I cannot leave the internal damage I am forced to cause to coagulate on its own."

Danos placed the utensils on a tray offered by a nurse.

"Rod, please."

The nurse passed on a bright grey rod the size of a littlefinger. Danos gently dabbed with a gauze and pressed the rod on the bleeding brain.

"*Bioxos, tiron vosu Vothos.*"

The Broken Oath

Nym's eyebrows shot up as he saw the blood disappearing, flowing back *into* the vessels.

"Amyra, what material is the rod made of?"

"Silver, Doctor Danos," Amyra's confident voice boomed in the theatre.

"Why is that? Why not regular iron?"

"Silver is antiseptic, it fights decaying miasmas."

"That's correct!"

Nym took a moment to appreciate how all throughout the explanation, Danos' eyes had not moved away from the operating site.

It was then when Nym's ear picked up an almost imperceptible grunt from Danos. Suddenly, blood began pouring back into the site, dark red obscuring the brain.

Tiny beads of sweat appeared on Danos' temple, who shot a glance to Emya, the anaesthetist. She perked up, busying herself with a miniature Horvos device.

"Amyra, why don't you move to this side? You'll have better visualisation during the next part," Danos pointed to the other side of the table.

He pressed a lever with his foot and the table lowered, the view of Zemya's head blocked by Amyra's change in position.

Nym walked closer reflexively.

"This is a good lesson in the utter importance of keeping calm," Danos said, a slight edge to his otherwise always monotone lecturing voice.

"It appears I have nicked the superior sagittal sinus. It is a known risk of this type of operation."

Shit.

The superior sagittal sinus, a blood vessel that acts as a confluence of veins running between the two brain hemispheres. A rupture in it was the worst possible complication in that scenario. The best method to get an uncontrollable brain haemorrhage.

Emya walked over and whispered in Danos' ear.

"She's very unstable, blood pressure is plummeting. You need to stop the haemorrhage *now*, Levantios."

Danos grunted an affirmation.

"Iron rod, please," he said with apparent calm. The nurse instantly placed a finger-length of metal on his palm.

"Nym, here," he gave him a fistful of gauzes. "Press it here, gently."

Nym did so, trying his best not to think too much about the fact that the only thing separating the girl's brain and his finger was some absorptive piece of cloth.

Danos drove the rod into the growing pool of maroon liquid and uttered an incantation.

"*Bioxos, hothon l'Tormos thosi Rothos Phyrotic.*"

The rod glowed incandescent red and hissed upon being pressed. It was followed by a revolting tinge of burned meat, then nothing.

Danos looked at the nurse.

"My Biothotic Codex please. And a bottled of Athospos. *Quietly.*"

The nurse complied, hiding the bottle with dexterity. He squatted as though he was looking directly into the surgical site and downed the solution. His eyes searched wildly the Biothotic Codex, nostrils flaring and sweat running down his temples.

"*Bioxos, doperon'Ios Voston.*"

Danos' Smaragdos started vibrating as Danos closed his eyes, guiding the incandescent rod again, this time blindly.

A hiss, repulsive smoke that tickled Nym's nose, and the bleeding ceased.

"*Bioxos, seruin vosu aktos.*"

Danos blinked a tad too slowly, his movement sluggish as he looked at Emya on the other side of the table. The anaesthetist was busy with her stethoscope and Horvos device.

Could it... is she...?

Emya gave a curt nod and Danos expelled a soud of relief.

"Good. That's very... good."

His words were slightly slurred.

He's drained.

Both Emya and the nurse must have been very familiar with Exios exhaustion in surgeons. The efficient anaesthetist pushed her stool behind Danos as a precaution and the leading nurse gestured to the rest of the staff. They swarmed around Levantios, replacing the bloodied tray with a clean one, containing an assortment of silver plates.

Camouflaged by the careful dance of moving staff, Danos drank another bottle of Athospos. Not a single person from the audience had caught on.

The doctor observed the pulsating brain, narrowing his eyes to slits. He was grabbing onto the edge of the table.

"I do believe there isn't any overt inflammation. We will proceed with the prosthesis and keep an eye on her intracranial pressure during the post-operative period."

Danos selected a silver dome from the tray and fitted it on the girl's skull, muttering another set of incantations that fused metal to bone.

Nym thought he heard the physician's voice waver toward the end. When he finished, he was breathing deeply with eyes closed.

"Any of you... knows... deep mattress sutures?" he asked between ragged breaths.

"I'm afraid not," Amyra said, looking down.

"I do."

Danos nodded slowly, putting his hand on Nym's shoulder. It was a meaty, heavy contact. Nym was being used for support.

"Fantastic. Emya will supervise you. We will debrief later."

Their tutor took a long, preparatory breath and straightened up, smiling for the audience.

"Thank you very much for coming! I will be in my office for the rest of the day. I will be available to answer any questions after a brief recess."

With that, Danos walked out of the theatre amidst a shy smattering of applause.

Emya moved closer to Nym, nurse offering the sutures, forceps, and needle driver.

He swallowed hard, struck by the unexpected responsibility of the situation. There were still people in the stand, attentive to his every move. Truth be told, he had indeed practised deep mattress sutures. On a dead pig.

Don't think. Do.

The first couple of stitches took an eternity and a half. His hands seemed to have lost all dexterity, jittering and trembling. He pushed on, focused on the task at hand. Eventually, nerves faded away and a year of training kicked in. Before long he threw the last knot and he wished he had more wound to suture.

"Well done," Emya smiled at Nym. He nearly cried tears of joy. He had never felt deserving of such praise, but what he had done was overwhelming. Assisting in his first operation, and he had *sutured*.

"You two get some well-deserved rest, I'll finish up here," Emya said with a warm smile.

Amyra and Nym sauntered over to the scrub room, a sober adjacent with washbasins and linen towels. They began washing away all the blood and pulverised bone from hands, arms and face in complete silence.

"How did you know how to do that? We are not taught how to suture until—" Amyra started, drying her face on the towel. She paused, clear eyes surverying Nym.

"Nymor, I don't know why Danos has overlooked this issue, but I certainly cannot keep quiet about it. Are you a medical student?"

Nymor smiled. It was a fair question. A question he knew would be asked and yet he had found no credible answer for. Tysides Romos hadn't implied any secrecy to it, stating more than once how unorthodox Danos is. However, he was less than inclined to scream his status to the four winds. A low citizen from the Slums who isn't formally enrolled in the University doesn't have particularly promising prospects if discovered.

His panic increased directly proportional to the ever-stretching silence. It was evident Amyra would not let the matter go.

"I am a student, and I study medicine under Levantios Danos. Ergo, I am a medical student," he shrugged, drying his hands on a towel.

That was shit.

"Let me change my question," Amyra walked up *very* close to him. Close enough he was able to see the faded freckles in her dark skin. To feel her exhaled air, count the creases of her full lips.

What is happening?

"Are you enrolled in the School of Medicine?"

Nym stared into her eyes, lines of gold in a field of green. Confusing things occured inside his chest. He found it impossible to lie to those eyes.

"No, I'm not."

She stepped back.

"A Doctor in the Rich Quarter owed my father a favour, so he took me in as understudy. He saw something in me, I guess, and told me Doctor Danos was looking for someone with a... *different* sort of intelligence."

No conscious thought went into deciding to tell her everything. He just did. Amyra held his eyes before silently walking toward the door of the scrub room.

She lingered by the doorframe.

"Will you teach me how to do that?" she nodded to the operating theatre, the previous harshness in her gestures fading away. Nym smiled.

"I would love to."

Amyra held the door open for him.

"You know, I consider myself a very capable student," she chatted on as they walked the long, empty corridors of the University Hospital. "But I am far from the best of the class. What you did in there, though? Stepping up like that? I don't think any of us would have done it."

"And yet I lack all of what goes on in there," Nym gently tapped his finger on her head. She laughed, prompting that strange feeling in his chest to return.

"What are you on about?"

"Are you oblivious to what you said during the interview? The thing about Somnos syndrome? Incredible," he shook his head in disbelief as Amyra looked away. It was difficult to tell under the lacking light of the oil lamps and the obscure tone of her skin, but Nym could have sworn she was blushing.

"Trust me, you do *not* want to know what goes on in here," she said.

The corridor took them to the central space of the Main Building, dying light reflecting through the glass dome.

"I am constantly amazed by this Hospital," Amyra continued as she approached the balustrade at the edge of the empty space. "I cannot believe how fortunate I am to be educated inside its walls."

Nym hummed an affirmation and joined her in admiring the multiple galleries from the heights. He asked a question on whim.

"You know," he started, surprised there was a bit of a knot in his stomach, "I could teach you how to suture now. We could grab the material from Danos' storage room, I'm sure he wouldn't mind."

Amyra looked away.

"I would like that Nym, but I am meeting a friend, I'm afraid."

"Ah, I see."

"In fact, there she is."

Nym turned in time to see a girl with her head down, reading a book whilst walking. She tripped over someone's legs and apologised profusely.

Nym laughed at her expense, then laughed doubly at the realisation.

The girl read on as she approached them, blind to her surroundings.

"Haleana!" Amyra called. Head buried in the book as it was, she was going to keep walking past them.

"Oh, Amyra, why did you take so long? I—" she looked up from the pages and trailed off when she saw Nym.

"Xhalenfros," he said, a smile as wide as the Sylvari river.

The girl. The one in the tavern. The one with eyes the colour of the morning sun, the kind face, the smart words, the painful leave. She looked at Nym twice over. She smiled with a reciprocating smile that gripped his heart tight.

"Xhalenfros, it seems."

CHAPTER 10
✱ ✱ ✱
The Sharp End of the Blade
Damyra Pinarios. School of Law. Guilds Association University.

THE FEVER HAD nearly taken her.

After her audience with Lord Uthos Astia and Senator Pamyros she had returned to the University, arriving to the Residences with the rising of the Heladian sun. She had been incredibly weary, each step made more difficult than the last, as though she had bagfuls of stones tied to her ankles, arthritic bones paining her with unfamiliar might. Her exhaustion-addled brain had made the mistake of thinking the weariness, clattering teeth, and tremoring limbs, were nothing out of the ordinary for her aging body after the journey.

Naively, she had dragged herself to her empty bed and collapsed. Restless sleep had descended upon her, a suffocating blanket of darkness, and she had plummeted into a maelstrom of twisted nightmares. The febrile dreams had interwoven with each other in the troubled night until she was awoken, drenched in sweat, by the midday bells of the nearest House of Nok.

Beating the pounding in her head, she had liberated herself from the sodden sheets wrapped around her, binding her to the bed, and stumbled to her cabinet. Vials and jars tumbled to the floor as her shaking fingers sought something for her inflamed body. She had drunk the medicine avidly and folded down. There, sat on the floor with her back to the cold wall, she was only concerned about pushing air in and out of her lungs. After a torturous while she had recuperated enough to take account of her sorry state.

The Broken Oath

It became clear she was suffering from no simple medical ailment. There was only one plausible explanation, and so she had limped out of her residence, crawled into the lifts and made it to the reception to arrange a carriage to the School of Law.

Presently she wobbled across the main square, feeble hands grasping the eroded handle of her stick. It had taken a clever combination of antipyretics, analgesics and stimulants to simply be able to stand up straight, then a monstrous amount of will and obstinacy on top of that to move at all.

"Nok take me swiftly," she exhaled, staring at the stairs leading up to the monolithic building.

Every joint complained, eyes welling with tears as she climbed those steps, and then she only managed half of them. She sat down, her back to the pillar of stone that climbed to the skies. With cane between her legs, she used an embarrassing shuffling that swapped pain in her knees and ankles for pain in her buttocks and lower back, and she made it to the top with only her pride scathed.

She anchored her cane firmly to the ground and grabbed onto it with her whole upper torso. She heaved herself back up to her feet with great difficulty, like a Sylvari silverback climbing up a vine.

"For fuck's sake, couldn't I have just died during my sleep?" she grunted, looking up. Who was she talking to? Nok? Pavaras?

She produced a kerchief from her toga to wipe her tears and dab at her emaciated face.

"Sod it. This is as presentable as I'm going to get."

She hobbled forth.

The inside of the School was an enormous, unwelcoming cube. Devoid of any furniture or adornation, except for a glass urn in the centre and a bizarre chandelier high above her head. It was like the distorted result of the imagination of a deranged mathematician. Perfect prisms of stone forming a stiff, geometrical spider of harsh straight lines and right angles. Grease lamps were attached to the many vertices and projected a weak orange light.

"Hello. May I offer some help?"

The disinterested drone of a woman behind a desk. Her eyelids fluttered, as though she had some trouble keeping them open in the time it took to address Damyra.

"You may. I'm looking for Professor Tamyros' office."

The woman stopped ruffling papers and looked up at Damyra. Her eyes widened.

"Cyrosi, are you quite alright?"

A question that truly spoke more for Damyra's conspicuous terrible state than the receptionist's compassion.

"Yes, yes, I'm fine. Professor Tamyros' office?"

The woman blinked.

"Do… do you have an appointment?"

The receptionist's low tone echoed many times over, each iteration nagging at ther like nails driven through her temples.

Damyra approached the desk labouredly.

"Listen carefully. I am Doctor Damyra Pynarios, Head of the School of Medicine. Professor Tamyros is… an old friend. I am quite convinced he won't mind my unexpected visit," she spoke each word slowly. The woman worked her lips up and down before re-adopting her expression of disinterest. She pointed behind Damyra, past the central urn.

"Ground floor, follow the far corridor. Last door before it turns right."

Damyra shut her eyes and exhaled.

Thank Nok Almighty, the Primal Roamer and the whole bloody Elder Council.

She would rather be stabbed in the eye with a rusty dagger than climb more stairs.

The clacking of her stick was multiplied many times over in the spacious hall, irritating her greatly as she walked past the glass receptacle. It contained a big leatherbound book propped up on a pedestal. A replica of the Foundation Charter, the constitutional document that cemented the origin of the Noktanian League. The original was under lock and key, somewhere in the Library of the Senate.

She walked by the solid walls of the cold, impersonal building, and surprised herself reminiscing. Last time she had spoken to Phanon was a lifetime ago. The conversations and interactions, the moments when they were together were all but covered under a thick fog of forget. One thing she did remember, they hadn't departed precisely amicably. Of course, she had peripherally kept tabs on him one way or another, seen him during the Signing of the University Charter, heard of his rise in the Guild of Lawyers and his subsequent retirement from politics to become a Law professor.

The fatigue and nausea that had been battling constantly to grab the reins of her being reached a climax and she had to stop before Phanon's door, right hand on the dark wood and left over her abdomen.

This was a physiological coup d'état, a rebel confederacy of her viscera to wreak havoc in her body, burn it from the inside out.

"Oh Nok," she muttered, bent over. The crumpled contract in her travelling toga shifted position, digging into her tender belly and reminding her of the purpose of her visit.

Let's get this over and done with.

She breathed in deeply, suppressing another wave of nausea, and knocked on the door.

"Come in."

The Broken Oath

Phanon Tamyros, sat behind his desk, head buried in a book. Time hadn't been kind to him. The top of his head was a wispy clearing, temples populated by silver-grey. He was fatter, skin oily and wrinkly. Those beady eyes interred in his round face, however, retained every bit of the intelligence that had drawn her to him in the first place. He held his left index finger up as he scribbled.

"Phanon."

He looked up. For a comically long minute he stared at Damyra. He blinked several times, fumbled with his desk drawers, and extracted an oval-shaped case. He produced a pair of glasses, small round lenses, and rested them over the bridge of his flat nose.

"Fuck me bloody."

Damyra emitted a pained chuckle.

"Good to see you too. May I?" she said, pointing to an armchair close to the entrance. She took Phanon's stunned silence as an affirmation.

"You look fucking terrible," he said from the desk. His shocked countenance was slowly regaining its normal expression.

"Your honesty warms my heart. You haven't fared the long decades excessively well either."

He reclined back, fingers intertwined over his bulging belly.

"Mighty grand of you to seek me out when you're moribund. What better way to rekindle an old acquaintance? Shouldn't you be in that precious little Hospital of yours, being looked at by one of your clever friends? You look right about to take a one-way trip to Bashork's Hall."

Damyra would have probably laughed if she weren't in so much pain.

"Are you quite alright?" he asked again, serious now. He was leaning forward, a semblance of concern on his brow.

"No. I'm not. That's why I'm here, Phanon. This… this is beyond medicine."

The Professor stood slowly and walked over to a series of cabinets and shelves on the right wall of the room. More bumbling than walking, he reached down into a cabinet and opened a hatch to a drink stand.

He pointed to a decanter glass with Portosi. She shook her head. He pointed to a glass bottle of Tunedosi blonde beer. She shook her head again.

"I see. I wasn't having the most productive of days anyway."

He grabbed two glasses and a bottle of hard Tynar liquour, the kind used by tribal leaders of the Tynar forest to challenge each other to see who was worthiest.

He filled the bottom of her glass and offered it to her.

"Thank you."

Phanon placed a clammy hand on her forehead.

"You're burning up, Damyra."

She moved her head away and nodded, relishing in the warmth crawling down her gullet.

"I know. I… Huh. I don't know where to start."

She took another sip of her drink as Phanon sat back behind his desk.

"Beginnings are not necessarily the best place to start. I find that people often confuse conception with importance, when the most prominent thing in their mind is what probably requires attention."

"Fair enough. I signed an *Akitos 'i' Legos* that binds me to assassinate Supreme Consul Kahmaos Blongatos and now I'm dying because of some unknown effect of Nokmollos," she said. Except, she didn't. No words came out. She felt aphasic, physically unable to speak. She tried again, only to emit unintelligible gurgles.

Phanon crossed his hands on his chest, forehead creasing.

"I can spot the effects of a Secrecy Clause from a stadium away."

Again, her tongue swelled and wedged in the opening of her throat. Nothing came out.

"But of course, you wouldn't be able to answer that."

A silence descended between them. Even the thought of attempting to tell him about the Agreement made her insides upend.

"Hmmm. Yes, that's why you look like utter shit."

"Once again, thank you for your candour," she said, glad she could speak at all.

"*Nokmo'mathar* is no laughing matter."

The worsening tightness in her chest, her guts churning, her knees screaming, the lost edge in an otherwise sharp mind. This had to be *Nokmo'mathar*. The cruel grip of Nokmollosi incantations that had begun poisoning her.

She writhed. He raised a hand.

"Please, stop. The harder you try to break a Secrecy Clause, the more severe the effects of *Nokmo'mathar* become."

He stood and began pacing the room, hands crossed on his back.

"Let's talk facts in isolation. You came here because you needed help, non-medical help that is. What kind of help would you get from someone with a keen interest in Binding Agreements? You can't tell me about any of it, which only points to the signing of an *Akitos'i'Legos*."

He stopped pacing, a smile as wide as his face.

"This is why Binding Agreements and Secrecy Clauses are so fascinating! You see, you can prevent the disclosure of information, but it is virtually impossible to craft an incantation to properly limit all actions carried under free will, actions that will inevitably point to an obvious reason for those with the necessary expertise!"

He pointed to Damyra, unable to hide his excitement.

"You have it with you, don't you? The Agreement? Wait no, stop! Absolutely do not tell me that!"

He looked around, deep in thought. He narrowed his eyes into slits and walked over to Damyra.

"Don't dare move a finger," he said, moving the flaps of her travelling coat. He patted the insides and fished the roll of papers out. He bounced to the desk with a near-childish radiance, extracting a reading loupe from a drawer.

Damyra was in trance, thoughts stagnant. She had never felt like that before, trapped in her own befuddled mind.

"Hmmm," Phanon murmured as he scanned the lines of strange legalese. "Yes, this is an utterly basic encryption."

He took a Smaragdos from the same drawer, cinched it around his neck and leafed through a blue Nokmollosi Codex.

"*Exios, rat'uhma oskonti Oter'ces.*"

Damyra was unsure what the result of that unknown incantation would be, nothing overtly changed.

"Ah, much better," Phanon brought his lens up again. His head moved hypnotically side to side as he read. Damyra jumped on her seat when he banged his fist on the table.

"Lashos bloody Domenikos! The bastard owes me three thousand drakmas!"

Damyra raised her eyebrows.

"You lost your right to judge thirty years ago, Damyra. I am aware of Domenikos' reputation. Lately I have been frequenting… unsavoury establishments."

"Brothals?"

"Betting houses."

Phanon rubbed his forehead with his knuckles and poured more liquor on his glass.

"My love for Underground Games will be the end of me… Anyway, what did that snivelling son of a serpent want from you? Don't answer that, purely rhetoric," he said as he carried on reading.

Before long, he paled. Minutes passed while he remained still.

She could see his eyes darting to and fro, his lips drawing out the words. She could read them from the armchair. The meticulously laid-out instructions.

On the night of Pavarios, immediately after the twelfth bell is struck, Supreme Consul Blongatos will use the back door of The Tethimosi Maid, unescorted. You are to wait in the adjacent backalley and act quickly. Kahmaos Blongatos must meet his demise by meeting the sharp end of the blade.

Phanon picked up his glass and downed all of its contents.

"Damyra, what have you done?" he said with disgust.

She held his stare.

"How… why…" he trailed off, shooting paranoid glances to the door. He pushed his bulk up from the desk and walked over to the door. He opened it, popped his head out in the corridor and then threw its three locks.

"Listen Phanon, I… agggh," her tongue flopped to the floor of her mouth. She was still unable to speak.

He raised his index finger.

"I have only decrypted it. The Secrecy Clause still stands," he said, returning to his desk.

He took off his glasses and produced a pouch from his pocket.

"But I'm not entirely sure I want to undo it, Damyra."

She simply kept staring. Phanon thumbed the hole of his pipe, eyes lost in the distance. He began filling it with Tobos leaf with mechanical movements, packing it with a spoon and lighting it with a candle on the corner of his desk. He inhaled a couple lungfuls of the smoke, his face turning more and more sour with each draught.

"How *fucking* typical of you. I haven't seen you in *three decades*, Damyra. And now you waltz into my office, throwing this… this contract," he lowered his tone to a hiss, "to commit the highest of treasons! Murder, Damyra! What do you expect of me?"

"I'm not asking for you understand what I'm doing. I just need help with the *Nokmo 'mathar*. I have no one else to go, Phanon."

"And who's fault is that?" he spat.

She had nothing to say. Her only recourse was to continue looking at him pleadingly.

He smoked the whole pipe in silence. An expectant silence that was only broken when he sighed. He shook his head with a rictus of disgust and went back the blue Codex, tracing the pages with his finger.

"Right. *Exios, Eytur' Des' Oter'ces Kolos.*"

Phanon's Smaragdos vibrated loudly. He closed his eyes and grabbed onto the edge of the desk. The contract on the table seemed to bend by its own will, the edges folding inwards. He strained for a few seconds and then released, sighing a quick *hmpf.*

As much as Phanon looked drained, Damyra felt much better. The fog extending to every recess of her brain receded, the sting in her eyes now bearable. The tightness in her chest and revolting viscera didn't vanish, but they faded into the background.

"I must assassinate Supreme Consul Kahmaos Blongatos" she tested, nearly cheering at being able to speak the truth in front of the lawyer.

"Chssst! Have you gone mad?" Phanon sprung from the table and lunged for the door. When he realised it was bolted, he pressed his back to it, looking to the sides.

"Bashork's Hall! I have a family, Damyra! I am in no mood to be detained by the Intelligence Corps, or the *Inquisition!*" he whispered madly.

Damyra bowed her head.

Vysios doesn't need to know. What's another lie or two for our sham marriage?

"I very much doubt they're listening to us, Phanon."

She stretched out her arm, holding the empty glass to him. The lawyer emitted an exasperated sigh. Soon enough, he wobbled over to the table and refilled it.

"Damyra, maybe start from the beginning. Just this once."

"A hexad ago I was approached by Domenikos. He came to the morgue, demanded to speak to me. Said I should sign a Binding Agreement with the thinly veiled threat that I wouldn't want to be on his employer's bad side. The catch was, he couldn't say what the Binding Agreement was about."

"And you listened to him?"

"He said they knew about Zar'Aldur."

Leaning against the desk, Phanon stared at his feet.

"Alda. Right."

"I wasn't going to sign it."

"Then why did you?"

Damyra looked away.

Phanon sipped at his drink, emptying the glass again.

"So who's Domenikos' employer?"

Her jaw locked instantly before she could open her mouth. Once again, her tongue didn't respond, swelling to an unnatural size, filling her whole mouth uncomfortably.

Phanon frowned. He read the contract again, shaking his head repeatedly.

"I see. Don't bother. I didn't break the entire Clause. Upon closer examination, it looks as though half this contract was written by Domenikos, the other half by someone much more intelligent than him. Or me, as implausible as that is. I won't risk any further questions."

He left the empty glass on the desk and rubbed his forehead with the knuckles of his right hand.

Damyra sunk deeper in the armchair, swallowing a wad of sour spit. A wave of unpleasantness crawled up her spine, making her shiver, insides jolting of their own accord. She wiped her forehead and her hand came wet with cold sweat.

"Is that why I still feel like utter shit?"

Phanon removed his glasses, crossed his arms, and tilted his head.

"Do I have to spell it out for you, Damyra? You are a Doctor. A *Guild-certified* Physcian that swore an Oath. Four, to be precise."

Damyra looked up to the ceiling and closed her eyes. Her upper back muscles pulled tight downwards, stiffening her lower back, hips and making his knees scream.

Hal'Gamac be damned.

"The Four Pillars of Hal'Gamac are one of the most ancient forms of an *Akitos 'i' Legos*. A primal contract bound in Titillation, compelling you to follow it. One without documents or Nokmollos, or lawyers. One more *far* more powerful."

He grasped the bottle of liquor and drank straight from it. He passed it to her.

"Can you break it?" she asked before she took a long swallow.

Phanon laughed.

"Can I *break* it... Can you stop a tidal wave with your hands? Fly around the moons and swallow the sun? Blow a hurricane with only the air in your lungs?"

"Simple *no* would have sufficed."

He lifted his right index finger for the umpteenth time. Thirty years and he still retained his astoundingly irksome mannerisms.

"There is something we can do, but I'll tell you in terms you'll understand. It's palliative. A patch, like scrambling to tar a hole in the hull of a sinking ship against the torrent of water."

"What are you trying to say?"

Phanon shook his head slowly.

"I can tar the hole, but it will burst through. It's only a matter of time before the ship sinks."

Damyra's head bobbed up and down unconsciously as she considered his words.

"I understand. Do it."

The lawyer grabbed his Nokmollosi Codex and approached her. Damyra's eyebrows knitted together when he knelt next to her with a guttural grunt. He placed the Codex on the wooden floor and his hands on hers, meaty and cold against the burning skin.

He read the open pages in front of him several times before tightening his grasp, forehead creasing.

"*Exios, Ko'Her Pan'Kos. Re'Tae tyr For'Zos.*"

Relief, cold and numbing, extended from Phanon's fingertips. It chased after the aching joint pain, eased her fever, vanished the taste of vomit from her mouth, pushed against the fire in her organs.

Pushed, not erased.

Just as the lawyer had warned, the *Nokmo'mathar* was still alive within her, she noticed. Buried deep in her abdomen, hiding down in her pelvis. Coiled and dormant.

Eitherway, the reprieve from the pain was enough for her.

"Thank you, Phanon."

"Save it," he said, standing with difficulty. He was out of breath, wheezing and sweating profusely. "Let's just say I've reached my lifetime quota of favours. Now, please leave."

He stepped over to the door, unbolted it and held it open.

"Leave to never come back again."

CHAPTER 11
* * *
Run Red
Nymor Strethos. University Hospital. Bamoria. The Fist of Nok.

"I WANT YOU each to find an acutely unwell patient and present them to me. I'll be in my office. You have until full-bell."

Danos gave the orders and absquatulated, leaving a bewildered Nym staring at the empty staircase landing.

That's not even a quarter-bell! How... what...

Amyra had already gone into the ward. He looked to the sides an alarming number of times before a pair of uniformed nurses descended the stairs. He followed his colleague and entered the ward proper to make some room, bumping into a pharmacist carrying a tray of vials.

"Watch it!" the man shouted, deftly moving the tray to the sides to stabilise the wobbling containers.

"I'm so sorry!"

"It's alright, lad. Just watch your step," he said without looking, walking into one of the bays.

Nym plastered himself to the wall, observing with panicked eyes the maddening choreography of nurses, doctors, pharmacists, and other specialists. They were wearing different togas, colours, and arrangements, denoting their position. Nym felt like being thrown into the middle of a stage during a play he didn't even know existed.

"Nymor?" Amyra called him from further down, where the corridor widened. She was standing next to a row of shelves and several chests, boxes missing the upper lid. He casted his eyes at her with a look of utter terror.

"Have you been to the wards before?"

"No. Please help."

She emitted a crystalline laughter.

"Thought so. Come over here, this is where they keep the records. It's not an exhaustive history, for those you have to go down to the Archival Department, but they have admissions notes, observations and current presentation," she explained, fingering the thin wooden flaps that separated the documents.

"Right."

"Great. There you go."

She grabbed a set of notes and patted him on the shoulder.

"You're enjoying my conspicuous discomfort a little bit too much."

She smiled and shrugged her shoulders.

"Maybe I am," she said, heading towards one of the bays.

"Amyra, wait! What in Bashork's Hall did Danos mean with 'acutely unwell patient'? We're in a hospital ward, every patient is acutely unwell!"

She laughed again.

"Astute observation. Read the name of the unit at the top of the notes," she said, tapping the papers on her hand before disappearing behind the curtains.

Admissions Unit for Acutely Unwell Patients.

He grinned.

"Excuse me, doctor. Would you please review this patient?"

He turned to the nurse proffering some notes, furrowing his brow.

"Pardon me?"

She waved the notes about.

He looked down at his borrowed white toga.

"Oh. Oh, no. *No.* I'm not a doctor. These are borrowed, you see. I'm just a student."

"Well, just-a-student, I'm Nithia and I'm busy. I don't care if you are the Supreme Consul. Review the patient and talk to one of the doctors, please. I've got things to do," the nurse said, shaking her head and thrusting the notes in his hands.

"But I'm…" he trailed off. She was already gone.

He looked through the notes.

Patient in mid-forties, of mixed Noktanian and Peninsular descent, presenting with icterus, epigastric pain, febrile, generally unwell.

He shrugged.

Guess this'll do.

Conscious of time, he headed for side room six as he delved into the notes.

"Cyrosi Khervanos Garvios," Nym said, closing the door to the private room. His eyes were still skimming the notes, squeezing in as much information in the brief moments before the patient acknowledged his presence. That brevity kept stretching and stretching.

Nym rose his eyes.

The man on the bed was a vivid picture of sickness. He was emaciated, head rested to the side, skeletal torso, protuberant clavicles and fibrous neck. He looked eerily similar to an anatomical drawing, skin removed, no fat and only wasted muscles. The grey light of an unusually clouded day casted phantasmagorical shadows on those harsh lines, made his sick skin glow even yellower against the background of pristinely white bedsheets.

Yet, despite his obvious poor state, the man struck a profound impression on Nym. There was no doubt of his Peninsular heritage, he was a hirsute man with thick eyebrows, manicured to fit his anatomy perfectly. He had an equally well-presented beard, black as coal and ending in a round point, shaped by four rings. One bronze, one silver, one golden, one made of a glowing black material.

Nym remembered his lessons, allowing plenty of time to observe the room and surroundings during his inspection, as it could offer many clues about the patient. He saw a carefully folded toga, exquisite Ei'Tulahi fabric, the most expensive Smaragdos he had ever seen with an intricately patterned metal he did not recognise, likely forged with incantations by Guild-certified Metallurgists, and a diamond embedded on its centre.

More than that, their mere unguarded presence, left unattended in the room, was astonishing.

Nym understood this man had a different sort of power. One born into, lived in, power and man one and the same.

Nevertheless, he painted such accurate image of illness that Nym wondered whether he was still alive. He let a few more seconds pass before he began panicking.

Nok save me, he's dead, isn't he?

He ran through the list of things needed for cardiopulmonary resuscitation and who he would need to call, the protocols that needed activating, the paperwork required as first responder to the medical emergency.

The patient moved his head, slowly opening his eyes.

"I do apologise, Doctor. I was resting my eyes for a moment."

Nym was taken aback by the deep, carefully inflected voice. Even in his unexpected awakening, bound to a hospital bed, wearing plain grey robes, he conducted himself regally, poised.

"I'm not a..." Nym trailed off, furrowing. Something told him this patient would not respond very well to a mundane medical student. He decided to leave that mistake uncorrected.

"I'm Nymor Stre... mos," he changed mid-sentence. That something also told him the patient would not respond very well to a *Strethos*, a Street-born, asking impertinent questions.

"Stremos. Curious name, Doctor. Is it Tunedosi?"

In more ways than you think.

"It is, Cyrosi. From Miramor."

"Beautiful city. Good business is conducted in Miramor," the man grimaced, one hand over the stomach.

"How are you feeling, Cyrosi Garvios?"

The man looked through the window with glassy eyes, taking a long time to conjure up a response. A gritty laughter, short bursts before he stopped to grimace.

"I appreciate the sentiment behind the question, Doctor, but isn't it *painfully* obvious this is not my finest hour?"

Nym blushed furiously.

"Certainly, though I never dare presume, Cyrosi," Nym said, recovering quickly. Garvios smiled, nodding. So simple a gesture, yet it made Nym feel buoyant.

"I'll change my line of inquiry, Cyrosi. What brings you to hospital?"

"Last night I found myself suffering the most excruciating pain. So terrible I folded, vomiting ceaselessly. My wife noticed then the yellow tint in my eyes and my skin. We thought best to come to hospital."

"Most sensible decision, Cyrosi. Was this pain brought on by eating?"

"Not precisely, no."

Nym nodded.

"And is the pain radiating anywhere?"

Khervanos Garvios took a few moments to think.

"Yes. It sometimes spreads through to the back, as though I'm being stabbed."

"Did it come on suddenly?"

"I suppose I have been feeling rather under the weather recently."

"I see. Have you been given any analgesia yet, Cyrosi Garvios?"

"I have indeed, though I must say its effectiveness is far from ideal."

Nym gave the notes another look.

"I see they haven't issued any Myrphinoids. I will make a note of that and have them review your pain management."

"Much obliged, Doctor."

Nym continued with his questioning, a rehearsed enquiry ingrained in his brain after countless practice sessions with Doctor Romos. An exploration of the patient's past medical history, surgical history, detailed list of medications and potential allergies, hereditary conditions running in the family and eventually, social history.

The Broken Oath

"I hope you do not find the next questions impertinent, Cyrosi, and that you do not dismiss them as inconsequential personal gossip. I simply need to know to provide the best possible care."

"Ask without vacillation, Doctor."

"Do you have a current employment?"

"I manage sundry businesses and financial directives. I'm sometimes involved in politics." There was a momentary playful glint in the Cyrosi's eyes.

"Do you smoke any Tobos' leaf?"

"I haven't for a very long time, ironically, despite having numerous stakes in Peninsular Tobos plantations," he said, giving a pained smirk as he glanced out the window.

"Any other recreational substances?"

"No."

Nym braced before asking the next question. If his medical knowledge was up to par, this would give a clear favourite in his list of differential diagnoses.

"What about alcoholic beverages?"

Cyrosi Garvios kept looking through the window with sober expression, yielding time to a settling tension, a pause that grew tauter every new second that passed.

"Occasionally," he conceded. Nym had taken enough medical histories to realise there was more behind that response.

"Would you be able to quantify that more concretely? Let us say, in the day of the hexad when most alcoholic beverages are consumed."

Again, another pause. A melancholic smile.

"Portosi red, Noktanosi ale. Rum, mead, any liquor under the sun. Even that Krossosi poison they call wine." Garvios stopped looking through the window to address him directly with stern eyes.

"This is but a variation of a conversation I have had many times, Doctor. Always the same questions, and I have had enough of them. I must know. Am I dying?"

Nym was infused with that borderline delusional confidence that he always felt when caring for someone. He was fully imbued by his role as a Doctor.

"Can I be frank, Cyrosi?"

"I would expect nothing but that, Doctor. I have asked an honest question. I demand an honest answer."

"Do you have a family, Cyrosi?"

That was an opening often used by Romos. It could be misconstrued as emotional manipulation, but devious Tysides preferred to call it 'forceful motivation'.

"I do."

"And do they matter to you?"

Seriousness permeated Garvios' face, a frightening change in his expression.

"Interpret without exaggeration, Doctor, when I say rivers would run red with the blood of those who dare cross anyone in the Garvios family."

Nym swallowed, wavering in his approach to this particular instance of 'forceful motivation'. If this went wrong, he would likely be forcefully motivated to leave the premises and the School of Medicine never to return. He plunged on, too late to back down.

"I am afraid your only enemy is yourself, Cyrosi. You will not die just yet, but you will soon enough if you do not stop drinking."

Garvios eyes weighed him for several tense moments.

"Pardon again my frankness," Nym felt compelled to add.

The man began laughing, hearty guffaws interspersed with spasms of pain.

"I cannot recall the last time someone spoke to me quite so… *frankly*. Refreshing. So, this is directly caused by drinking?"

"I believe this is a bout of acute pancreatitis, Cyrosi. Alcohol is toxic for humans after all, and the pancreas is an organ very sensitive to those toxins. After drinking copious amounts of alcohol over prolonged periods of time, it can become inflamed. This inflammation can also stop your bile, a digestive juice, to move through your intestinal tract and its components accumulate in the skin, giving you that characteristic yellow colour. We call it icterus or flavinism."

Garvios nodded solemnly.

"I understand, Doctor," he said, before returning his eyes to the overcast sky. Nym considered his perhaps morally dubious method of prompting a lifestyle change successful.

"What happens next?"

"I will do a quick abdominal examination and convey my findings to a senior doctor. Then, we will initiate treatment."

"Thank you, Doctor. I must congratulate you in your resolve."

Nym looked down. Resolve. He smiled. Resolve is all he truly needed.

"You're late, Strethos. Lateness is thoroughly unprofessional."

Nym was breathing heavily by the door, the full-bell having tolled some time ago. Levantios Danos was stood behind his desk, hands crossed in his back. Amyra was looking down from her chair.

"I apologise, Doctor Danos. I was pulled aside by one of the nurses and I had to do an intake form for a patient, then report to one of the doctors in the ward."

Danos held his eyes for a couple of tense seconds. He then nodded, sitting and gesturing to the empty chair next to Amyra's.

"I assume it was the case you will be presenting now?"

The Broken Oath

"Yes, Doctor," Nym said, rushing to be seated. He wrestled with his notebook, uneven lines he had scribbled as he ran through labyrinthine corridors.

"Very well," Danos interlaced his fingers on the table.

"I saw a man in his forties, Peninsular descent. He presented with epigastric pain, vomiting and icterus. These symptoms started—"

Nym stopped. Danos had raised a hand.

"Part of your task as a clinician is being able to identify what is the chief complaint, and what are associated symptoms. What is more important here, in your opinion?"

"Epigastric pain."

"Very well, then focus on that."

Nym bowed his head.

"Epigastric pain, though common for the patient, it exacerbated greatly last night to the point of being unbearable. It radiates through to the back, characterised as being 'stabbing' in nature and accompanied by vomiting and icterus."

"Does that complete your presenting complaint and history of presenting complaint?"

"It does, Doctor."

"Right. Now I would like you to imagine I'm on my way to a surgery and you need to capture my attention. Knowing his initial presentation, what other factors point you to a suspected diagnosis?"

Nym scanned his notes, juggling and rearranging words in his head.

"The patient acknowledged excessive alcohol consumption for an extended period of time, pointing to acute pancreatitis."

"Good. I want both of you to read up on other differentials for epigastric pain, as well as treatment and management of acute pancreatitis. Now," Danos said, standing. He stretched his hand up, grasping a handle near the ceiling and pulling down a chalkboard that covered half of the ample window. "Amyra," he continued, drawing a shape with white chalk. "What is this?"

"The liver," she answered promptly.

"And Nymor," the doctor drew on, tube-like structures extending downwards from the liver. "What is this?"

"The... hepatic duct?"

Danos shook his head.

"Not quite. Amyra?"

"The common bile duct."

"Correct. What structure does the common bile duct connect into, Nymor?"

"Pancreatic duct."

"Be more specific."

Nym's forehead creased.

"I... don't understand what you mean, Doctor Danos."

Levantios Danos looked at Amyra.

"The common bile duct and major pancreatic duct fuse together to form the hepatopancreatic ampulla, also known as Ampulla of Vathas."

"I don't suppose you know the name of the sphincter that separates the hepatopancreatic ampulla and the duodenum," Danos said to Nym.

"I…um…" he trailed off, rubbing the back of his head.

"Sphincter of Odos," Amyra chipped in.

Danos sat back down, propping his head with his right forearm, pondering.

"You're lacking important foundational anatomical knowledge, Nymor."

Amyra again avoided his eyes.

"I must apologise once more," he said blushing, looking down. The excitement of the previous interaction with Garvios turned into the ashen taste of shame and embarrassment in his mouth. "Doctor Romos has a more… *hands-on* approach to medicine."

Danos emitted an affirmative grunt.

"Whilst that is undoubtedly good, you must learn the basis. There is no point in continuing this lesson before that is remedied. We will have to take care of that."

"Yes, Doctor."

"Take the rest of the day off for self-study, I must see to some things," Danos told them. He lingered by the door before leaving.

"Out of curiosity, what was the name of the patient you clerked in, Nymor?"

"Errr, Peninsular family name, Garvus or Gartios, something of the sort."

"Khervanos Garvios?" the Doctor asked, a hint of strain in his voice.

"Yes."

He dashed away without another word, door ajar after him. Nym frowned.

"What's the matter with him?"

Amyra's eyes were two big pools of white and golden-green.

"Nymor, you took the history of Khervanos Garvios. The Garvios family owns the hospital."

Pieces fell into place.

"Oh. I thought the University fully funded the hospital."

"How do you think this massive complex was built in so little time? It was a joint venture. The Guilds Association only owns half of it, the other half is all Garvios wealth."

"How about that…" he murmured as they closed Danos' office door. Aeros waved at them from the reception, smiling unctuously.

"Have a great day!"

"You too, Aeros," Amyra said, chasing after Nym who had swiftly exited into the main corridors.

"What's the rush?"

"I just can't stand that smile. He must be on something. Perpetual happiness is suspicious, don't you think?"

Amyra elbowed him.

"Oh, stop. Not everyone is as miserable as you. It's part of his job, anway."

"If that was part of my job I wouldn't survive the first day, I'll tell you that."

The clouds had shifted enough for the sun to peek through the glass dome, rays bouncing playfully in the central hanging lattice of crystals.

"How about that suturing teaching now? I can offer some anatomy tutoring in exchange, remedy that unacceptable gap in your knowledge," Amyra suggested, leaning against the veranda.

"I would love to, but I was... going somewhere."

Her expression changed subtly, so subtle it escaped Nym's attention entirely.

"You're going to see her, aren't you?"

Nym smiled.

"I'm furiously hoping I'll do something more than just seeing her. Speaking to her again should be a good enough start."

The Red River Tavern wasn't enjoying an exuberant number of patrons on that lazy Aesios afternoon. The main grounds of the School of Law had been largely empty as Nym had approached the otherwise popular establishment, harbouring the far-fetched hope to stumble upon Haleana, aided solely by the capricious hands of chance. Barely a quarter-bell past one, faculty and students were still locked inside the windowless monolith.

Nym was met by the bar in the centre, empty. A grim premonition for his fragile wishes.

The left side of the tavern was comprised of several tables and private alcoves arranged around a raised pedestal for performers. There were only a few students and a robed professor populating the area, a roaring crowd compared to the completely barren opposite side.

Of course she wasn't there.

Nym's shoulders sagged instantly, lips curving into a sad smile.

"How foolish can one really be?" he whispered. He vacillated in the entrance, tapping his side-hip, feeling for the purse concealed behind his dirty trousers. Considering the weight satisfactory for some much-needed consolation, he approached the bar.

The barkeep was busy wiping the impolute surface, making it glisten with the shaking light of the torches. He was the young helper that had been wrestling with a barrel during Nym's first fateful visit to the tavern, he remembered. Intense red hair rendered even more distinctive by his pale Limthosi skin. Kothos, his name was.

He stopped wiping to address him, both hands on the counter. Nym couldn't help but notice he was a rather handsome fellow, clear eyes a promise of assiduous mischief.

"What will it be? Another round of Krossosi wine? You gotta be careful with that stuff, it'll burn a hole in your stomach if you don't pace yourself."

Nym laughed sonorously.

"Am I that memorable?"

"Embarrassing spectacles are always expected when students try to chat up each other, but yours was particularly striking. I will be frank, I didn't even know we stocked Krossosi wine," Kothos said, grabbing a pint glass with lithe fingers. He started polishing it.

"All I'm hearing is that I'm memorable."

Kothos winked.

"That you are. So? Have you come here today only to distract your fidel barkeep?"

Nym let the sack of drakmas fall heavily on the bar.

"I have enough funds today to afford your best ale."

"Bold. After all, how expensive can ale really get?"

Nym narrowed his eyes into slits. He opened the sack and deposited two drakmas before returning it to his toga.

"Do you see right through everyone as much as you do me, barkeep?"

"Occupational hazard. One grows rather perspicacious after a while. All I do is read people, daily."

Nym pulled one of the stools and sat down in front of Kothos, leaning onto the bar.

"Read me, then."

Kothos rested the pint glass under a tap connected to a tube dangling from the ceiling. He opened it, amber liquid pouring into the tilted glass. Masterfully draughted, all ale but for a finger-width of foam at the top.

"If I remember correctly, you were besotted by that girl when you decided to buy the rat poison. You came again today in the hopes you would see her again," he said, thrusting the pint in front of Nym.

"You are *good*."

Kothos waved his right hand in an exaggerated flourish before bowing.

"Yours to serve. Sadly, she never comes on Aesios, I'm afraid."

Nym hunkered over the pint, eyes lost in the distance.

"I see."

Kothos snickered.

"She's got a real hold on you, doesn't she?"

"It appears as though she does," Nym said, puckering his lips, eyebrows meeting in the middle. He felt a strange sort of relief when admitting that aloud. He was surprised by the inscrutable power of those vocalised thoughts. "Never mind that," he continued, "I was enjoying our conversation anyway, barkeep."

Kothos bowed his head.

"Again, here to serve."

"Please, do continue with your readings. What am I studying, then?"

Kothos continued to polish glasses, piling them in gravity-defying patterns on the back shelves.

"You see, despite my undeniable talents, the colour-coded togas and robes help a lot. You, on the other hand, have none."

"Quickly falls the curtain hiding the puppeteer," Nym said, scrambling to find a plausible excuse. "There was an issue with mine, I'm still waiting for them. You don't strike me as someone that would cower from the challenge, though."

"Ah," Kothos said, tilting his head slightly backwards. "If I were to hazard a guess, I'd say you are a Humanities student. Most of our students don't have such a beautiful grasp on Neokahmirian. I find they have an abhorrent reluctance to crack open a book."

It was Nym's turn to bow his head pronouncedly.

"You flatter me so, but no. I am but a humble medical student."

"Ha! Humble, you say. Yes, now that you say that it does make sense. You do look like the medical type."

"Why do I feel like that is a veiled insult?"

"Oh, my mistake. I didn't mean to veil it at all."

Nym opened his mouth mockingly, feigning shock.

"Careful there, barkeep. You'll lose a clie—"

"Well, would you look at that," Kothos interrupted, tossing the rag on the bar surface. "I never am, yet it looks as though I was wrong on this one occasion. Do excuse me, I have a new customer to attend."

Nym followed Kothos' eyes to the entrance, where a silver-grey robed law student had entered the tavern. Her slightly wavy hair was the colour of fine Sylvari wood and her breathtaking eyes, two globes more resplendent than the sun, were fixated on the page of a book.

Mouth half-agape, Nym's eyes followed Haleana's serendipitous figure as she walked to the far end of the bar, the very same spot where he had seen her first.

Kothos was already pouring wine from a decanter into a tall, thin glass.

Nym stared dumbly, hand coiled around the half-empty pint. She was still reading the same book, he was sure of it.

She rose her eyes from the page, they locked eyes.

"This can't possibly be another coincidence," she said.

Returning to the other end of the bar, Kothos pointed in her direction with dissimulation. A subtle, beckoning shake of his head.

"No, you're right. Alas, providence does have its limits," Nym said, walking over to her side of the bar. "May I?" he asked, pointing to the stool next to hers.

"You certainly may, yet I must disappoint you again. I am studying."

She sipped wine from the cup handed by the barkeep and returned her gaze to the page.

Nym shot a glance to Kothos. He was busy serving new clients. As the hour neared the end of lessons, more and more students had begun arriving at the Red River Tavern. The barkeep did have enough time to shrug his shoulders nonchalantly at Nym.

Cheeky bastard.

Nym scratched his head.

"Studying is good. I myself do some of that from time to time, you know."

Haleana rose her eyebrows without lifting her head from the book.

"Do you, now?" she said with minimal interest.

Nym drafted a hearty gulp from the pint.

"So how do you know Amyra?"

Once again, Haleana spoke without pulling her eyes away from her book.

"We grew up with the same tutors," she said succinctly.

"Interesting. How come you chose different career paths?"

"I don't know. That's life for you, I suppose."

"Ah, yes. Life. A most fickle orchestrator. Let me ask you something, why do you come to study here? In a tavern?"

Haleana stopped reading. She looked at him with those golden-brown eyes. Ineffable, surveying, and ponderous.

"Alright..." she trailed off, gesturing at him, encouraging him to say something.

Realisation hit, heart dropped in his chest.

She doesn't remember my name.

"Nym."

"Nym, yes. Are you always this loquacious, Nym?"

"Only in the presence of those capable of handling the wit of my loquacity, of course."

She stared at him for several charged breaths before breaking her serious countenance with a genuine smile.

Aha! Got you, elusive Haleana.

She reclined with her back against the wall, rising her glass between them.

"I enjoy a glass of wine or two, makes Kahmirian Law go down more easily."

Nym raised his own glass to the toast.

"Fascinating, seldom do I find another who truly exploits the sharpening effects of alcohol," he said, downing the last of his ale. He pushed the pint glass away and signaled Kothos for a second round.

"Virtue is in the middle, Nym," she scoffed, "and by the laws of exponential growth, that sharpening will soon turn to stupor if you keep up the pace."

"You underestimate me, Haleana. I know my limits," he said, welcoming the second pint that Kothos gave him with open hands.

Haleana analysed his movements, observed him over the rim of her glass. She nodded.

"Yes. I see now what she meant."

"What's that?"

"No matter, thinking out loud."

Nym wiped the foam on his lips, letting the ale extend a pleasant warmth all over his body.

"Don't let me stop you, do share with the class. What are you thinking?"

"Conversations. That's all I think about sometimes. Conversations, how the most inconsequential little chats can carry a world of weight. How is your tutelage under Levantios Danos?"

"He is much like setting a dislocated shoulder back into its original position. Necessary, but brutal. He is a rather good teacher, but quite frankly, let me put it this way, my bowel movements have been more numerous since I started studying with him."

"Intense."

"Very much so. You wouldn't even know, Haleana."

"Yes, that's come up in a chat of two with Amyra. I am friends with her, remember?"

"Right, right," he pushed the pint away. "Maybe I do have to pace myself," he joked, though the harsh reality was that the effect of having that conversation with Haleana was a hundred times more inebriating than a dozen pint. He could easily do without beer.

"What happened to the sharpening?"

"Alas, you've rendered me edgeless. I submit to your superior knowledge."

She flashed that maddening smile before finishing her glass. The one that tugged at him, made him *want* her.

"Well, Nym. As much as I find you amusing, I still have work to do."

He looked down at the bar, nodding slowly as the momentary oasis disappeared, reality settling. She was not interested. He grabbed his pint and stood.

"I understand. I will take my gentle insistence away before it morphs into outright pestering."

"Mighty optimistic of you to think it hasn't already morphed," she said, smiling.

He offered a smile of his own and turned to go.

Yes, perhaps she wasn't interested. Perhaps she was conveniently using her studying to swat his unwanted attention away.

Or perhaps she *was* interested, but needed to work, nonetheless.

He would hate himself if he didn't try one last thing. He whirled to face her again.

"Before I leave, I do have an offer to make. I have yet to prove that I do indeed study. Would you like to accompany me some time to a location more conducive of the profound concentration we require, say, the University Library?"

She cocked her head.

"Aham, I see. But what if I say no?" she said playfully. Nym puckered and stomped on the floor, spilling ale, and eliciting some looks from the growing crowd.

"Then prepare to be responsible for the lives of everyone here! My ire knows no bounds! I will make rivers run red! Then, and only then, this tavern will truly earn its name!"

Her melodious laughter drowned the merry cacophony of the tavern.

"Alright, alright. I do not want to bear that on my conscience."

"Truly?"

"Yes, yes! Now settle down, or the University Guard will come for you. What will you have to say then, loquacious Nym?"

He rose his index fingers, smile beaming.

"Nothing but the truth. That it will have been worth it!"

CHAPTER 12
* * *

Pen and Paper

Phanon Tamyros. School of Law. Guilds Association University. Fist of Nok.

"ARE YOU LISTENING?"

Phanon blinked, refocusing on the man's reprobatory countenance. Enkir Mesopos' perpetual scorn was coming perilously close to angry snare.

"My apologies, Enkir. I find myself uncharacteristically distracted lately."

"May I suggest you remedy that? We have a frail situation in our hands, and I need your help," the Head of the School of Law said.

Phanon sighed, rubbing his forehead with his knuckles.

"Is there truly any reason to worry?"

He stood and wobbled to the shelves.

"You tell me, Phanon. You wrote the Nokdamned thing."

Tamyros waved his hand dismissively, fencing his index finger forward.

"I was the Scribe, nothing more. The University Charter was agreed upon by all Guilds. Besides, I seem to remember you were there with Xeno Dionos and the rest of his cronies."

"Don't condescend me, Tamyros. I remember the Signing very well. Spare me the history lesson and tell me how to make this go."

Phanon grabbed a book and returned to his desk.

"If memory serves right, I'm afraid you can't."

"Every contract has a loophole."

"Not if I wrote it," he said, flipping pages. "I believe— yes, here it is. 'A referendum can be motioned by any member of the University, student or staff, backed by representation of at least five other individuals sharing said status from every School, in any meeting of the Intercollegiate Council.'"

"It must be submitted to vote in the Council, though," Mesopos said, wriggling in his chair to lean forward. He was rubbing the fingers of his right hand together compulsively.

"Yes, but it only has to pass a simple majority."

"Bah! Preposterous!" Mesopos pushed his chair back. He began pacing Phanon's office.

"Are you entirely sure that we must vote on it? Isn't there a disqualifying clause for being a… crude, fanatical nincompoop?"

"Not quite. That's why it must be backed by five representatives from each School. Did Kalavis submit the necessary signatures?"

"He did."

"Then it must be," Phanon announced as he closed the book.

"Unacceptable."

Phanon laced his fingers together over his protuberant abdomen.

"Eupides, *please*. So what if Kalavis wants to play politics and run his little campaign? The referendum won't pass."

Eupides Mesopos collapsed on the chair, burying his face on his right hand.

"I can't allow even the faintest uncertainty, Phanon. You don't understand the pressure I'm under from the Association."

Tamyros ran his knuckles across his forehead.

"That I can't help you with, Eupides. There's a reason why I retired from politics long ago, University or otherwise."

"I could use some of that famed Tamyros political intuition right about now."

Phanon grunted.

"Here's a little pearl of Tamyros wisdom. Democracy is an illusion, a pretty lie we tell ourselves to soothe our weak moralities and sleep at night. Who will vote in this referendum?"

Mesopos frowned.

"Students and members of staff."

"Exactly, and students will always be more numerous. Have you seen the students we're getting lately?"

Mesopos shrugged his shoulders.

"Point being?"

"They're terrible! Lazy, spoiled bastards that don't attend half their lectures! We've become glorified childminders for the Cyrosi of the League who dump their useless offspring on Campus ground. They'll do whatever their teachers say, like the stupid mindless sheep they are! Even if the Council vote allows it, all you need to do is... *persuade* a few key professors and the rest will follow."

Mesopos rose his head.

"Yes. Yes! That might work."

"It will, trust me. If it told you—" Phanon stopped, tilting his head. He thought he had heard something. An almost imperceptible creak. A gentle change of pressure? A trick of his mind?

"What is it?" Mesopos asked.

Phanon raised a finger. He dashed to the door and opened it, heart pounding in his chest.

There was no one on the other side.

Surely not.

He turned his head several times. The corridor was empty.

"Phanon?"

"It's nothing. I thought I heard something, must have imagined it."

He remained by the door, eyebrows united in the centre of his forehead. Eyes lost somewhere in the distance without seeing. He screwed his eyelids together.

Not again.

"Are you quite alright?"

"Yes, yes. I've had a taxing day, that's all. If you will excuse me."

"Of course. Thank you for your help," the Head of the School said, joining him by the door and offering his hand. Phanon shook it distractedly. He waited a few seconds after Mesopos disappeared around the corner, casting his eyes back and forth, before he returned to his office.

The neck of the decanter clinked against the rim of the glass, dark red Portosi flowing into it. It clinked many times before the expensive wine reached the brim, then overflowed.

"Shit."

Phanon left the glass untouched and sat down. He started drinking from the decanter, ignoring the spillage seeping into strewn papers, staining them red.

Damyra's visit had been entirely unexpected, he hadn't seen her for close to thirty years! Why would he be listened to? He was not unfamiliar to the unforgiving tendrils of paranoia, the most toxic poison of the mind, and he knew the inherent risk for those who spend too much time travelling the confusing grooves of the brain.

"Yes, that must be it. I'm overthinking again."

He drank the last of the wine in big, avaricious gulps and pushed the decanter on the desk. It slid across, halting when it collided with the glass and sprayed more wine. He paid no mind.

He grabbed his leather case from under the table and extracted a worn-out journal. He fished out a pen from under the papers and began writing.

It's happening again. That nauseating sensation, the doubt of whether something is a figment of my imagination or indeed real. Real to others.

He took a big breath.

I trust Doctor Mephistos' method, I do understand this is panic. I must be rational. All I saw was a brief fluctuation of light, misinterpreted by my tired brain, marred by worry.

I have spent inordinate amounts of time in this office, working and pondering. I have stared at the floorboards long, memorising its patterns, the way they bend when people walk by. How that one with a darker vein appears to curve under weight on the other side of the door, pointing to the adjacent board.

Just like it was doing then.

Phanon placed the pen on the page, eyes bulging out of his skull. He was not a fast man by any definition of the word, yet the fear conferred him feline agility. He sprung from the chair and rushed to the door, opening it brusquely. He realised only then he was holding the decanter by its neck, brandishing it like a weapon.

Once again, the corridor was empty.

Except, when he looked to the right, he saw the waning light at the end of the hallway shift. And was that…? Indeed, the sound of steps, tailed by someone's shadow. It was unmistakable.

He vacillated by the door, pivoting left and right. He threw the decanter on the armchair and plunged to his desk. He started opening drawers arbitrarily, pulling so hard the frames broke and they flew across the office, dropping their contents on the floorboards.

He found a sheathed blade, roughly the size of his forearm. Fine leather hilt, new and unused, a fine emerald embedded in the hilt. Trembling fingers secured it around his waist.

Fat load of good it'd do against an incantator SCI agent.

That thought gave him pause.

He remembered a box gathering dust under his desk, given to him by a friend in a fundraiser in the School of Engineers. He squatted and grabbed it. It was heavy. He lifted it, growling, and pushed it on the desk. It displaced the papers and books which in turn knocked over the glass, spilling wine all over.

It still had a scribbled note attached to it.

I thought you ought to look at this after our conversation about checks and balances of incantators. It's designed to incapacitate, not kill. It's only a prototype though!

Perios

P.S. Not sure whether this project would pass ratification from the Association. Don't show anyone. And remember to aim for the neck.

Phanon opened the crate. The inside was cushioned, lined with silk. Resting on its centre, a device made of wood and metal. A bow dovetailed into a length of fine Tynar timber, hooks and levers along its surface. It was folded to occupy less space, and next to it a single bolt, shaped like a horseshoe.

When he picked up the device it unfolded on its own. One didn't have to be a weapons expert to understand its functioning. There was a circular gear on its left and a protruding lever. He gyrated the crank and a mechanism retracted the thin filament of the bow, until it clicked into place and he couldn't turn the gear anymore.

Intuitively he held the butt of the wood against his shoulder and took aim at an imaginary incantator. It even had a circle of metal with a wire cross, facilitating the aiming.

There was a trigger underneath, placed where his right hand sat naturally. He pulled and sharp twang accompanied the release of the cord.

"Nice."

He folded the device, grabbed the bolt, and stashed them in his case before he left.

"Ilyra. Ilyra, wake up, please. Get dressed. We need to go," Phanon said, gently shaking his wife's shoulder. The sheets rustled when she turned, the confused furrowing of sleep on her brow.

"Phanon?"

"Yes, dear. Get dressed, please," he said with urgency, leaving the candle he was carrying on the bedside table before moving to the windows of the room.

He drew a sliver of the fabric, carefully. The oil lampposts lining the street below the Faculty Residences flickered weakly, creating shifting shadows in the night that fuelled his paranoia. The horses drawn to a carriage formed particularly grotesque silhouettes, long limbs and moving torsos that made his saliva dry and glue his throat shut, his heart pound harder.

His wife covered her eyes from the candle flame.

"Phanon, it's late," she said, turning away from the light.

"I know it's late, but you need get to up."

He sat on the bed and helped Ilyra to sit up reluctantly.

"Why? What... what's happening?"

Phanon took her face in his hands, caressing tenderly.

"Ilyra, you know I'm not one for hysterics. There is no exaggeration when I say if we don't leave right now, we won't see the light of day *ever* again."

"Leave where, Phanon? What are you talking about? You're worrying me," her voice grew harsher. She shook her husband's hands off and moved away, right hand on her distended abdomen. He clenched his jaw.

"Worry is a good start. Worry is warranted, trust me," he said, pulling a trunk from under the bed. He began opening drawers and haphazardly throwing clothes and jewellery inside.

"Phanon, what in Bashork's Hall are you doing?"

"I told you. We must leave now. I'll explain on the way."

Her face softened momentarily. She shuffled her bottom to the edge of the bed and used the night table to prop herself up. She waddled around, right hand still on her bulging belly and left hand on her side. She squatted next to her husband and placed a tentative hand on his forearm, caressing his skin ever so slightly with her thumb.

"Phan. Is this about your... um, paranoia?"

His muscles grew tense. Ilyra quickly withdrew her hand and returned it to her belly before he relaxed again. He carried on packing things away.

"I... At first, I thought that might be case, but... I was in my office, and I heard someone eavesdropping, I'm certain... and I saw... something. And after Dam... No, it can't be a coincidence. Just can't."

Her lips painted a straight line.

"Phanon, listen to yourself. You're not making any sense. Isn't it possible that this just a bout of your illness?"

He stood up brusquely.

"Fine. Fine! Don't believe me. Let's say this is all an acute deterioration of my mental condition. If you humour me, just this once, I swear to Nok, Helad and the entire *fucking* Kahmirian Pantheon that I'll go to Doctor Mephistos and let him pump me with every anti-psychotic known to man until they seep out of my arsehole. Now, please. Get. Dressed."

Ilyra grasped the bedframe and helped herself up. She began wrapping a travelling toga around her without uttering another word.

"Thank you," he said, relieved. He drew the curtains again, barely a crack.

He surveyed the street again, then the road beyond connecting the Residences and the Main Campus. It traversed the Serpent's Spine in a segment where the mountains didn't reach quite as high. He also glanced north, unable to distinguish the School of Medicine in the obscure distance. He had been careful to keep to the shadows. A journey that didn't normally require far past a full-bell on horseback had taken him hours, but he had been careful he was not being followed.

A heavy knock came on the front door. Three solid, reverberating blows.

Ilyra looked at him, mouth half agape, face furrowed.

Something dropped inside Phanon, as though a suctioning void had appeared deep inside his ribcage. A void that extended its tendrils and gripped his viscera, pulling inward, imploding. His ears became full of his heart pounding, his vision swam. After a few seconds, his trembling hand reached for his hip. He unsheathed the dagger, glint reflecting over Ilyra's terrified eyes.

"Put on your Smaragdos," he whispered.

She nodded.

He blew the candle and moved into the corridor with short, measured steps, using his hand against the wall to guide himself in the darkness. He lived in the lowest floor of the Residences, a humble accommodation consisting of a long corridor connecting kitchen, room, and washroom. Despite being barely a few steps long, the hallway seemed to stretch to infinity. A macabre illusion of his mind, like two mirrors confronted creating an interminable projection.

He swallowed with difficulty, worried about the mad galloping of his heart in his chest. He was sure it was audible, loud as the pattering of hooves in the dead of night.

He stopped a few paces away from the door, silence hanging like an executioner's axe. Yearning to be broken.

Nothing happened.

He raised the wavering blade in front of him.

"Who goes?"

"Herios, at your service, Enkir Tamyros."

He dropped his arm to his side. His back released the tension and his shoulders slumped. He emitted a squeal of a chuckle.

Of course.

He opened the door to a young boy in his late teens, rubbing his reddened eyes.

"Apologies for the delay, I... dozed off. Your carriage is waiting, Enkir Tamyros. As requested."

"Damyra paid me a visit yesterday."

Ilyra stared at the night through the window of the carriage as they entered Guilds Way. Hundreds of feet below the waters of the Eye of Nok lapped peacefully at the bases of the columns, massive pillars that bore the weight of the aqueduct-like path connecting the island of Katadia and the eastern shore of the Eye of Nok.

Normally they would be able to see the reflected moons on the peaceful surface, observe the mighty walls of Noktanos come closer, the Forbidden Citadel looming nearer as they approached the capital city of the League. They couldn't tonight. Pregnant clouds clustered in the sky, menacing discharge, rendering the night dark and ominous.

Herios had followed orders suit, spurring the horses to an all-out galloping, hooves clattering loudly on the cobblestones as they dashed in the night.

Ilyra's lips puckered. Phanon could see she was working her tongue inside her mouth, caging it, repressing it.

"I thought you said you hadn't seen her in thirty years."

"And I hadn't. Until yesterday," he said, shuffling forward. He rested his hand on hers.

"Ilyra, sweet, it's not like that."

"Then what is it like?"

She still refused to look at him. He sat back.

"What did she want?"

"She needed some legal advice. I think it's safer if I don't tell you all the details. Suffice it to say she disclosed some… *dangerous* things."

She locked eyes with him.

"Dangerous?"

"She has become involved with the wrong sort of people."

"The Factions again?" she asked, disappointed grin on her face. She shook her head. "How do I believe you, Phanon? You said you were done with Slum business."

He pressed his fingers against his forehead.

"And I am! This is different. Worse than the Factions. It has to do with Alda, and Nok's Voice."

"Worse than the…" Ilyra trailed off, shaking her head. "You know I love you, but I can't help you if you are set on destroying yourself. Your career, your *family*," she grasped her belly tighter. "You know what she did to you, Phanon."

He looked down.

"I know, and I told her to never seek me out again."

She pursed her lips. They sat in contemptuous silence, swaying to and fro with the carriage's movements.

"Let's do it," he said abruptly.

"Let's do what?"

"Fuck the School of Law, and the University, and everyone! I am done. Let's go to Parthos, let's retire to your Father's estate. Raise our baby in peace. Away from the Factions, Damyra and that pit of vipers," he said, gesturing toward Noktanos.

Ilyra glanced at him. Over him, rather, indignation tugging at the edges of her face.

"I'm serious, Ilyra."

"You might think you are, but I have been disappointed enough times. I'll believe it when I see it."

"I said I was sorry about—" Phanon stopped. He raised a finger.

"Did you hear that?"

"No, Phanon. I didn't hear anything, because there's noth—"

"There again!"

A distant thud. Ilyra turned to face the night. She had heard it as well.

The carriage swerved, wooden wheels screeching as they drifted across Guilds Way. The right side of the cabin suddenly rose, as though the carriage had gone over a huge bump. Both passengers struggled to remain seated. Ilyra was thrown to the floor back-first by the sudden deceleration, both hands across her belly. Phanon was tossed to the opposite wall, landing painfully on his right shoulder.

After a few seconds, the carriage righted itself, picking up speed.

"Are you alright?"

Ilyra's breathing was rapid, eyes wide with fear. She looked unharmed but for a few bruises.

"The baby?"

"Moving."

Phanon banged his fist on the roof.

"Herios, is everything alright, lad?"

There was no response from the driver.

"Herios?"

Phanon stuck his head out in the night, blinking profusely. It had started raining heavily. He craned forward, grabbing onto the frame. He could see the four horses, galloping ahead madly. Only one lamp remained lit, orange hue revealing an empty plank, whip discarded on it.

There was no one on the driver's seat.

It was then when he caught a blurry flash out of the corner of his eye. He didn't think, his reaction visceral, subconscious. He threw himself on top of Ilyra.

"I love you," he managed to whisper in her ear before the cabin exploded.

Cloudy night, fire, smoke, and splintered wood alternated before his eyes. Eventually, he found himself face down on the wet cobbles of Guilds Way.

He wriggled pointlessly. He was trapped under one of the wheels and a mountain of debris. Too numb to feel his broken ribs, his bruised legs and torso. A patina of sweat and rain marring his vision.

He rubbed his face against his shoulder and took account of his surroundings. He was lying under the destroyed carriage, his case and trunk obliterated, upended contents across the cobblestones.

"Phanon! Phanon!"

"Ilyra, I'm here!" he cried.

"Watch out!"

He ducked his head as hurricane winds blew savagely, moving the debris trapping him.

"Can you stand?" Ilyra shouted once the winds abated. She was wearing her Smaragdos.

"Are you alright?" Phanon grunted, limping beside his wife.
"I'm alright. What was th—"
"Down!" Phanon pushed her to her knees as plume of fire burnt past them. Its hot light let him see the incantator perfectly. A cloaked figure, some dozen paces away. Phanon dove for the contents of his case. He fumbled with the crank of the device, which had unfolded, turning the gear with slippery fingers. The cord quickly retracted and he mounted the U-shaped bolt.

Before the incantation ended, he turned swiftly and took aim, resting the butt of the weapon on his shoulder.

When he pulled the trigger springs, pulleys and levers screeched and moaned as they were activated. The bolt flew in the night, striking the incantator on the neck.

Fire ceased immediately and the hooded figure emitted a pained squeal before collapsing to the ground.

Phanon looked at the device, dumbfounded.

"Huh."

There was no time to rejoice at his unforeseen marksmanship. His wife was shouting incantations in his direction.

Two cloaked figures had emerged from the edge of the elevated pathway, landing gracefully on the walls. Yet another one appeared on the opposite side, behind Ilyra.

"Behind you!" he screamed, dodging the wheels and splintered wood Ilyra had sent hurtling toward their assailants. Ilyra turned to face them.

Phanon limped precariously to the other two, throwing the device with all his might at one of them. He put his back to his wife and unsheathed his dagger.

The assailant on the right lingered back, slowed by the hurled device, whilst the other had a naked blade poised for attack.

Phanon met the steel with the awful realisation he would be quickly overpowered. Regardless of the quality of his dagger, it was just a dagger. His attacker was taller than him, swinging a Senate-issued xyphos.

He grunted, blade coming closer to him. He was using both his hands on the small hilt, knowing it was not enough. He let his left hand go and pressed it on the blade, sharp metal biting deep into the skin of his palms.

Pain like he had never known burst in his hand, fired up down his forearm as blood seeped profusely. He shrieked, struggled, imprinted all his dwindling force in resisting the man.

He didn't last long.

The other attack had caught up, swinging the hilt of their xyphos hard to the back of Phanon's head. He collapsed, thrashing in semi-consciousness. He felt a needle puncturing the side of his rear.

Pain and sound washed away as a cold, unwelcoming unconsciousness took him.

"Up, you fat prick."

The voice sounded inhuman to Phanon, impossible to match to a body. Genderless and hoarse, it switched between deep and high-pitched tones.

"See? I told you I didn't mess up the dose. He's waking up," another voice said, this one clearly a woman's.

Ilyra! Where's Ilyra?

"My... wif..."

He received a brutal slap across the face, rattling his teeth and forcing his eyes open.

"Save the talking for now. Methia, go fetch the others. Our illustrious guest is awake," the first voice croaked.

Consciousness returned to him staggered, small bursts at a time. First blurry contours, shaky lights. Torches, they were, a hundred of them, then dozens, then two when his eyes finally focused.

A red-haired Limthosi woman stood in front of him, a knotty scar splitting her pale and angry countenance. She had a nasty-looking bruise on her neck, greenish-purple blotches all over. She slapped him again, twisting her hips and putting the strength of his upper back. She knew how to hit.

"That one is for my bloody neck, you bastard."

Spittle mixed in with speckles of blood flew out of his mouth, staining the circular walls of the small empty room. Apart from the chair he was bound to, the torches were the only other adornment.

"Good thing I couldn't find that damn weapon, or I would have shoved it up your fat arse," she said, rubbing her neck.

Before long, the door opened and the woman whose name must be Methia entered. She was followed by three men, one of them so tall he had to bow his head lightly to stand upright in the room. Phanon's head lolled to the side unbidden, and he saw a fourth man, gesturing to a child to stay out of the room.

"Pasho, this is your customer," the Limthosi said to the fourth man that had been speaking to the boy. He was short and wiry. Brown Peninsular skin, bushy eyebrows, and keen clever eyes.

"Enkir Tamyros, damn shame we couldn't resolve our issues through the intermediaries."

The woman Methia walked up next to him, grabbed a fistful of his hair and pulled his head up.

"Arghh," Phanon whimpered.

"Well? Ain't got nothing to say for yourself?"

"Please... My wife..."

"Shush. Your wife is safe. She put up quite the fight, unlike you. She ain't going anywhere. Where's me money, Tamyros?"

"Your... money?"

Working up the effort to form more than a word was like walking through mud. Why would the Senatorial Intelligence Corps demand money? The Limthosi slapped him one more time.

"Have we smacked your tongue off? Where is our money, Tamyros?"

"Ease off, Althera. Let him catch his breath," one of the men said. He was short of stature, grey eyes, and black hair. His skin was leathery brown, different from the Peninsular named Pasho, though. The old sort of tan that had been cultivated after many hours walking in the sun.

"We have no time for your... compassion, Tanor. We *need* the money," the woman spat.

"See, you would normally deal with Argos or Merios, not even Pasho here," a potent baritone interjected. It was the tall man that had stood toward the edges of the room. "I certainly never get involved in monetary issues, but Enkir Tamyros, understand our plea. Your debt has amounted to near twenty-five thousand drakmas, and as Althera as well put, we need that money."

He almost started laughing. He hadn't been detained by the fucking Senatorial Intelligence Corps.

"Boss Engos."

The tall man nodded solemnly.

"Precisely."

"I... I thought..." Phanon trailed off. The momentary relief was rapidly replaced with horror.

He certainly didn't have *twenty-five thousand* drakmas to pay them back. He swallowed.

"I'm... I'm afraid I don't have that kind of money."

Pasho sighed, shaking his head slowly.

"That's not the answer we were looking for, Tamyros."

"You put us in a precarious situation," Boss Engos said gravely.

Phanon's brain worked madly, thinking through the concussion. What would they do to their wife? He might not get out of there alive, but he had to find a way to buy freedom for his pregnant wife.

An idea formed in his head. Daring, so very daring. It just might work.

"I do have something else. Something worth more to you than drakmas."

"What could you possibly offer worth more than twenty-five drakmas?" the woman Althera asked.

"Information."

Pasho cackled.

"Spare me. Methia, go get his wife."

"Boss Engos, please! I assure you, this information cannot be priced!"

Another slap. He swam dangerously close to unconsciousness again.

"Please... if it doesn't... satisfy you, then you can do with me whatever you want."

Althera smacked him again.

"Speak, then," she said.

Boss Engos rose his hand.

Phanon spat a bleb of blood and saliva containing fragments of smashed teeth. He tried to offer Althera his most debonair smile, which was awfully difficult when one had teethless gaps.

"That'*ss* not how leverage work*ss*, my Limtho*ss*i friend. I *ss*hall need pen and paper," he said, air sibilating through the bloodied gaps of his denture.

Pasho frowned.

"What for?"

"To draft a contract, naturally. I need to make *ss*ure you hold up your part of the bargain."

"Fucking lawyers," Pasho murmured, shaking his head.

Boss Engos, however, smiled.

"Right. Methia, fetch a table, pen and some paper for our crafty little guest here."

The woman returned with a rudimentary stool-like table, a cheap replica of a fountain pen and rough paper. Althera released his bindings with blatant reluctance and he set to drafting a simple contract.

"You wouldn't happen to have a copy of a Nokmollo*ss*i Codex, would you?" Phanon said to no one in particular.

Althera reached to the back of her trousers and tossed an eroded exemplar on the table.

"Much obliged."

He took less time than he would have liked to write the document under the attentive eyes of Engos and his followers, but it would have to do under the current circumstances. He checked against the codex meticulously, looking for clear errors, making it iron clad. He included a Secrecy Clause to protect himself and his wife, though he planned to put as many stadia between him and the Noktanian League if he got out of there alive.

"Get on with it, Tamyros," Pasho said.

"Yes, yes," he nodded, pen hovering over the papers. They would ask how he came across the information, how it was legitimate. He would have to tell them about Damyra.

He grimaced, hesitating.

She doesn't deserve it.

But he wasn't like her. He added a clause to protect her as well.

When he was done, Althera grabbed the papers. She scanned them twice over.

"Nothing iffy, Boss. It's a simple Binding Agreement to release him and his wife without further harm if information worth more than the monetary value of twenty-five thousand drakmas is disclosed, said value to be agreed upon by every signing member of the contract. It also includes a Secrey Clause for the non-disclosure of the aforementioned information, regardless of origin."

Even in his state, Tamyros was thoroughly impressed. That was *exactly* what it was, written in complex Nokmollosi. It would seem the Limthosi could do more than slapping him senseless. She had been trained by a member of the Guild of Lawyers, no doubt.

Phanon waited patiently until every man and woman in the room signed the contract. Althera then threw the papers in front of him with abject disdain. Unfazed, he picked them up and stacked them neatly before reading it slowly and carefully.

"Very well, all in order. Now, Boss Engos, exactly how much do you like our Supreme Consul Kahmaos Blongatos?"

CHAPTER 13
* * *
A Powerful Feeling of Dissatisfaction
Nymor Strethos. The University Library. Guild Association University.

EVER SINCE TANOR had returned to his life, he had made sure Nym was fluent in Neokahmirian, all dialects of Nokator, Tunedosian, Krossosi and Peninsular. Even among Roamers, Nym had received an extensive education in an incredibly short period of time. All things considered, he was astoundingly good with words, one had to admit.

He had been to the ancient Archives of Ei'Tulah, the private collection of High Patron Elmiro of Portos, the Tablets of the Chieftans in Krossos. Stories, plays and city libraries all over Helados had given Nym access to numerous literary and academic works.

All of them paled next to the University Library. The biggest book repository in Virthos' history, bigger than Kahmir's own library during the most prosperous time of the Empire. All the books in the world, from every known and unknown author, dead or alive. Every possible, coherent combination of letters and symbols of every language.

Yet he found, for the first time, he had not the slightest inclination for any of them. How could he in the presence of Haleana?

The girl was reading her book, the very same she had been reading that first night in the Red River Tavern. She had an expensive-looking pen in hand, hovering over a piece of paper of equally exquisite craftmanship. The two suns on her face brightened her expression, and his existence. She had taken him down to the seventh level, through countless identical shelves and into a retired alcove with a table and some chairs. He was convinced he wouldn't be able to find the way out without her, lost forever in the labyrinth of ledgers, tomes, papyri, rolls and every other word-containing format.

Lost without her.

Was that really possible after just meeting her? After speaking to her on barely three occasions? Another question ensued in his head. Was it also possible that she was stealing the colours from the world, leaving everything greyer in favour of the intensity of her auburn locks, her perfect hands, long elegant fingers, the map of freckles on her skin like stars on the night sky?

Nok take me, she just accepted to come here with you. Snap out of it, Nym.

He blinked, realising he was unsure of how long he had been staring at her.

He tried and failed to remind himself the peril of emotions and looked away, opening the closest book to him. Horvos' *Basics of Clinical Medicine* as it were, he began reading without reading.

Haleana looked up, frowning.

"Glorious Nok, you finally pick up a book. It has been almost a full half-bell since we got here."

Nym raised an eyebrow.

"I take great pleasure in allowing sufficient time to find the right source of information."

She stared at him.

Steady on, Nym. Steady on.

He patted the pile of books to his right.

"Besides, I like to start with a good variety of books. You, on the contrary, have been nursing that old dusty tome on Kahmirian Law since I first saw you."

"Kahmirian Law is not Noktanian Constitutional Law, my dear Nymor."

His heart skipped a beat.

Stop being silly.

He furrowed an inquisitive countenance.

"That is to say it is not easy."

"I see."

"Perhaps we should swap. I would venture… what's that?" she lifted the cover of his book. "You see, *Basics of Clinical Medicine* can't be as difficult. It says it right there, *basic.*"

"Be my guest."

She swapped the two tomes with agile fingers.

"Someone as dextrous as you should be a pickpocketter."

"Who says I'm not one?" she gave him a sly look that made a number in his lower abdomen. "Tuition is not cheap, I have to fund it somehow."

"I would have thought your family's affluence would pay for it without second thought."

"Now, now, that's awfully presumptuous of you, don't you think?"

Nym stapled his fingers over Haleana's book and leaned forward on the table.

"The fountain pen you are using was first crafted by the Guild of Metallurgists not two years ago, it has the new line of tips. I have seen Guild-issued pens going for as much as a couple thousand drakmas, and that one over there would go for more. The leather case you use to carry your ledgers around? I could sell it and use it to buy two houses. The silver pins in your hair? Finest Moxosi silver no doubt, and I could have sworn I saw a glint of diamonds. You stink of Cyrosi. A high one at that, my dear Haleana."

He couldn't stop the tirade. Why couldn't he? He had laboured on as the sinking feeling increased.

"Here I was, thinking I had rid myself of the stink after my morning bath. In my very expensive Tymavirian marble bath, mind you."

Despite the light tone, there was clear resentment in her voice.

"The only mystery is why you accept company of a low citizen."

What the fuck am I doing?

She cocked her head.

"I didn't know you were a low citizen."

Nym barked a despondent laugh. That irked him. He grabbed the tattered seams of his shirt and pulled.

"Spare me. Do I look like a Cyrosi?"

Haleana shrugged.

"Looks are deceiving. You would be surprised about the garments of choice from some Cyrosi I know. You certainly don't *sound* like a low citizen, which is a far more realiable telltale sign."

"Ha. My linguistic prowess extricates me from a most awful situation once more, it seems."

She regarded him with unreadable eyes, then looked down.

"My family's wealth enabled me to access to the best education on Virthos. That is the extent of its usefulness," she said, eyeing Nym's book. "Not the pen, or the pins, or the case. Those are gifts from my father. He... well. He truly is someone that believes the best use of money is to flaunt it in front of others."

"What terrible burden it must be, to be forced to flaunt wealth."

You have fully lost your mind.

"I didn't ask to be born in the cradle of a rich family," she cut in mordaciously, "nor did you in low citizenry I presume. Now, I'd like to move on from the subject."

Any remaining joviality abandoned the conversation.

Way to go, you utter donkey.

She snapped the book shut and asked for her tome back.

"According to Horvos there are seven different ways of treating an infected wound and I already got bored. I will stick to Kahmirian Law, thank you very much."

"I'll have wound dressing techniques over *Paradigm-shifting Legislations following the Kah'Mar-Par'Avios Dynastic Succession* any day," he said as he handed it over.

He was thoroughly confused how such a harmless conversation had turned sour so very quickly. He should rather feel complimented. She had looked sincere when she said he didn't sound like a low citizen.

Nym continued down the path of mental self-deprecation, words swimming in his vision without a shred of internalisation, before Haleana spoke again.

"I'm intrigued. How is it that you speak like a Cyrosi, and can afford Tuition?"

"Let's say I have persuaded someone high-up to take me under their wing, bypassing the more traditional routes of admission. As for the speech, my Trade required a certain level of fluency. People think you ought to be respected if you sound respectable."

Haleana placed the pen on the page.

"I must confess I have never met a Pharosi before. I gather your Trade is your occupation?"

"Peoples from all over the Noktanian League have different occupations, but only one is spoken of as the Trade. It's what Roamers do. Travelling all over Helados and beyond to collect Incantations, learn new Nokator dialects, and sell all of it to willing payers."

"I didn't know the profession of Roamers had a proper name. Do you Roam?"

"Roam*ed*. With my father. About a year ago he decided to settle down in Noktanos, cash in a few favours."

"Fascinating," she murmured. "Father has a big map that occupies a whole wall in his study. My family has merchant roots and Grandfather had a flotilla of ships that sailed all the Southern waters. I used to spend hours imagining all the places I could go… Alas, I haven't left the Fist of Nok since I was born."

"Name one," Nym jumped to the opportunity.

"Pardon me?"

"Name one place."

She smiled a thawing smile, somehow infusing Nym with a renewed sense of calm. She stroked her chin with her hand.

"The Pyrinosi chain?"

"Ah, I've been there thrice, once nearly died of frostbite during a blizzard."

Haleana narrowed her eyes and sat forward, elbows on the table. Nym was keenly aware of how close she suddenly was. He let himself swim in those golden-brown eyes.

"Have you seen the Death Crossing?"

He leaned forward conspiratorially, ever closer to her hypnotic face.

"Seen it? I've *crossed* it. Once. Only time in my life I have been convinced I was going to die."

She opened her eyes wide, lips drawing a small *O*.

It was maddening.

"So, it is true what they say."

"They don't call it Death Crossing for nothing. One thready bridge, dangling over the cliff, Bashork's Eye raging down below. Every gust of wind sent it crashing against the rocky wall. It was so unpredictable. Sometimes it would blow savagely from ahead. Look," he put his hands on the table. Haleana's fingertips followed the lattice patchwork of scars he had on the heel of his palms. Again, her touch was like holding those electrifying rods with Tysides when they had saved the Dionos boy's life. She thumbed the scars, her other fingers following the bulging white down his palms. Nym allowed himself to fantasise about holding those delicate hands, craddling them. They were so very close.

She retired them.

"I got friction burns holding on for dear life that day, held until they bled and then held some more."

"Nok, must have been terrifying."

"It wasn't pleasant, I can tell you that much."

Though her hands weren't touching his anymore, she remained close, head a mere handspan away from his.

"Ei'Tulah."

"Capital City of the Vast Peninsula. Some people call it New Kahmir, you know? I've lost count of how many times I've been there. So beautiful. Tall pyramids and exquisite gardens. But Haleana, there's *so* many people. Everywhere you look, packed. The city doesn't have an official census like Noktanos but when they say it is the most populated city in Helados, I believe it."

Passion seeped out as he spoke, casting his mind back at the marvels he had seen during his travels. He hadn't known he missed it that much until then.

"What about the Salt Mounds?"

He grimaced.

"Only from afar, I'm afraid. We were once travelling accross Salinos and I saw the crystallised mounds from the distance. The last person that lived in Yshkar died decades ago, so we didn't stop until we got to Kausanos."

"Kausanos! How is it, in the far north?"

"Cold. *Very* cold," he said instantly. Haleana's giggles were infectious.

"I would imagine. Umm," she moved even closer, as though she was going to tell him a secret. "I enjoyed tales of mythology when I was a child like any other person. You know, *Of the Wondrous Creatures of Hel'Adad* and all that. I know what is real and what is not, but I will regret it if I didn't ask. Did you see *Him*?"

Nym smirked. Gargenthios, the Serpent of the World. A sea serpent as big as a mountain range. Legend had it his home was deep in the waters of the Serpent Strait.

"Two weeks had passed since we had left Portos. The captain of the barge fumbled the provision count and we found ourselves without food and scant water. We barely made it to Retir, a port city by the strait."

He paused, placing his hands palm-first on the table.

"Whilst my father sorted the prices in an inn, I staggered to the fenced edge of the small town. I remember the salty wind, blowing hard from below, making me cold to my bones. Now, I hadn't drank for nearly two days and not eaten for a hexad. I don't know if I was hallucinating, but down there, I swear to Nok Almighty, I saw the waters of the Strait shift. The *whole* Strait, Haleana. As far as my eyes could reach. The surface turned from blue to scaly black green. Miles of it. Then back to blue after a minute or two."

Haleana looked enraptured. Eyes intent on him, lips half agape. His whole body churned at the outlandish prospect of kissing them.

"What a truly fascinating life. How did you end up Roaming?"

Nym's happiness cracked.

Mastress Zhemyra's face appeared in front of him. A shower of cold water, sobering and unpleasant. He had been in a trance for days, unable to think straight.

What am I doing? This cannot end well.

Her voice mingled with his own thoughts, a nauseating whirlwind.

Emotions are not good for business.
Sex is great until it stops being so.
Is that what you want from this girl?
Only that?

He swallowed hard.

"A troublesome childhood. In any case, you haven't asked me for my favourite place in Helados."

"And what would that be, Master Roamer?"

Would it be too much if I said Here, with you?
Yes. Yes, it would.

"Have you ever seen a Krossosi play?"

"I have indeed."

"I have seen a few myself, though one stands out. I saw *Written in Salt* in the grandest amphitheatre in Krossos."

Haleana's eyebrows shot upwards.

"The epic is not one normally acted outside of Krossos, it requires a lot of skill. The place looked more like the Ultimate Arena than a theatre. It had a big pond with an island in the middle, full of palm trees and buildings. And the narration... The water bulged and changed, the wind picked up and fire started with the most beautiful Nokator I have ever heard! It was like poems written with the elements. A love letter to the Titillation. You remind me of one the protagonists," he blurted.

Oh, child, Mastress Zhemyra's acrid voice chided in his mind.

In *Written in Salt,* a Krossosi ship is stranded in an unknown island. In it, a sailor, merely an indentured warrior of low birth, falls in love with the daughter of a Tribal chieftain. A macabre work of his subconscious. He found some momentary solace in thinking that it was unlikely that she knew about it anyway. It lasted until her face lit up with recognition.

"Hang on, doesn't she die a horrific death at the end of that play?"

Nym blushed profusely. Heat seemed to radiate outwards from his face.

"Oh. You know it. Yes, well, I forgot about that part. I implore you to focus on the breath-taking, love-letter-to-the-Titillation aspect of it."

Haleana stared at him.

"I've realised something, Nym. There is an edge to your voice. An underlying *something* that threatens to paint every word with sarcasm. It disappears when you tell stories about Roaming."

Nym was only half-listening, eyes barely able to focus on anything other than her lips.

"I... might have... *romanticised* it."

Their heads were so close. The hammering of Nym's heart in his neck seemed to push him forward, to greet her lips with his. Barely a breath it would take for him to just...

The low ring of a bell, hidden somewhere on the level, penetrated the walls of the alcove and vibrated down on them.

"Nok's Grace! What bell is that?" She held one hand up, eyes unfocused as she strained to count the tolls.

Seven, eight, nine.

She began gathering her stuff when it got to ten.

"Tenth bell! I was supposed to travel back to the city in the tenth-bell carriage! Father is going to skin me alive!"

He handed over her ledger and pen with care and she touched his hand lightly as she grabbed it, sending an electrical wave all over his body.

"I can take you, if you wish," Nym gambled. "I have a horse stabled in the Hospital. He's fast."

"Right. Because coming home on some stranger's horse would be any better."

Nym acted hurt.

"I've told you the abridged version of my life. I thought that would graduate me to, at least, acquaintance."

"No, you are right. I did have a good time, Nym. Thank you."

She latched her case shut and dashed toward the door.

"Bye," she muttered quickly as the door of the alcove clicked back into place.

"B... bye," Nym repeated, stunned. He stared at the old wood, contemplating the afterimage of her second abrupt leaving in his retina.

A powerful feeling of dissatisfaction and anguish settled in the pit of his stomach. The conversation muddled and replayed in his mind.

It's probably for the best. No more Haleana.

CHAPTER 14
***
Alive
Damyra Pynarios. Faculty Residences. Guilds Association University. Fist of Nok.

"I LOVE YOU, Alda."

"And I love you, Damyra, but that doesn't subtract from the fact that you still lost," she said with a cheeky smile.

The gentle waves of the Eye of Nok washed at the pebbles of the hidden cove as they stood opposite each other, breathing heavily. Damyra's muscles complained, her lungs burnt. Alda never gave quarter, not even when sparring.

"Your Nokturian incantations have come a long way. Remember our first training session?"

Damyra rubbed her left elbow, where a boulder had grazed her.

"I do. I have learned much over the years."

"You have, but you still have trouble with speed. The Nokturia developed their martial skills to be dynamic and useful, *not* pretty. You stumble over every incantation, mindful of respecting grammatical rules. Nokturian incantations are not like other dialects of Nokator. You don't need a Codex for a reason, they are half about summoning, half about intention."

They walked closer together.

"I was just in the mood to let you win," Damyra said. Alda smiled again, holding her face with her hands and placing a kiss on Damyra's lips.

"We both know that's bullshit."

Damyra stepped back, feigning indignation.

"How dare you."

"*Terros, domon vosu Exios. Arrantos!*" Alda said, lowering her centre of gravity. She thrust her right fist forward and a shower of pebbles flew from around them, raining down on the far side of the cliff surrounding the cove.

"See? I didn't have to specify I wanted more than one pebble. I *thought* of it, willed it into my Nokturian incantation."

"Your mastery enlightens me."

Alda gave her a gentle shove.

"Shut your big mouth and reset positions. We'll start again."

Damyra walked away from Alda, leaving again gap of two dozen feet. Except when she turned, she wasn't in the cove. They never were. They were of course in the Anathema, long before it had received its name. The statue of the Goddess Pavaras laid on the floor, destroyed, a crumbling mass of detached limbs and broken torso.

Alda was driving a knife into the thigh of one of three people bound to chairs, bloodied and whimpering. They had the distinctive leather armours and caramel skin of the Zereri.

"Not so gracious now without your beloved horses, are you? Do you feel the pain? The shift of power?" Alda cried out, twisting the knife. The Zereri squirmed, screaming desperately. Sanguinolent spittle dribbled out of his contorted mouth.

Damyra should have felt disgusted, shouldn't her? Instead, she turned to the Zereri woman in front of her and used the knife in her own hand to separate her thumbnail from its bed, digging, prying. She both relished in the rider's pain and was horrified by it. She was both astounded spectator and avid player.

"Was it you?!" Damyra shrieked. Had she really sounded like that? "Was it you that killed the ambassador and his wife, years ago, in the plains?"

The Zereri woman laughed weakly before answering with a heavy accent.

"You ask, who I kill. I don't know who I kill. I kill, and kill, and kill. If you no kill me, I kill again. I kill you!"

"AHH!" Damyra shouted, a scream that rattled her throat, as she plunged her knife deep into the woman's head.

Except she didn't have the face of a woman anymore. She had Guildmaster Imathios' face.

"Is this what you promised? Is this what you intended when you took the Chains and swore the ancient Oath?" he was saying with his tremulous voice, old jowls shaking madly.

"The Almighty Gods of the Pantheon will haunt thy! Nok will discharge all his fury upon thy! Smite thy! Turn into Bashork and give thy the welcome thy deserve in his most wicked Hall!" he shouted compulsively, trampling over words. His flesh had started to peel away from his bones, a putrefacient simile of the Guildmaster that kept ranting until it was nothing more than a skull with rotten blebs of flesh hanging from the bone, until his jawbone broke away and he couldn't speak any more.

Alda ran toward her in one fluid, unnatural motion. Grasped Damyra's head. Her face was all Damyra could see.

"Damyra! Damyra, I must go. I must go to never come back. You will never see me again, my love. Never again! Never again!"

Alda shoved her with strength, lifting off her feet. Damyra fell, but she didn't fall onto the ground.

She was plummeting down a pit, a cylinder with walls populated with sharp spikes, longer and longer as she fell, coming closer to her. She flailed uselessly in the air, saw the bottom of the pit. A red-orange circle, glowing, growing bigger with the uncontrolled descent. Larger and larger until she realised it was a pool of incandescent lava, bubbling, spurting noxious gases.

She fell in it, her whole body immersed, surrounded by searing pain that gnawed at her skin, breathing in a viscous substance that evaporated his mouth, and trachea, and lungs.

She emerged from a pool of her cold, rancid sweat, forming in her bed.

"Right," she whispered submissively, hyperventilating, heart rioting in her chest. The pain that the sudden movement of her awakening had caused in her joints caught up to her senses. She stayed immobile, screwing her eyes shut and breathing shallowly, withstanding the battering waves of pain as best she could.

She was very familiar with the inexorable approaching of death, and yet again, this wasn't normal senescence. The *Nokmo'mathar* had flared up during the night. Whatever Phanon had done was surely unravelling.

"Damn it to Bashork's Hall," she growled, clutching at her aching sides.

She focused on her breathing for endlessly long minutes, paralysed in the same uncomfortable position. She didn't bother trying nerve-blocking incantations, she had used all her arsenal the previous evening to no avail. She would have to bear this on her own. Until the ship sank.

Eventually, her muscles limbered up enough for her to roll out of bed. She sat up carefully, pausing long before every move, and reached for her cane.

She limped to the medicine cabinet. She would need an immediate concoction to spruce up or she would be late to class.

"Damyra. Just the woman I was looking for."

She saw the sillhoutte of the man leaning on the doorframe, cut against the weak orange hue of the morgue lamps. A man she would recognise anywhere.

"If it isn't Doctor Levantios Danos. I thought we agreed long ago I was precisely the woman you were *not* looking for."

Levantios bowed his head.

"I deserve that, but I am not a man that dwells in the past. In any case, you owe me a favour."

She sighed and bent precariously to rub her right knee.

"I thought I didn't either, yet recently I have found the past to be my only dwelling," she murmured with resignation as she moved to the storage room, gesturing with her head.

She sat down on a stool and offered one to Levantios Danos, who politely declined with a smooth wave of the hand. She extended her right leg, suppressing the omnipresent nausea.

"How have you been, Damyra?"

"Old. Don't betray your nature with banal chitchat, Levantios. We both know you are dying to get straight to the point, and I have a class to teach."

"As you will. I have taken a new student under my wing. I want you to bring him up to speed with year one and two curriculum. He is a fast learner, he'll be fine."

Damyra exhaled a long, exasperated sigh.

"Not again, Levantios. Who is it this time?"

"Nobody important, a Pharosi. An incredibly clever one, the right sort."

Damyra frowned.

"A Pharosi? Is he enrolled in the School of Medicine?"

Danos produced a scroll. She gave it a quick look as the physician explained.

"That's his Inscription Writ as of this morning, stamped and signed by yours truly and the Representative of the Rectorate."

"Where did a Pharosi get enough money to pay for tuition?"

Danos remained impassive.

"It was waived."

"Waived. You are seriously telling me that Rector Arthos 'waived' someone's tuition fees?"

Danos looked away. He sighed as he lowered himself on the stool that Damyra had initially offered.

"Fine. Call it an investment."

"Levantios, you can't keep doing this. Look what happened to the Surk'Imla girl."

Again, he looked away.

"That was a miscalculation on my part. I should have gone for her sister, but that has been corrected now."

Damyra stared at him.

"You are paying for Vivana's sister's tuition as well?!"

"No. The Surk'Imla pockets are deep. But I *am* mentoring both."

It must have been over seventeen years ago when Vysios had relocated to the Coalition Quarter to be trained as the highest-ranked Inquisitor, and for the first time in their marriage she had broken away from the inadequacy and frigidity and pursued Levantios Danos, the prodigy of the University Hospital. He had always been raving about his rights to mentor medical students. Magister Emti Surk'Imla's first-born daughter was the first to meet his very demanding expectations.

"What happened to Vivana?"

"I never knew, and it's common knowledge the topic is a taboo for Emti. She suddenly withdrew from the programme and disappeared. It was only later that I found out she was also enrolled in the School of Metallurgy *and* Natural Sciences at the same time, always excelling in everything she did. What a truly powerful mind. A terrible shame."

Damyra surveyed him, a pleading expression so uncharacteristic of him. He only showed passion for teaching his favourites. Only for them, and medicine. Nothing, and no one else.

"I'm not sure I will, Levantios. My relationship with the Rector has never been amicable. The last thing I wish right now is to have the Rectorate coming down on me if they find out."

"Damyra, you saw his Writ. I very much doubt Arthos will care about a lowly Pharosi in the School of Physicians. He has better things to do. Remember the little girl with constant seizures? He pretty much cracked the case and helped with the operation as well, sutured the wound perfectly. And Garvios? He is ready to stop drinking after he spoke to him. He just needs some of the basics. Can you please bring him up to speed?"

"Nepotism and favourcracy. The true bedrock of the Noktanian League."

"Damyra, please."

"Fine. Whatever ends your incessant grovelling. I don't want him disrupting my classes!"

Danos stood with a satisfied smile.

"His name is Nymor Strethos, he'll be an interesting addition, trust me."

Strethos?

"Pharosi *and* street-born in my morgue, no less," she huffed, shaking her head and rubbing her knee.

Danos lingered by the door of the dimly lit storage room.

"You know I can infiltrate that knee with my formulation of Myrphid extract and rid you of pain for a half-year?"

If it were just the knee...
"I might just take you up on that."
He gave a curt nod.
"You know where I am."
Damyra grabbed her stick and headed for the morgue. The truth of the matter was that a new student with shady admission was the least of her problems.

She recognised that Nymor right away, standing away from the main bulk of students. He wasn't wearing the regimented white toga, instead sporting dusty trousers and an airy shirt. Short and stocky, his bluish eyes were peering over the cadaver on the table with fascination. Only him and a few of the keener students stood close to the inanimate body. Nymor grabbed one of the skin flaps in the chest, incisions done in previous lessons, and opened it. His eyes glinted with curiosity at the internal structures.

He was so focused he did not realise Damyra had arrived the room and was slowly moving toward him.

"What is this?" she asked, pointing to somewhere inside the chest.

Nymor jumped back.

"My sincerest apologies, Doctor Pynarios. I'm afraid I got lost in my bewilderment. I haven't had the chance to study anatomy with human specimens."

She frowned.

He must be the most well-spoken Pharosi I've ever encountered.

"What is this?" she repeated. Nym looked at the cadaver and stepped closer, understanding the assignment.

"Based on the orientation of the fibres, I'd say it's the internal intercostal muscle."

"*You'd say*? If you want to be a doctor you must transmit certainty, for medicine is too uncertain as is."

"Internal intercostals."

"This," Damyra pointed to a raised portion of the breast, where the manubrium and sternum joined.

"It is known as the angle of Kyrkos, otherwise you can use the technical name, manubriosternal joint."

"This."

"That's just adipose tissue."

"This."

"Diaphragm."

"Be more specific, boy."

"Errr... costophrenic recess?"

Damyra stared at him.

"Costophrenic recess."

The whole class stared at that impromptu test. Damyra then shuffled to one of the sets of shelves and everyone initiated a dozen hushed conversations.

"Never mind that, I'm sure Nymor doesn't fuss over an audience," she grunted, straining to reach a jar with a murky liquid.

"Lad," she said to the tall boy she had healed a hexad or so back.

"Lysos, Doctor Pynarios."

"Yes, yes. Lysos. Give me a hand, will you?"

Lysos grabbed the jar and carried it to the table following Damyra's instructions.

She took the lid off and tilted it.

Nymor looked at the obscure liquid and raised an inquisitive eyebrow. Damyra nodded a *go-ahead*, and, to his credit, he plunged his forearm elbow-deep without a change in his expression and extracted a dripping heart.

"What's that?"

"A human heart, Doctor Pynarios."

A meaty thud came from behind. It appeared as though the sight of the bare organ on the boy's hand was too much for Lysos. The young lad was sprawled on the floor, unconscious.

She rolled her eyes and walked over, crouching with a wince.

"So much muscle and not enough wherewithal to resist the sight of a heart."

She made sure her Smaragdos was in place and slid her hands to either side of his back, several fingers below the lowest ribs.

"*Bioxos, hosin Kardia latn volo'oth.*"

She welcomed the slight pull of energy. Lysos grumbled from limp to awake and she intoned a terminal incantation.

"Take it easy, lad. Who wants to accompany him outside?"

A girl stepped forth from the crowding students.

"What the... How... Did I...?" Lysos mumbled as she helped him to his feet, walked him out with her arms around him.

Damyra couldn't help but smile.

"Ask Lymos for some water. We always get a fainter or two."

Mirth disappeared when she shot a glance to Nymor, still holding the heart aloft.

"The Tymavirians believe the heart is the physical manifestation of the soul. Certain Pyrinosi tribes think the heart is at its purest when it is still, so we can only achieve perfection when it stops beating. As Physicians we must respect custom and beliefs, but favour the study of Physos, of the matter that surrounds us. This follows no belief. It simply *is*. Nymor, what is the function of the heart?"

"It has two sets of chambers, two auricles and two ventricles that, in healthy conditions, beat in synchronicity to pump our blood in a dual circulatory system. One pulmonary, one systemic."

Not bad. Not bad at all.

Satisfied, Damyra tap-tap-clacked to a stool.

"Today's lesson will revolve around the heart and the major vessels in the mediastinum. But before that, I recall there was some pending work."

The chubby boy of nervous manners raised his hand. Phenyros, his name was.

"Yes, Doctor Pynarios. You tasked me with finding all the information I could gather on Biothos, more specifically on why it is more Exios demanding."

"And?"

"There was ample literature on the etymological differences with other dialects and how it was derived over the years. Multiple assertions on linguistics and the like, but I could not find a straight answer as to why the manipulation of living tissues is more costly."

Damyra nodded.

"You couldn't, because there isn't one. That is a question that has kept doctors and natural scientists awake at night for decades, and we are not any closer now than we were a hundred years ago."

Phenyros looked relieved.

"That shouldn't bar us from theorising," she continued. "If you were to venture a guess, why do you think that is?"

"There are multiple studies that establish different Exios expenditure based on the material. Manipulating the basic elements is easiest, but among them there are subtle differences. Manipulating earth is easier than water, that easier than fire and then air. Other elements, like metals, require more Exios. I would suggest living beings, perhaps, are made up of many different materials in differing proportions and that's why it is so difficult."

Damyra scoffed.

"Are you quoting my own papers to me, Phenyros?"

The boy's face exploded red.

"I... I... It wasn't my intention to insult you, Doctor Pynarios. I came across *On the Physos of Life: How We Are Shaped*, and... and... I have never seen so much clarity with regards to the origin of life!"

"Plagiarism is a serious offence," she smiled, though it turned into distorted grimace when pain shot up her insides. "I do get why you did it, though. It *is* a brilliant paper."

That elicited several forced laughters from the students. Damyra realised she was actually enjoying herself for the first time in a whole damned hexad.

She turned to face Danos' new toy.

"And you, Nymor? Thoughts?"

The muscular boy massaged his jaw.

"I suppose before that we would need to define what being alive really *is*. Just as Phenyros said, if there is different Exios expenditure within the basic elements, would Biothos expenditure differ with different types of living beings? The other day I saw Doctor Danos manipulating a brain and it completely depleted him. Is it because it is the organ that gives us sentience?"

She stared at him.

Damn you, Danos.

"That is... quite insightful."

He bowed his head.

"I also wonder whether our own conception of being 'alive' has any weight in the matter," he added.

Damyra cocked her head.

"Do elaborate."

"We say someone is alive when they are walking about. Talking, thriving in society. I visited Intesive Care in the Hospital and I was utterly dumbfounded at what I saw. I was told it was an experimental treatment, a woman that had received a very strong blow to the head couldn't breathe on her own and she had a Kytoshi tube rammed down her trachea, connected to some sort of Horvos-device-looking apparatus that expanded her chest."

Every student was paying close attention. They were still first years, hospital visits only a dream far in the future.

The procedure Nymor was describing was indeed extremely recent. A paper published by the Hospital's Board of Physicians was still waiting to be read on her office desk that very moment.

"The doctor in charge explained to us that, likely, the woman had lost all brain function. He said, *brain-dead*. And yet," he lifted the organ he was still holding in his hand, "her heart pumped blood, and the apparatus was infusing her with air. Can we say she was *alive*?"

"That is a very good point you bring up, Nymor. The traditional concepts of being *alive* or *dead* are rapidly changing with the recent advancements in medicine. We are approaching a point where even death can be treated, if it has occured in a short—"

That's it!

How could it have escaped her? The answer to the problem was so very simple.

The *Akitos 'i' Legos* stipulated how Kahmaos Blongatos was to die by the blade. Nowhere did it say she was barred from attempting to resuscitate him. In the grand scope of things, she was only doing a little bit of harm, because she would promptly remedy it. No Pillar would be permanently contravened. That was her way out.

She was suddenly starting to feel much, *much* better.

An intrusive thought barged into her mind.

Lord Uthos and his friend Senator Pamyros won't be too happy about that outcome. They won't tell me a single damned thing about Alda.

She closed her eyes.

But it's either that, or Death by Nokmo'mathar... I have no other choice.

"Doctor Pynarios?" Phenyros asked.

She opened her eyes. She had stopped mid-sentence, staring into the nothingness.

"Yes. I'm afraid I must call an end to the lesson earlier than expected. I have remembered there are some things I must attend to immediately."

CHAPTER 15
* * *
In the Act
Nymor Strethos. School of Medicine. Guilds Association University.

The students stared at the doors of the morgue after Doctor Pynarios' abrupt farewell. They swung several times before they came to a stop.

"That was... odd," Nym said, heart in his hand dripping embalming fluid over the dissecting table.

"Quite the contrary. That was remarkably customary of Doctor Pynarios," someone said from the other side of the table, far behind the group. A scrawny girl that barely filled the grey and white robes of medical students. Her eyes were actively avoiding the dissected specimen and the organ in Nym's hand.

"She's brilliant. We're lucky she finds the time to teach first-year students," Phenyros said. Nym found his face unnerving, an eerie blend of young and old. He moved up next to Nym and offered his hand.

"Phenyros."

Nym placed the heart on Phenyros' outstretched palm and patted him on the shoulder, managing to wipe some of the fluid on the boy's robe.

"Ah, thank you, Phenyros."

"What the—"

"I'm just not the kind of person that wears his heart on his sleeve, you see. You seem far more suited for that."

The girl at the back emitted a high-pitched giggle as Nym headed for the doors with wide strides. His forehead creased when he realised no one was following him.

"I'm sorry, is there some sort of protocol to leave the morgue? Do I shake the cadaver's hand?"

Phenyros put the heart back in the jar and grabbed a towel from a nearby tray.

"Our anatomy lesson is an hour long," he said, rolling his eyes and pursing his lips.

The uncharacteristic uncertainty of his age made Nym doubt whether to feel chastised or proud for getting on the spoiled Cyrosi's nerves.

"We are allocated morgue time for an hour, and it hasn't elapsed," Phenyros continued.

"Well, something tells me whatever is occuying the brilliant mind of Doctor Pynarios right now will take longer than an hour."

Still, no other student moved. Nym waved at them.

"Very... *loyal* of you, I suppose. I shall see you all in our next lesson. Do enjoy the thrilling company of the long deceased," he said, and exited the morgue.

"Does money make you lose common sense?" Nym whispered between closed teeth when the doors stopped swinging.

"It does. Is she off again?" a man's voice startled him.

Nym jumped and turned his head quickly. He saw the hunched figure of the morgue caretaker approaching in the corridor.

"Yes."

Lymos looked at him up and down. A penetrating stare. Nym felt a sudden urge to run away.

"Students normally stay for the entirety of their allocated morgue time," he grumbled.

"So I have been told, but it becomes fairly useless without a teacher to guide you, doesn't it?"

"Hmmm."

Nym turned to go.

"We have textbooks."

"So does the Library!" Nym yelled from around the corner, actioning the lift lever. He couldn't get out of the depths of the School of Medicine soon enough. Once the Doctor had left, the adrenaline had worn off and the crude reality, and weight, of having millions of cubic tonnes of rock between his head and the open skies had hit him.

After an unbearably long time, the lift reached ground floor and he almost broke off into a sprint across the School's reception.

Once outside, he let the warm Heladian sun bathe his skin, shutting his eyes. He took a long lungful of the pure breeze, tinged with the crisp cold of the Serpent's Spine and felt instantly better.

He looked around and smiled.

Can't be past second-bell.

The prospect of a free afternoon filled him with unparalleled joy. He descended the grand staircase with a spring on his step and set off for the School's stables.

"Nymor!"

Someone had been waiting for him further ahead on the path back to Bamoria. A girl patting the neck of an impressive Peninsular stallion.

"Amyra, what a pleasant surprise."

The girl approached him unceremoniously, took his hand in hers and slapped something on it. Nym furrowed his brow.

"What is this?"

"I trust you know how to read," she said derisively. She returned to her horse and mounted in one smooth motion.

"I… Amyra!"

She heeled the sides of the stallion and took off without another word.

Nym stood still, his countenance a field of bewildered creases, as Amyra's figure rapidly grew smaller and smaller on the horizon until she disappeared through the tunnel.

Did I do something wrong?

He opened his hand. She had given him a note. The small piece of paper had elegantly traced, flowery handwriting that said:

Meet me at Pavar Park in the Base at eighth-bell.

Hal.

He did a quick mental calculation and grunted. His boots smacked the cobblestones as he ran madly toward the stables. He lacked the necessary lexicon to thank Boss Engos enough for giving him the fastest horse in the Slums.

Nym dangled from the scaffolding, swung and used the momentum to propel himself upwards. The planks creaked and bent, the whole structure staggering. He moved deftly with it, unfazed by the shifting. The faintest breeze could make it sway so he had adapted, like a sailor to its ever-moving ship.

He walked the length of several scaffolds on the western side of the hill, looking over the city. From there he could see the outline of the Senate Building and the closest of the Four Avenues.

He turned hillside and drew the thready curtain of his dwelling.

"Nym?"

"No. It's your other secret son."

"Ah. Which one, though?"

Nym snorted and patted his father's back. Tanor sat on the floor, crosslegged and stirring the contents of a metal pot on the hearth.

"I wasn't expecting you home so soon."

"The lesson was cut short. Teacher was being weird. She is an odd one. Clever, but odd."

"Most clever people are, son."
Nym tossed his rucksack to the side and sat next to him.
"Sylvari infusion?"
"Please."
Tanor grabbed two grubby mugs from a wooden crate and served the steaming concontion. He left the mugs on the windowsill to cool down and shifted about to tidy.
Nym stared at the rivulets of vapour, dancing and mingling with the backdrop of the Slums.
He pressed his hand to the side of his trousers, feeling the shape of the folded piece of paper.
"How do you know when you're in love?" he suprised himself saying on a whim.
Tanor was stashing cans of herbs and roots in a wooden crate. He stopped and turned.
"That is quite the question. You'd probably be better off asking a Philosophy professor. Or a poet. I speak seven languages and yet lack the words to tell you, son. Such is its nature."
"Have you ever been in love, then?"
There was a long pause. Nym half-expected a negative. A scorn for asking silly things. Tanor's lips curved into a nostalgic smile.
"Yes. Once. Her name was Myra. Lovely Myra. The first time I saw her we were in some festival in Unamor. I was bound for Miramor the next day, but I extended my stay because I wasn't man enough to approach her that first day. But I did the second. She was dancing with a friend, not a worry in the world. And her smile. Mischievous. Clever."
He scoffed, shaking his head.
"That extra day turned into a hexad, then two, then three. I had never stayed in a place for so long since my Cruk'Ix days."
Nym noticed his father fiddling with a metal spoon, eyes set in the horizon across the hills.
"What happened next?"
"Love happened next. The world faded, blurry, and Myra was the only thing that was clear. Roaming was my entire life and it all suddenly seemed so... *pointless*."
"Why didn't you stay with her?"
Tanor stared at him. The pieces fell into place.
"Oh."
His father bit his lip.

"I could say I didn't know she was with child, she never told me. But I knew, Nym. I knew somehow. One day, her father came where I was staying. It wasn't a pleasant encounter. The daughter of an important merchant, frolicking with a dirty Roamer, and foreigner. That couldn't stand. He challenged me to a Kontivos Doxos, and I lost. I left. I chose the easy way out, even though…" he trailed off. Tears were rolling down his cheeks, his voice cracking.

"I just left. It is not easy to say, but that makes it no less true. Even though I loved her. Even though a part of me knew she was pregnant with you."

Nym shut his eyes tight, his own tears now falling.

The rest of the story he could gather. His mother, repudiated by his family when she was found to be pregnant, shunned without mercy. Living in squalor with a baby, dying after contracting the plague, leaving the child to the streets. Thieving and hunger the child's most loyal companions. It wasn't the happiest of stories.

Nearly five years had passed since his father had gone back to Unamor and recognised him. Five years since Nym had reluctantly agreed to Roam with that stranger only to escape the claws of Mastress Zhemyra's cruel tutelage. A stranger that kept saying he was his father.

It had taken a long time to believe him.

In that moment of mundanity, of fire crackling in the hearth and steaming infusion on the windowsill, Nym found the heart to forgive him.

He swallowed hard.

"Thank you. For telling me, dad," he whispered. They fell into a shuddering embrace.

"Right," Tanor sobbed lightly as they came apart, wiping tears that had waited for years to fall.

"What's the name?"

Nym gave a sad chuckle, blinking the last teardrops away.

"Doesn't matter. Emotions only bring trouble."

"Love *is* hard, Nym. So is climbing a mountain. Yet, when you summit it, you get to take in the astounding views. Remember Teidos?"

Oh, he remembered. One doesn't easily forget climbing the tallest mountain in the whole continent of Helados.

"Haleana."

"Haleana. Beautiful name."

Tanor stood again and rested a hand on his shoulder.

"Love is hard, but it's worth it. For even if it fades away, at least you got the chance to feel it."

Feelings are bad for business. Sex is great. Until it isn't.

He grimaced. He was not Mastress Zhamyra's property anymore. He had made a choice. He had escaped. He *could* feel if he wanted to.

"Thanks for that, dad."

He grabbed his rucksack and dashed to his room. He needed to get ready. Haleana was waiting.

"I must say, I was not expecting your note," Nym said, patting his trouser pocket unconsciously. Haleana looked him in the eyes, smiling confidently.

The warm light of the setting Heladian sun inched close to the west, slowly finding a hiding place behind the tall towers of Dytalis. They casted a shadow that crept towards them, sat on a bench across the park and facing the intimidating walls of the Citadel.

"Bold choice. Meeting in the richest neighbourhood of Noktanos. At sundown. With a Pharosi."

Please, don't ruin it again.

"It's always like that with you, isn't it? Always about social status."

She shook her head vigorously.

"You know, I despise Supreme Consul Blongatos for what he did to this city. I am not stupid, I know how societies work. I know there will invariably be a tacit stratification based on wealth. We can argue on its ethos, but it is a fact of life. Something very different is to etch it in Law and segreggate the inhabitants in Cyrosi, Demiosi and Pharosi based on the amount of drakmas they have accrued and stashed away. Non-sense! Giving foreigners the permanent title of low citizens simply because they were born outside of the League? What's that!?

"Nym, when we founded the Noktanian League we did it on the principles of democracy and inclusivity. A League where a miner from Moxos or a landowner from Parthos have an equal chance to sit in the Senate, if they have the support of the people."

Nym hadn't seen that emotion in her before.

"Blongatos has pushed us back to the days of the Old Regime!"

She caught herself in the fires of the rant, blushing slightly and shaking her head.

"I apologise. I am imbued by indignation when I talk about politics. It can get ugly."

"Maybe you should be the Supreme Consul. Listening to you, we would be much better off."

She averted her eyes.

"Maybe. One day."

An awkward silence settled between them. Her beliefs were loable and certainly not commonplace among the Cyrosi, but Nym remained cynical. It was easy to complain about a system from a position of privilege within it.

"That moving plea will not dissuade the Watch if they catch me gallivanting on the streets of the Base, though."

"That's why I brought this," she flapped her cloak open and showed a sack tied to her belt. It clinked when she moved her hips.

Nym burst with laughter.

"The language every person speaks, from Ei'Tulah to Kausanos," Nym said with a jovial shrug of the shoulders.

"I don't see status, Nym," Haleana said, shuffling to the side and sitting on top of her right leg to face him. "I see a person, that's all. One with a fascinating story."

Nym looked at her, drinking her golden eyes and luscious lips, letting his mind soar with the chest-ripping possibility of kissing her.

She stood suddenly, startling him out of his fantasy. She offered him a hand.

"Come, let's go for a walk."

Nym stared at her hand as though she was showing him the Prima Codex. He furrowed his brow.

Is this a trap?

When he finally took it, he was pleasantly surprised Haleana didn't let go.

They strolled through the park holding hands, crossing a paved walkway guarded by pristinely groomed hedges. They were interrupted by the occasional manicured tree, never fully blocking the views of the sprawling city below.

"I have been in Ei'Tulah, Tymavir, Unamor, Miramor, Kausanos and Portos. Every major city in the whole continent," Nym started gingerly, eyes on the sea of buildings. "Nothing quite compares to Noktanos."

The Nym that was convinced he must leave seemed like an entirely different person. To think he would have missed on meeting Haleana…

"Not once in History such a prosperous metropolis has been erected in so little time. Not once a truly democratic government has been instated. Not one civilisation has received Nok's Gift but us. Noktanos *is* special," Haleana elaborated.

"That's right. Except Nok's Gift is not limited to the Noktanian League. I have seen Codex Games in Ei'Tulah and constructs helping in the fields outside of Portos."

Haleana smiled, cocked his head, and wagged the index finger of her right hand.

"None of them is his Seat, though."

Nym rolled his eyed.

"Alright, Supreme Consul of Etymology. That's like saying, Ei'Tulah is unique because there is no other city that is called Ei'Tulah."

Haleana giggled.

"Potent rebuttal, Nym. Are you always so good at demonstrating fallacious statements?"

"Only most of the times."

They laughed as they exited the park, hands clasped and gently swaying. Nym let Haleana guide him, walking by tall-gated mansions and estates. Though they encountered several stern-faced Watchmen, warily eyeing Nym up and down, none said a thing after glancing at Haleana.

They walked northward and upward, following the shape of the hill.

"So, do you speak anything other than Nokmollos?"

"I manage with plain Nokator, but no other dialects. My Father wanted me to be a Physician like my uncle, but I never learned Biothos. What an absolute nightmare, I do *not* envy you."

"I'm surprised, in all honesty. I had heard the Cyrosi are rejecting Nok's Gift more and more to pander to the Old Regime."

"Fools. My Father is cleverer than that. He would never reject power. He is a fairly good incantator himself."

Silence ensued as they walked on, an abscence of words that was different. It wasn't awkward. Nym relished it, still riding the waves of euphoria every time he glanced at their entwined hands.

"Have you been to this place before?" Haleana broke the silence. Nym looked about him, couldn't see anything other than high walls, clean streets, and the looming presence of Dytalis.

"Huh, can't say I have?" he said, frowning.

"Not here, *here.*"

She turned right and pointed to an alleyway between two tall walls. There was a natural ceiling of branches from trees either side, perfectly framing a small blue rectangle at the end.

Narrow as it was, they had to walk separately. He had to restrain himself from shouting *No!* when she let her hand go and entered.

He thought of himself as a man of manners, so he focused his eyes on her locks of auburn hair rather than openly staring at her rear.

When they came out the other side, Nym emitted an audible gasp.

The Great City of Noktanos like he had never seen it before.

The alleyway led to a small round balcony tucked between two estates, a watchpoint from which they could see the sunset-bathed Noktanos in its entirety.

He walked over to the edge of the marble bannister, flabbergasted.

To the far right, the disorganised mountain of improvised dwellings of the Slums, like a gigantic sleeping hedgehog. To the left, the sober Coalition Quarter of grey walls and buildings, crowned by Nok's Steading, the cathedral of towering spires. Down in the valley surrounded by the three hills, the classic cylindric buildings of blue and white intermingled with the harsh lines of modern Gigos architecture.

Everywhere he looked he was captivated. The perfect semi-spherical shape of the Senate building in the centre of the City. Nok's Steading, the Ultimate Arena, the Four Avenues flowing with tiny specks, the waters of the Eye of Nok. The clouds had disappeared, yielding an evening so clear he could see Guild's Way, disappearing in the distance like a fading arrow pointing to the Serpent's Spine in the horizon.

"This is truly incredible."

Haleana rested her hands right by his side, elbow brushing his forearm.

He met her eyes.

"So? Exactly how long were you planning on waiting before you kiss me?"

It wasn't long. He might have fumbled the first moment in the library, where their eyes locked and their lips longed to be together. He would not fumble a second time.

"How's that for a Pharosi?"

Her smile zapped his heart.

"Not bad. Not bad at all."

After that, time and perception stopped working for Nym. Somehow, they had left the viewpoint and stumbled along the streets, running from shadow to shadow, hiding behind trees, walls and statues, kissing passionately. Before he was sure when or where he was, it was night and Haleana was guiding him through the backdoor of a walled estate.

He didn't ask where they were going. His mind was too occupied.

Haleana, Haleana, Haleana. Why are we not kissing right now*?*

She locked the door with a key, stashed it in an inner pocket of her cloak and walked ahead along a path, guarded by marble statues and meticulously groomed bushes. Under the dim illumination of the moonlights he saw exquisite flowers he had only seen outside of the Fist, decorating stone arches and fountains.

The path curved to the left, revealing a small arena, two small platforms, Rods, and a central pond.

"What the... Where are we?" he mumbled as Haleana hurried him along. The answer was obvious, it toyed with his logic at the edges of his distracted brain. He needed confirmation.

"I told you, Father is a good incantator. He's quite fond of the Codex Games, he even has famous incatators to spar with him sometimes."

"You are taking me to your house?!"

"Shh! You'll wake Mother. She is ill and needs her rest. Nok forbids the help hears us. They'd have gossip fodder for days."

The path wound away from the miniature arena and he was soon close enough to see Haleana's stately home.

He had never seen such a tasteful use of Gigos architecture, blended with the traditional Noktanian style. They had managed to make the surface boil and freeze in time. Blue-and-white circular walls that contorted in mesmerising way only made possible by Nokator.

"Haleana, Nok Almighty and the Primal Roamer. I knew you were a Cyrosi, but this?" he gestured. "Wait, what is your family name?"

She turned and pushed up against him without breaking eye contact. When she was but an inch away, she gently hooked her hand behind his head and pulled his lips closer, delivering a torrid kiss.

Nym's heart was on the brink of bursting.

Is there such thing as lover's myocardial infarction?

"Does it matter?" she said, her voice a low sensual purr. He shot a glance at the building, then at her clever eyes.

"No. It does not."

And they kissed again. And again.

Nym's hands begun moving of their own accord, first a genteel touch on Haleana's cheeks, moving slowly to her back. Down and down her lower back.

She emitted a groan that was maddening before she placed her hands on his chest and peeled herself away, laughing a throaty giggle.

"Nymor, Nymor. Do you have no patience?"

"I usually have, though it does seem to be momentarily impaired," he said, going in for another kiss. Haleana kissed him back only once before she stepped back. She led him to the back of the house, shooshing him quiet.

He thanked Nok for the intermittent darkness of the night. Running was an awkward enterprise with a bulging erection, it certainly would have been quite the spectacle in the light of day.

Haleana extracted another key from the many pockets lining the cloak, slowly to avoid any clinking. She grimaced as the key turned in the lock, putting her weight against the movement, as though she was lifting the door. The lock slid open silently and she breathed out.

"My room is at the top," she whispered, barely more than a breath. "Keep quiet until we get there."

It was pitch black inside, but Haleana moved with astonishing speed. Nym held tight to her hand and tried not to trip over with the turns and steps. They ascended a spiral staircase that in Nym's impatience appeared to be extending to Nok's own bloody dwelling in the Heavens and when they finally reached a landing, Haleana stopped and tugged him into a small hallway and through one of two doors.

Nym stood aimlessly near the entrance as Haleana rustled about in the dark room, handling something on some sort of desk. After a brief moment, a *skk* sound preceded a tiny flicker of flame, a match she used to light an oil lamp hanging from the low ceiling. The weak orange hue casted soft shadows that accentuated her sharp features, made her eyes more ponderous.

The room was quite modest. A desk, some shelves bursting with books, a window on the ceiling above her bed that faced the night. The bed was perhaps the most ostentatious thing in the room. It looked well-built, a mattress of utmost quality, clean white linen and plump pillows likely filled with goose feathers.

"Do you mind shutting the door?" she said with a mischievous smile, undoing the knot on her neck and dropping the cloak on the bed.

"Not one bit," he whirled to shut the door. When he turned back, Haleana had undone her belt and placed it gently on the floor, taking special care the sack of drakmas didn't clink.

Beltless, cloths shifted loose as she leaned down. She straightened and one of the folds lazily slid down her arm, revealing the tantalising curvature of her right breast.

She stared at him expectantly.

Nym approached her slowly, intently, regarding every inch of her body.

He slid his hand under the bundle of cloth still hanging from her left shoulder and shuffled it down. A gentle tug was all it took to unravel, cloths dropping to the floor and leaving Haleana completely naked.

She smiled confidently, cocked her head and her rose her eyebrows.

Nym's fingers found her neck, he pulled her against him. They kissed. She pressed. Somehow his shirt was lying on the floor, and then his trousers, and then he was naked, and they were in bed.

"Wait!" she gasped, pushing him away.

"Why, what's wrong?"

His voice sounded strange in his ears.

"Nothing. Just wait. You really need to work on your patience," she scorned playfully. She walked over to the desk and started mixing some herbs in a small vial with water.

Aertramor root, that's reassuring.

She drank the concoction and re-joined him in bed.

"Where were we?"

Nym was overcome with primal need, familiar yet never this strong. He hooked his right hand to the small of her back and neck and pushed down. Seeking more contact, he needed every available square inch of her skin on him.

"Ah…" she moaned, scratching, biting.

The door banged open.

"What… is THIS?!"

Haleana scrambled away from Nym, falling maladroitly from the bed, dragging the sheets around her. Nym panicked and lunged for the cloak before quickly shuffling up against the headboard. He bundled the cloak and pressed it on his otherwise exposed crotch.

A man stood at the door, eyes darting madly between Haleana and Nym. His fists were clenched so hard his forearms looked like the ropes of a ship.

"Nok Almighty, Father!? What are you doing here? You said you'd be at the Association's Headqu—"

"WHO ARE YOU?! YOU BASTARD, WHAT ARE YOU DOING TO MY DAUGHTER?!"

The shouts reverberated in the room. Nym didn't know whether to put his hands to his ears or hide under the bed.

"Right, I understand this situation is far from ideal," he managed.

"Father, it's alright. He's not…"

The man closed the door with such strength that splinters flew from the segments close to the frame. The hinges disassembled and the whole thing fell with a sharp *plang*.

"You little *shit*."

Haleana stepped forth, putting herself between the bed and her father. Nym shuffled back even more, standing on the bed.

"Father, please!"

He shoved her aside.

"I'm going to skin you alive like a fucking deer you… you…" he jumped toward the bed with blind rage.

What the fuck do I do?!

The rabid man was blocking the only door to the room. There was only one way left.

He took a big breath.

"*Eysos, domon vosu exos!*" Nym felt the air around him change behaviour, solidify, shield him. Without wasting another second, he crouched.

"Hartos!"

A swooshing sound overwhelmed his hearing and he welcomed the sudden levity. Just as Haleana's father was about to close his hands around his ankle, he shot up in the air.

His back met the small window on the ceiling and crashed through, sending splintered wood and shards of glass everywhere. He was propelled up into the night sky, realising with terror he had perhaps used too much intent behind the incantation.

Nym began hurtling down toward the building.

Fuck.

He racked his brain for the best Nokturian command to slow his descent. Much to his despair, nothing came.

Instead, he bunched the cloak against his right shoulder.

The air was knocked out of him upon contact with one of the domes of the building's protuberances. Before he had time to recover, he began sliding down. Gasping for air, he rearranged the cloak under him and used hands and feet to guide himself. He got to the ground only with a healthy assortment of bruises and friction burns.

Freedom regained, he wobbled down toward the path, heart beating fast in his chest. He stayed low, shuffling by the manicured hedges.

A shout came from behind. He glanced back just in time to see a marble statue hurtling toward him.

"Ah! *Arrantos!*" he said, thrusting his right hand forward.

The air stirred in front of him and exploded forth, blowing hard enough against the statue to stop it mid-air.

A nauseating wave of fatigue hit him.

Not now.

Grunts and shouted incantations persecuted him as he forced himself to press on. He ducked another flying statue before he saw the backdoor ahead.

He shot a glance over his shoulder.

Haleana's father had closed on him. His body was shining red.

"Well, shit."

"*Phortos!*"

A plume of fire birthed from the man's hands, lighting the night and hitting Nym with a heat that felt as physical as a rock. He dove, fire roaring over his head. It stopped after a few seconds, only managing to singe his hair. The back wall was not as unscathed. It was covered in black and the door aflame.

Haleana's father started sprinting toward him.

Nym wrapped himself with the cloak and tackled the door with savage desperation. Luckily, the fire had debilitated the integrity of the sturdy gate and he was able to crash through without much difficulty.

The streets were blessedly empty. He rolled over the cobbles and jumped to his feet, running and avoiding the pools of light from the lampposts.

He stumbled into a side alley and hid in the shadow, casting a look back at Haleana's backdoor.

The man was on the street, still tinged red, heedless of the curious stares from nosy neighbours. He vacillated, shouted some incoherent curse and returning inside his estate.

Nym wasn't overly keen on staying much longer to formally say his farewell. He stopped channelling and aware of his advanced state of nakedness, he put Haleana's cloak on and kept to the shadows as he walked away from the Base.

Only when he reached the edges of the Slopes did he afford a half-stifled laugh of victory.

He was mangled, barefoot, burnt, dirty and stark naked under the cloak, but he still strolled toward the Slums with his head held high. All things considered that had turned out to be a great night.

CHAPTER 16
***
Thwarted
Damyra Pynarios. Guilds Association Headquarters. The Great City of Noktanos.

DAMYRA DREW THE the transparent liquid under the light of the oil lamp, squinting as she held the syringe up, observing the fluid inside the glass.

She flicked the surface with her fingernails, a few bubbles creeping up and accumulating at the top. She then pushed the embolus and squirted some of the liquid out.

I'm sure Danos' formulation is more effective, but this'll have to do.

She took a big breath as she lied down, the pain in her knee excruciating. Flexing the joint into a right angle without shrieking took every single drop of self-control.

It felt like having a spiked wheel inside, creaking and clicking as it moved.

Once in position, she palpated for the edges of the kneecap, gritting her teeth, and found the fleshy area on the external side. She squinted hard again, wishing she had the clear light of the operating theatre.

She exhaled, then drew a sharp breath as she drove the fine needle in. An explosion of fire inside her knee followed and she produced a muffled growl, teeth grinding on teeth. She pushed the embolus slowly until all the liquid was gone and extracted the syringe, pressing a gauze against the minuscule puncture wound.

She waited.

A second passed. *Pain.*

Another second passed. *Pain.*

Yet another second. *Pain.*

Blessed cold birthed from inside the joint and spread all over, making the pain disappear instantly. She blinked tears away and stared at the gauze with a single red pinprick.

The relief was indescribable.

She mobilised her knee, flexing and extending fully and smoothly. She hadn't had a painless range of motion in nearly a decade.

She put the syringe away and changed her clothes. The airy gown would be no good for the night's tasks.

She moved carefully in the study, trying her best not to make a sound as she moved to the bundle prepared a few hours ago. She didn't need a lamp, the Pynarios domicile was high enough in the Headquarters so that the line of buildings was far down, the light from the moons entering uninterrupted through the big window.

She removed the gown and tightened a fitting toga, then donned her pitch-black cloak on top of it. It had an ample hood that hid her face completely.

She grabbed a case from under the desk and extracted a dagger from one of its drawers. She secured its sheath around her waist and rolled it backwards so that the weapon rested on her left, hidden in the cloak.

She had a quick look around before leaving and heading for the front door.

"Damyra?"

Piloted by adrenaline and focus, she had missed a subdued Vysios putting Sylvari powder in a pot over in the hearth.

She screamed, hand flying from the half-turned doorknob.

"Nok Almighty, you nearly startled me to death."

"Where are you going? What's that?" he pointed to the case.

"House call."

He frowned.

"That's not your case. And what kind of house call is this at past eleventh-bell?"

Her heart skipped a beat.

"I left mine in the University. An emergent case, a favour for a friend."

Vysios' eyes lingered on her for several more seconds. His lips drew a straight line and he returned to his pot.

"Why are you making Sylvari infusion at this hour anyway?"

The boiling water hissed as it touched the metal.

"Special assignment. Can't really tell you much beyond that."

"Of course. Coalition's business."

Does he know? How would he know?

Vysios grunted an affirmation, stirring the embers with an iron rod, sparkles fluttering about. He seemed satisfied with his questions and paid her no further attention.

The Broken Oath

Damyra clutched the handle of the case and left.

Full moons followed their curved path across the skies above the spheric shadow of the Senate, an unmissable reminder of the Government of the People.

Unaided by her cane, Damyra walked briskly around the circumference of the Central Square, keeping the glistening silhouette of the Forbidden Citadel in the distance as reference.

It was a quiet night, a Pavarios like any other in the lull of the mid-hexad. Damyra couldn't but envy the throngs of Noktanians that had returned home after the last mass of the day. Ignorant of what she was about to do.

She went over the plan in her head one more time. There was no such thing as too much preparation.

The instructions had been clear. Supreme Consul Kahmaos Blongatos was very difficult to track down. He was on a different place every day of the hexad, spending his days between Noktanos, the other constituent cities of the League and his estate in the outskirts of his home city of Tethimos. Always guarded by the most elite Praetorion.

However, every Pavarios after the Senatorial session, Supreme Consul Blongatos would unwind in The Tethimosi Maid until very late. According to Lord Astia, after his... *unwinding,* he would exit the establishment through the backdoor, eager to enjoy his post-coital pipe smoking in the solitude of an alley.

In *complete* solitude.

She was to hide in a nearby overhanging bridge, joining the two sides of the backalley, and wait for the perfect moment to jump down and strike.

She exhaled a long, weary sigh. How had she got herself into that situation?

Oh right. The contract.

She soon reached the Rich Quarter and followed the memorised grid of streets provided by her employers, avoiding the City and Quarter Watch patrols, heading toward Astis Way.

The Tethimosi Maid was no flea-riddled Slum whorehouse. The Tethimosi Maid was an impeccable playground for the wealthy, a renowned brothal of utmost class and place of sanctioned debauchery, frequented by Cyrosi and Senators alike.

Damyra had been there twice herself.

Once during her brief tenure as Guildmaster of the Guild of Physicians in an event organised by the Association. The nature of the other occasion she would rather always remain secret.

The moons lingered lazily near the tallest spire of Dytalis, the Dark Fortress, Eternal Shadow. The home of House Astia and old seat of power in the Fist of Nok.

She shivered at the memory of being in that room, looking at Uthos and Senator Pamyros from the lifting platform embedded in the walls. The city she had been born and lived in, cut against the men. Another not-so distant night when her fate had been sealed.

She made it to Tovyrant Street south of Astis Way unnoticed and crept forwards on a half-crouch until she distinguished The Tethimosi Maid in the distance.

Further ahead, big oil lamps with tinted red glass offered the only hazy light in the street. The establishment was strikingly different from the soft curves of the Noktanosi architecture or the harsh lines of Gigos. A building made of a big stone wedge supported by multiple columns. Fashioned after a pagan pre-Kahmirian temple, Damyra always thought it was the perfect choice for the brothel.

She saw two Silencers and four Quarter Watchmen near the short staircase leading to the entrance. There would be plenty more inside. Safety was paramount for Juntos and Morkos, owners of the Tethimosi.

Time to get crafty.

She locked her Smaragdos in place and turned left between two buildings on the far side of Tovyrant street, wedging herself into the U-shaped space formed by their curved façades. She adopted a wide stance, feet at shoulder length and squatted lightly, marvelling at the absence of pain. She then faced slightly to the right.

"*Eysos, domon vosu Exios. Hartos!*"

A gust of wind rustled the hem of her cloak, suddenly building up around her feet and propelling her upwards in a violent current of air. She flapped up, angled straight for the wall, and just as she approached it, she turned with the momentum and repeated the command. She bounced upward in a coordinated zigzag, soon reaching the top of the building.

Breathing hard, she kept low and made sure the cloak was covering the case and her whole body.

It was exhilarating.

She could barely remember the last time she had felt so free. Years. Decades. Air still coalesced and crackled around her.

"*Tarasos!*"

Wind picked up from behind as she sprinted, irrespective of the rapidly approximating roof edge. She jumped high, wind carrying her across the full width of the street.

"*Hartos!*" she said as she descended on the flat roofs, soaring, cloak flapping madly. The upwards current she summoned was timed perfectly for her to land softly without breaking stride.

She used the same basic air elemental incantations to lower herself down onto a bifurcation of smaller streets that demanded a careful pause.

The Broken Oath

She looked left and right, trying to imagine the croquis in her head, and decided for the left. She was relieved to see a steep slope crawling up and right. A bridge connected the two sides of the street just ahead, hiding the source of a faint red light.

She was in the right place.

The midnight bells struck, each toll a weight pressed down upon her.

She masked her steps with the loud ringing and snuck underneath the bridge, hiding under the wooden awning of a loading bay from one of the businesses of Tovyrant street.

She placed the case on the ground with the last toll of the bell and waited for the only part of the plan that couldn't be calculated.

She was unsure how Uthos and Pamyros knew about Bonglatos' comings and goings with that level of detail, but they were adamant he would come down those tortuous steps to smoke his pipe.

Only problem was, no one could predict exactly when he would be done with his night of carnal diversion.

A door opened with a screech, letting raucous laughter and histrionic moaning into the night, bringing her back to reality. Heavy footsteps descended lazily, thudding.

She recognised the orotund figure, the superior half of the Senatorial toga rolled around his waist, his prominent gut hanging over it in the night. The red light painted the jiggling rolls of fats with a sanguine shine as he wobbled precariously down the steps, drunkenly singing vulgarities that didn't precisely follow Senatorial decorum.

The Supreme Consul.

Such was his advanced state of stupor Damyra worried he would topple down and break his neck, rendering all her efforts utterly pointless.

She tensed, shooting glances up and down the alley from the shadows as Blongatos staggered down. He wrestled clumsily with the folds of his toga until he produced a squat pipe made of gold and marble. Pressing his voluminous abdomen against the short wall facing the alley, Blongatos kept digging in the fabric until he found a round receptable with the Tobos herb.

He was standing barely a dozen feet away.

Damyra stood still, hoping his inebriation combined with the cloak would conceal her. Her hand moved back, slowly, gripping the hilt of her dagger.

Blongatos threw the herbs in the pipe, spilling out an equal amount, and pushed it down using a small metal spoon.

Wind rustled in the alleyway, drawing circles with the dust and making her cloak flap. A shadow leaped in the darkness, landing behind Blongatos.

Damyra looked at the scene unfold with mouth agape and face furrowed, dagger half-unsheathed.

"What in the f…" she exhaled susurrously.

"Wha... hmpf?" Blongatos mumbled, turning very slowly.

It was a man, short and muscular, face hidden by a hood. He was holding a dagos in his right hand, a short blade halfway between a dagger and a sword.

"Who the f—" the Consul began, but the man rushed forth, coiling his left hand around Blongatos jaw, smothering the question. He drove the dagos up, blade against his neck, wavering. The Supreme Consul didn't try to fight, he simply sagged against the wall, fat rolls folding over the edge.

Damyra contemplated the scene with disconnected confusion. As though she was calmly watching a play in the amphitheatre.

What is happening? Who is that?

The door at the top of the stairs opened.

"Halt at once!" a Praetorion shouted, running down the steps. Three more Praetorion appeared behind him.

"Fuck," Damyra whispered.

The surprise assassin shoved Blongatos on the ground.

"*Terros, domon vosu Exios!*" he spat. He lowered his centre of gravity, squatting, and threw his fist toward the steps, shouting "*Korron!*"

A big fracture scaled up the back of the Tethimosi, splitting the steps in half. They started to crumble.

The first Praetorion displayed inhuman reflexes.

He jumped down before the structure collapsed under him, and even though he cleared an entire floor with the stunt, he landed with precision, standing nimbly.

"*Prysos, domon vosu Exios,*" he said with clenched teeth as he unsheathed his sword.

"*Prendon!*" he shouted. As he swung his sword, it caught flames. A fiery arc descended upon Blongatos' assassin.

Damyra closed her eyes. She had to focus. The constant lurking in her insides reminded her it didn't matter who that was.

There was no time left to look at the incantations in her Codex. Simple Nokturian commands were not enough for what she was planning. She clicked her Smaragdos around her neck, hunkered down and pressed both hands to the ground.

"*Exios, hosn thosi Pontos volfon!*"

She felt the Titillation tugging at her, depleting her as the ground quaked under her touch. She could sense her fingertips impressing her will down on the earth. A grinding noise clung to the air, then the bridge overhead *broke* off from the walls. Damyra looked up toward the fallen debris of the staircase, where the other three Praetorion where shuffling to their feet, and the bridge flew toward them.

The Praetorion lifted their round shields with rehearsed coordination and intoned protective Nokturian commands in unison. They thrusted their shield at the same time, driving a wall of grey wind against the bridge. To her astonishment, it was repelled back.

"Shit."

She grabbed her case and abandoned her shelter, diving for the ground just in time to dodge the bridge. It crashed against the buildings, demolishing the loading bay and the surrounding structures.

She stood, unsteady on her feet. The incantation had been sloppy and ineffective, taking too high a toll.

"On her, I've got him!" the Praetorion with the flaming sword shouted. He was the one giving orders.

The element of surprise had catastrophically faded away into non-existence. The fighting had called upon plenty of bystanders, observing the confrontation in the back-alley unfold. Cyrosi and half-clothed customers of the Tethimosi poked their heads out of the many windows, displaying the same sort of putrid and blatant curiosity as any Pharosi or non-citizen in the Slums.

She quickly threw her hood back in position.

"*Terros y Prysos, domon vosuere Exiosi!*" shouted one the Praetorion, channelling a dual Nokturian incantation.

Damyra smiled, recognising the grammatical error in their summoning.

I just need to keep them channelling that for long enough.

"*Terros y Eysos, domon vosuere Exiosi,*" she said in response, calm and precise. A faint halo of dusty clouds appeared around her. She advanced, each step distorting the ground under her feet.

Defensive stance. You have the advantage here, numbers don't matter when you whisper to the Titillation.

She separated her feet at shoulder length and squatted.

On a foolish whim, she raised her right arm and motioned with her hands, taunting the baffled soldiers.

Sure enough, they unleashed a barrage of incantations in her direction.

Big chunks of the Tethimosi broke away from the back, the stone wedge, and the columns, and flew toward Damyra, with the added danger of being incandescent. She saw with horror how the battered brothal started crumbling, screams filling the darkness.

"*Arrantos! Arrantos!*" she thrusted her fists forward. Boulders broke from the street and the buildings behind her and were propelled forward by a powerful rush of wind.

The momentum carried them through the flaming rocks and though slowed, still managed to land near the Praetorion formation. The barrage continued, and so did her defence, yet with each wave her boulders landed ever closer to the quickly tiring trio.

They decided to change strategy and unsheathed their swords, joining their tips.

"*Terros y Eysos, holtos!*" she terminated her channelling, anticipating their next move.

"*Prysos, arrantos!*" they shouted.

"*Prysos, domon vosu Exios,*" Damyra intoned as a column of flames roared toward her.

A wave of blistering heat punched her face and arms, but it didn't deter her from carrying out her risky move. She moved slightly to the right and whirled very close to the fire, so close she felt her skin burning.

"Arrantos!" she said as she gyrated.

The fire coiled around her and was *redirected* at the wide-eyed Praetorion.

Though adrenaline coursed through her arteries and veins, numbing her from the pain, the manoeuvre had costed her second-degree burns all over her arms.

It was worth it.

Her incantation had reinfused the flaming pillar and it now raged with streaks of blue toward her foes. The Praetorion scrambled to mount a defence, badly pronouncing incantations to reinforce their shields with rocks.

The fire hissed upon contact and hid them from view. It enveloped them.

When it dissipated, two of the Praetorion were on the floor, ashen, twitching. The third staggered, using his sword as a cane. Exios-exhaustion had finally caught up to them.

"*Prysos, holtos.*" she said.

She had a purpose there.

Blongatos needed to die by the sharp end of the blade.

She looked for the unexpected attacker in the ruins of what had been a perfectly normal back-alley several moments before. She saw him on the ground, his back to her. He wasn't moving.

Something changed on the left side of her vision, attracted her attention. She stepped back.

The leader of the Praetorion was staring at her from up the gentle slope, blood dripping from his sword. She returned his stare before glancing to a writhing body closer to her.

She unsheathed her dagger.

Blongatos was five paces away from Damyra, exactly halfway between her and the Praetorion.

She screamed, lounging forward with her naked blade. So did him.

The night was suddenly illuminated like it was day. Time seemed to stop in the blinding, searing white. They were tossed aside from their trajectories by the loudest explosion she had ever heard.

She turned on the rough ground, debris digging into her skin. The ringing in her ears was so very loud. Disorientating for a short while, she promptly remembered where she was.

She had been projected further up the slope by the shockwave.

"*Blaggh*," she curled on her side and vomited, convulsing. The Myrphid infusion of her knee was all but gone. She was shaking, feverish, her body fighting against itself.

Blongatos was still alive.

She looked around her.

The Tethimosi Maid had fully collapsed, portions of the stone wedge spread across the nearby buildings. There were charred segments of marble that had rained down on them, the smell of burnt flesh lingered in the air, accompanied by shrieks of pain and desperation.

Her head moved slowly to the other side.

Up ahead, the body of the Praetorion rested face down near the short man, who was now trapped under a pile of rubble.

Her dagger was still gripped tightly in her hand, Blongatos close within reach.

She coughed up blood.

Unable to rely on her legs, it took her a forceful heave to push her weight onto Blongatos' expansive torso.

"*Hmpf... wha...*"

Eyes buried in excess fatty tissue opened as much as they could. He tried to push her away with feeble shoves.

"Don... don... don't! Oh N-n-nok, please... d-d-don't kill me!" he sobbed.

She truly despised him in that moment. Yes, he was Kahmaos the Flaccid, a self-indulgent, depraved little man. An imbecile that had built a big wall and hid behind it, lost wars and sucked on the Senate like a bulbous parasite. Someone that had had the power to avenge the pointless death of her parents and had done *nothing*.

But he was a human being.

He despised him most for having to die by her own hand, after all.

First, you shall never do harm.

Her insides gave another powerful lurch.

"It'll be over... soon," she said, voice catching.

"Oh no... No!"

She plunged her dagger into Blongatos' chest. A single, accurate stab that pierced flesh between his ribs and into his heart.

"Ah... ah..."

Damyra extracted the dagger. His whimpering stopped.

She tossed the bloodied blade aside and waited. Waited for the man's life to spill out of his body.

The Nokmo'mathar wreaking havoc inside her seemed to split in half, both a wave of relief washed over her and pain stabbed at her innards at the same time. The ripping sensation brought her to tears.

There was no need to check for a pulse.

She knew then Supreme Consul Kahmaos Blongatos was dead. The *Akitos 'i' Legos* fulfilled. There was now an Oath to uphold.

"Time is heart," she muttered to herself.

She stood with renewed vigour, limping down the alley. Her case had been miraculously spared with only a few singed indentations.

She dragged it up next to Blongatos and opened it. She took a glass vial and pressed it against one of the multiple cuts in the Supreme Consul's body to collect a few droplets of blood with her right hand, palming a smaller black case with her left hand. They worked as though commanded by two different brains, completing different tasks at the exact same time. She placed the black case on his chest and opened it as she rested the vial next to the Kytoshi bags simultaneously, shooting a quick glance at the portable rods to make sure they were connected to the thin chains.

She held a hand in the air.

"Sca—" she stopped. She was *not* going to have an assistant for that particular operation.

She grabbed the scalpel from the black case herself and made an incision on the centre of the thorax, above the breastbone.

The blade slipped away from her hands, clattering down on the ground.

Something had bludgeoned her on the back of her head. She collapsed on the shattered cobbles.

Deep darkness ensued.

CHAPTER 17
* * *
Don't Think
Nymor Strethos. The Base. Rich Quarter. The Great City of Noktanos.

THE HOUR WAS late. Nym pushed aside the patient histories and piled them on the edge of the narrow table. More time spent in the University Hospital meant staying in the clinic until the hour was so to catch up on ever-increasing mountains of paperwork.

The archives were located on the lower ground, though Nym thought calling it 'archives' was a tad euphemistic. More like 'dingy room behind reception without any semblance of ventilation'. He was convinced there was some sort of forbidden ancient incantation in there, because when he sat behind that flimsy desk time refused to flow. The utter stagnation hammered away at his sanity.

He grabbed the oil lamp at the corner of the table and hung it on a naked hook on the ceiling, waiting for the oscillation to stop before putting his quill to a blank piece of paper.

My dearest Haleana.

He came away with hands on the table, staring at his scribbling.

He grimaced. He crossed it out and started over.

Dear Haleana,

As extraordinary as it may seem, I find myself bereft of words. It is not every day I must apologise for evoking the grandest of wraths and instigating the complete destruction of a beautiful garden. In retrospective, it was unduly short-sighted of us to engage in such activities in your family home.

He sighed.
What is it I want to say?
The quill lingered on the last word, soaking the paper through with ink.
He wrote at the bottom of the page.
My heart is inflamed with the prospect of seeing you again. If only to give your cloak back and extend my gratitude. It was an act of theft that saved me from public nudity.
He pondered, tickling his jaw with the feathers.
How paradoxical, as I wish, nothing but to be naked again. Perhaps in a more private fashion.
He held the letter in front of him, two paragraphs at either end with an intimidating blank middle.
It would remain so for the time being. Tysides Romos burst into the room, Kymos sauntering after him.
Well, fuck.
Romos stared at him from the door, nostrils flaring. Kymos shoulders slumped as he approached one of the tall chests of drawers and leaned against it.
Nym stood and took a few steps back.
"Doctor Romos. Let me explain. I… It wasn't my intention. I believe there was…" Nym glanced at Kymos. The boy's eyes fixated on the floor. "A connection. I thought… *we* thought it best to call it off because…"
"Nymor. I don't remotely care that you two shared a bed, he can lay with whomever he pleases." Romos crossed his arms across his chest and turned to Kymos. "As long as he fulfils his Cyrosox."
Kymos didn't look up.
"That was precisely why—"
"What exactly did you tell him, Nymor?"
"Whad did I…"
Nym shut his eyes tight, realisation dawning on him.
"Kymos, tell Nymor here what you told me."
The boy sighed, blabbing some incoherent answer.
"Speak up."
"I want to become a Priest of Nok."
Oh, Kymos.
"A Priest of bloody Nok!" Romos roared, slamming his hand on a nearby drawer. Kymos retreated within himself, chin to his chest, legs buckling.
"Of all the positions in the Coalition, he wants the *only* one that enforces celibacy!"
Romos squared up to Nym.
"Who do you think you are to meddle in my family matters?"

"I... I... Doctor Romos, I assure you, I suggested nothing of the sort. I merely said that I... understood the predicament but... that he should... *think* of what he wants to do."

"What he wants to do!" the doctor threw his hands in the air. "If we all did what we wanted, the Noktanian League would collapse!"

Romos shoved the table aside, books and letter falling to the floor.

Nym retreated to the back wall, chased by the waggling of the Physician's index finger.

"That's your problem, Nymor. That's why I was so reluctant to take you on! You do as you please, regardless of the consequences. When will you learn we have to do what we *must*!"

"Father, he only gave me the final push. This is what I *must* do. I feel Nok's Calling in every bone of my body."

Romos turned from Nym.

"Fanatic non-sense, Kymos. You have a Cyrosox to..."

"Enough! Mother would have wanted me to do what makes me happy!"

"Well, your mother is dead!"

The scream stung in Nym ears. Kymos' eyes turned glassy.

"Your mother is dead," the doctor repeated, softer now. "I'm old, Kymos. I'm old, fat and abrasive. I will die alone, and if you don't fulfil your Cyrosox, the Romos name dies with you."

Nym had never felt the need for *not* being in a place as strongly as in that moment.

Kymos slumped to the floor, cradling his face on his hands. He began weeping.

Doctor Romos sighed and walked away, squatting next to his son.

"I'm sorry, Kymos. Your mother wanted the best for you. She fought hard to earn her Cyrosi status. For her and other women in Noktanos. It hurts me deeply to see you rejecting it so."

"I know... I know," Kymos sobbed.

Nym seized the moment, shifting slowly and heading for the exit.

"I'm not done with you, Nymor."

Nym's head lowered.

"I'll wait in reception."

The hour was indeed very late. Lena had long gone home, the oil lamps were almost extinguished. Past midnight, well into the second or third morning bell by his estimations.

He yawned, rubbed his eyes, and collapsed onto the secretary's chair. She had all papers and ledgers neatly arranged on the left, quills, and ink pots in a row on the right. He smiled, pulling some of the drawers to corroborate his suspicions. Everything in Lena's workstation demonstrated her impeccable organisation.

A blinding flash of light came through the glass panes of the entry doors.

Nym whirled to face it, bringing his arm up. He couldn't see anything past the searing white.

It was followed by the loudest explosion he had ever heard. The whole building vibrated madly, windows rattling until they shattered. Nym's jaws clattered of their own accord before he was propelled away from the seat by the shockwave, shards raining down on him.

He blinked several times, struggling to breathe air into his lungs.

"Wha... th... f..." he panted sharply.

Blurry with white, his vision slowly revealed the reception. All lamps had fallen, oil pooled on a carpet of broken glass. Lena's desk was not neatly arranged anymore.

Romos and his son staggered in the darkened room.

"What happened? Are you alright, lad?"

The physician helped Nym up, assessing him for any clear fractures. He pried open his eyelids to check for signs of brain damage.

"I'm alright, Doctor. Just winded and sporting a few minor cuts. I think it must have been some sort of explosion."

They stomped out a few lingering flames on their way out of the clinic, boots on crystals creating a sickening crunch. Yevia was trotting from the main entrance. Back tense and straight, she was poised to fight.

"There is something off, Doctor. As far as I can tell, that was in the Central Square, but something tells me it was no accident."

As though conjured up by the guard's concerns, a heavy knock came from the barred entrance gates.

"I'd recommend you get inside but I know you doctor types have to know everything."

She walked with a powerful strut, shoulders wide apart. Hand on the hilt of her sword. She was already wearing her Smaragdos.

"Who goes?"

"The Watch! Open up!"

"City or Quarter?"

Nym heard some muffled arguing on the other side of the wall.

"This is Squad Leader Koryos, of the City Watch. May we be granted entrance?"

The City Watch?

Yevia looked up with a fleeting rictus of fear that worried Nym more than the explosion. Doctor Romos nodded.

She heaved the bar and pulled the gate open.

A group of sixteen men waited on the street, clad with the white-and-blue armour of the City Watch. They each carried spears, shields, and a belted sword.

"My apologies for the inconvenience, Doctor Romos," said the closest to them, the man named Koryos. "We've been sent by Command to important enclaves to ensure no one comes in or out."

Nym looked down toward the valley. There was a faint glow in the distance. Changing, shifting, and projecting strangely thin shadows in the Central Square. That, and the sounds of screams and the clash of steels.

"Why would that be, Squad Leader Koryos?" Romos asked.

"The Noktanian Senate has been attacked. We don't have much information at this moment, but multiple revolutionary militiamen seem to be launching a coordinated attack."

Nym observed the city watchmen, some of them of his very same age. Some of them were shaking.

"Not to worry, though. We have responded quickly. The City Watch and the Senatorial Guard has been deployed and the Legions have been called into the city. The situation will be contained by sunrise."

Romos frowned.

"If you kick a dog enough times, it'll bite back," he muttered.

"Pardon me, Cyrosi?" Koryos barked, seeking no clarification with his tone.

"No matter. What will you have us do?"

"Stay inside. No one comes in unless injured. Tyos, Mosyos, Okos and Denos will stay with you for protection."

"We are protected well enough already," Yevia contested, puffing her chest.

Romos rose a conciliatory hand.

"We'll do so, Squad Leader. Every bit of help counts, should the situation... remain *uncontained*."

Koryos stared at him. After an uncomfortably long silence, he motioned the named men forth.

"Stay safe," he said, marching away with the rest.

"Men, I will leave you in Yevia's capable hands. I'm sure you understand, she is head of security around here."

They nodded dutifully.

"Good."

Romos strolled back briskly, Kymos and Nym trailing.

"Nymor, I want you to prepare the surgery room and run a quick inventory. Things *will* get ugly. I will bring more supplies from the storage. Kymos, you come help me."

"What did you mean, father? The 'kicking a dog' thing?"

"The people of the Slums have been seggregated and oppressed for a long time. Ask Nymor."

Kymos had avoided Nym's eyes ever since entering the archives. He now waited for his answer. Nym gave a single terse nod.

He chose not to disclose he was receiving protection from the Faction Boss likely responsible for the attack.

Nym rushed into the surgery room, mind storming. He couldn't stop thinking about the throngs of Slum dwellers pressed into Engos' Grand Hall. Their rabid screams, their fists in the air, their savage chants for Cyrosi blood. Was it truly any surprise? He had no personal stake in this or any revolution, after living his fair share of low citizen revolts in Miramor, Unamor and Tys he knew how futile they were. How many lives invariably lost.

Yet he had happily accepted Engos' money, protection and aid all the same.

His hands were clammy, his heart galloped uncontrollably in his chest.

Am I a part of this?

All his organs seemed to drop inside him. His saliva turned into glue, his breathing hitched as he backed up against the door. What was his father involvement in all this?

He shook his head.

He knows better. He is a Roamer. He will be fine. I will find him when things quieten down.

One way or another, uprisings always ended.

The gates of worry had already been blasted, preoccupation now flooding his senses. He could almost feel his arteries exploding when he thought of Haleana. He had to find her.

He rested his hand on the doorknob, clamped his fingers, the muscles on his forearm taut like rope.

What good would that do? She's either on Campus or safe within the walls of her estate. Her father knows full well how to defend himself.

He released it and screwed his eyelids shut. His hands spread over his face, thumbs anchored in the line of his jaw and fingers the edge of his skull, pressing, willing the pounding in his head away.

No. No. No.

He opened his eyes.

No. *I'm needed here.*

He moved away from the door and lit the lamps on the walls and one behind a big lens. It had serpent oil mixed with a powder made from Athospos and upon a simple incantation, it would shine powerfully white and steady. The waxing and waning of the normal lamps was far from ideal when operating.

He busied himself with the menial task of opening drawers, checking the gauzes, vials, plasters, syringes, scalpels, sutures and a hundred other pieces of equipment against the inventory.

He heard a clear thud outside the room.

He stopped and raised his head, brow furrowed, fists clenched. The surgery room was close to the eastern wall of the clinic, and it almost sounded like…

Like someone had jumped over the wall.

His stomach curled unto itself.

"Who's there!" one of the watchmen shouted outside.

Nym left the room, dashing across to the reception. Once there, he poked his head out of the gap left by the broken windows.

He couldn't see a thing, but his ears picked up the rustle of clothing, some grunting.

Then a shriek preceded a tangled mass of blue and white flying in his direction.

He had just enough time to react, falling back into the building. He skidded several feet on the slippery oil, shards painfully breaking into skin as Yevia and the rest of the watchmen ran past the front, lances and swords drawn.

"Identify yourself at once!" Yevia was screaming, voice shrill.

In that moment, Nym decided he would feel much safer with his Codex in his hands. He extracted it from one of his pockets and fitted his Smaragdos on his neck.

Doctor Romos came down the stairs carrying boxes, Kymos behind him.

"What was that?"

"There's someone outside."

Before any of them could do anything, one more thud came from outside, louder.

The space in front of the door was still empty, shaded by the night.

Then another thud. And another.

"Yevia?!" called Romos.

There was no answer.

Suddenly, a man in an exuberant red toga and gold-plated armour stepped inside. A Senatorial Guard. Sword in hand, his hard eyes surveyed the reception.

"Are you the Physician?" he pointed to Romos with his sword, blood dripping on the floor.

"Yes."

The Senatorial Guard nodded and gestured with his head. Three other Senatorial Guards entered the reception carrying a large body, white toga splattered with blood.

Romos dropped the boxes.

They were carrying the body of Supreme Consul Blongatos Kahmaos.

Doctor Romos was in stasis. Nym could see he was swaying slightly, back and forth. Like a spring that had been tightly wound. After a few seconds, just as one when it's released, the doctor burst into action.

"Follow me!"

The tallest Guard and the three that carried the Supreme Consul ran after Romos.

The Supreme Consul of the Noktanian League... In the Clinic.
Nym was stunned.
Medicine does not care about titles or stations. Bodies are bodies all the same.
"Bodies are bodies all the same," he whispered.
Romos is going to need help. Don't think. Do.
He trotted down the corridor toward the surgery room.
"Nymor! Where in Bashork's damned Hall are you?"
Romos was hauling instruments from the drawers onto the tray as the Guards lowered the inanimate body onto the bed.
"Vitals! Now!"
Nym quickly washed his hands in a nearby basin and grabbed a stethoscope. He squeezed through the three armour-clad soldiers, dumbly standing around the operating table.
"A little room, please," he said, emboldened by his role in the care of the Head of Government.
Romos moved next to the tall Guard and observed Nym as he took the patient's vitals.
"How may I address you?"
"Caput Major Lyontos Pyrdos of the Praetorion, Cyrosi."
Caput Major.
Nym didn't recognise the title, but he did the Praetorion, the most elite branch of Senatorial Guards, charged with the protection of the Supreme Consul and the Heads of Department. He could only assume there weren't many more titles above Caput Major.
"Caput Major Pyrdos, I am Doctor Tysides Romos, Guild-certified Physician, but I gather you already know that. I need to know exactly what happened."
"We were guarding Supreme Consul Blongatos during his nightly recreations at The Tethimosi Maid. He stepped out for fresh air around half-bell past midnight and was attacked by a man and a woman. My men... They were distracted by the attack on the Senate." Pyrdos clenched his jaw. "So was I. A distraction the assailants seized and repelled us for long enough to stab the Supreme Consul."
"Stab where?"
"In the chest."
"Where *exactly* in the chest, Caput Major?"
"Front of the chest."
"How many times?"
"Only once."
"Any other injuries?"
"Scrapes and bruises."
"Does the Supreme Consul suffer from any medical conditions I should know?"
"No."

"Did he consume any intoxicating substances during his nightly recreations?"

"How dare you..."

Romos was quick to interrupt the incipient irate tirade.

"I do not seek to insult the Supreme Consul with my impertinent curiosity, Caput Major Pyrdos, neither will I run to the city papers for a meaty exclusive. I need to know to ensure best medical care. To avoid using medications that might interact with any intoxicating substances."

"Fine. Portosi wine, Tethimosi tobacco and liquour," the Praetorion said through gritted teeth.

"Mostly alcohol, I see. Any Myrphid plant derivates? Horod or Bashork's Leaf?"

"No."

"Kausanosi powder?"

"No."

"Syldenaphil root?"

Nym could see Pyrdos' muscles tightening in his jaw and temples. His eyes looked about to fall out of their socket. Nym's eyebrows shot up, but he refrained for any other reaction. Doctor Romos' words etched in his mind.

Never judge a patient. You are a carer, not a Juror.

Syldenaphil root extract helped with impotence, causing vasodilation of penile capillaries precipitating a potent erection even in old men past their prime.

"I... do not know. He... has in the past."

"I will presume he did. For safety." Romos said nonchalantly. He rubbed his hands and addressed everyone in the room. "Right. In that case, we need space to work, Praetorion," he said in that tone exuding both confidence and urgent adamance. "I ask you to leave the room."

Caput Major Pyrdos shot a glance to the other three and they filed out instantly without a word of protest. He however remained by the door.

"I will not leave Supreme Consul Blongatos' side. That is non-negotiable."

"As you please," Romos conceded. "But do not interfere, for the Consul's sake."

Though still imbued in his task, Nym had enough room in his brain to listen to the exchange and relish the sour face of Caput Major Pyrdos. The Caput Major of the Praetorion ordered about by a civilian.

"Nymor?"

"I can't find a pulse, Doctor Romos. No respiration either. The patient is in cardiorespiratory arrest."

"Understood. Probably hypovolaemic shock. We must act quickly."

Romos positioned himself on the other side of the table, two fingers feeling for the Supreme Consul's carotid pulse. He then retired the bloodied toga.

There were some superficial lacerations that weren't life threatening. However, as Pyrdos had said, there was a puncture entry wound on the left side of Blongatos' sternum.

All in all, Nym had seen far more gruesome injuries. He was surprised.

"How can it be shock? There's barely any blood."

"On the outside there isn't, Nymor. We have plenty of cavities *inside* our body to drain the blood from our vessels."

Of course, internal haemorrhage.

Nym nodded.

"This is very odd," Romos said.

Nym looked at the doctor's fingers. They demarcated a laceration down the exact centre of his chest. It was different from the others. A perfect straight line of bright red.

"What is that? It looks like a scalpel incision."

"No time to ponder. Infusing blood will be pointless if we don't repair the damage caused by the blade. Bring four bottles of Aesthospos and my Biothotic Codex."

Four?!

Nym put the rounded viles of the yellow-green liquid, the Codex and Romos' Smaragdos on the tray and wheeled it over to the physician.

The physician deftly placed a cannula in one of the Consul's veins and injected a liquid from a glass syringe.

"Hetarinas anticoagulation infusion?" Nym asked. The doctor emitted an affirmative grunt.

Blood stasis would lead to coagulation. Clots lodging everywhere was the last thing they wanted on top of whatever was going on.

"Do you have your Biothotic Codex with you?" Romos asked, placing the syringe back on the tray and cinching the Smaragdos around his neck.

"I do. Always in my pocket."

"Good."

The doctor took two bottles and pushed the tray toward Nym. He guzzled both in a matter of seconds and looked at him expectantly.

"Those two are for you, lad. We are both going to channel the incantation. Bottoms up."

Nym paled.

I am not ready for this.

"Doctor Romos, are you sure I am advanced enough in my training for... *this*?"

"Most definitely not. But there isn't any other option. I must *see*, and I need help."

He nodded slowly and placed his own Smaragdos around his neck.

No thinking. Doing. Just doing.

He drunk the vials and welcomed the exhilarating energy, surging to every cell of his being.

"Visualising Incantations, the last one in the section. Look up Master Incantations in the index."

Nym flipped the pages, eyes darting between the lines. He was reaching the end of the small booklet, skimming pages he had never perused. Pages with incantations only a medical graduate would know how to intone. Some of them not even that. His unstable confidence wavered even further.

"Nok save me."

"The only one that needs saving tonight is Supreme Consul Blongatos here, Nym. You *will* be alright."

He grabbed onto Romos' words like a drowning man would a rope.

"Found it."

He scanned the incantation, recognised some of the words. It was similar to the one used by Doctor Danos during the hemispherectomy operation, only more complex.

"Are you ready?"

No.

"Yes."

"It does not need repetition, once shall suffice. Also, note the necessary change from the first singular person *ios* to the plural *nosos*, or we'll waste Biothos. On my mark."

Nym wiped his forehead free of sweat. He tried to swallow but his mouth was drier than the Remnants.

Romos had both hands on the tray, focusing intently on the Codex in front of him. Nym placed his with shaky hands on the table and took a big breath.

Romos bowed his head.

"*Bioxos, myntaron'Nosos onos Anathomos y doperon'Nosos Voston yntos,*" they intoned in unison. Nym thought he had done it correctly, as both voices had echoed perfectly.

He felt a massive pull and Biothos fled from him, sucking his chest inward and stopping him from breathing. He staggered, knees buckling.

The sensation went away, leaving only the familiar afterburn of Exios usage.

Nym looked around. Nothing had changed. Then again, he wasn't entirely sure what would change.

"Did I do it wrong, Doctor Romos?"

"Close your eyes, Nymor."

Nym did so and gasped.

Everywhere was dark except for Blongatos' body, which had come alight with a thousand shades of amber. It was like a shroud made from a million pinpoints of light. Nym found that the more he looked at one part of his body, the more detailed it became.

"Very well channelled, Nymor."

"Thank you, Doctor Romos, but, if you don't mind me asking, what is the purpose of this? I see what I see with open eyes, only glowing."

"You are the most adept student of Nokator and Biothos I've ever had. Translate the incantation to Neokahmirian."

Show me all the Anatomy and allow me to see inside. To see inside.

He realised the doctor's and his own body were covered with the lights. He rose his arms in front of him and focused on his right hand, *willing* to see beyond the exterior ocean of swarming lights.

They shifted. Soon he was looking at a mesh of blebs. He smiled.

Subcutaneous fat.

He willed more, wanting to see deeper. The fatty tissues disappeared and he saw muscles and tendons, vessels and nerves. He flexed his fingers and saw the muscle fibres tensing and relaxing, saw minuscule lights in a line travelling up and down the nerves, and saw the flowing of the blood in real time.

"This is astounding!"

He kept turning his hand over. He saw as deep as the bones and ligaments. He was flabbergasted.

"It is, but it is also astoundingly taxing. We have limited time and Biothos. Now, focus."

The gravity of the situation made his excitement dwindle. He heard the tense shuffle of Caput Major Pyrdos.

"Look at the chest, observe the heart."

He focused his intent on Blongatos chest, using his own anatomical knowledge to centre on the right plane and axis. He visualised the Consul's heart.

It was obvious something was profoundly wrong. It was still, and *massive.*

"That is swollen."

"Not so much swollen but *congested.* What you are seeing is actually the pericardial sac, not the heart itself. The blade perforated the base of the ascending aorta and blood rapidly accumulated in the space between the sac and the heart, compressing it."

Romos walked over to Nym's side. He lowered the table and grabbed a saddle stool.

"Cardiac tamponade."

"Precisely. We need to cut the sac to relieve the pressure, repair the aorta and shock the heart into functioning. We don't have much time. I don't know how long he has been in cardiorespiratory arrest."

Romos turned toward the door.

"I must warn you, Caput Major Pyrdos. There is a very low chance I can save his life. Even if I do, he probably has sustained irreparable brain damage."

"Just do your job, Physician."

Nym was starting to feel the effects of exhaustion after channelling the incantation for so long. The lights began to blur and lose nitidity.

Romos pronounced a series of incantations and with the aid of a scalpel, he had opened the chest, performed a sternotomy, and exposed the heart in a matter of minutes.

"Let's halt the channelling, Nymor."

They intoned the terminal incantation. Sighing of relief, Nym opened his eyes.

The ability to see inside one's body without laying a finger on it was truly remarkable, but he preferred the real, fleshy thing a hundred times over.

"The puncture was true, causing just the *right* amount of blood to flow into the pericardial sac without compromising the integrity of the aorta. If I didn't know better, I would say it is deliberate. Gauzes, please."

Romos palmed and handled the forceps and needle driver as though they were extensions of his body. He patched up the big vessel at dizzying speed.

Nym took the instruments back and handed him a silver dish the doctor positioned near the bulging organ. He used his scalpel to make an incision in one swift motion.

The sac opened upon itself from the seam and dark blood poured out into the dish.

The defect in the aorta repaired, Romos used a syringe with a saline solution to clean the tissues and soaked up the blood with a fistful of gauzes.

"Now we need to shock."

Nym already had the insulating gloves and rods in his hands.

"Well done, lad. The best helpers are those that anticipate what you want."

Nym thanked Nok he didn't have to do any channelling this time as they took positions. He was utterly exhausted.

It meant he had to be the one placing the rods against the heart.

"Put the right one here," Romos pointed to the right atrium of the heart. "And the other one lateral to the left ventricle."

Nym breathed hard, trying not to think about the trembling. Romos placed a solid hand on his shoulder.

"You've got this, lad."

Romos dashed to the other side of the table and stepped on the wooden stool.

"Now, Nymor."

He placed the rods in their respective spots.

"*Exios, hosn Elektros kidon sinon-dor trovos thosi Kaukhos.*"

Controlled lightning surged through the chains and rods.

Blongatos' whole body convulsed violently.

"*Exios, seruintin vosu aktanon.*"

The Supreme Consul's body stilled. Romos jumped down and dashed to Nym's side.

"Nothing," he observed, looking at the static heart.

He repeated the incantation and came down a second time.

Still nothing.

With a sullen expression, Romos tried one more time.

Nym had seen that face in the doctor countless times before. A grim preparation for what came next. For the *I'm deeply sorry* that would irreparably break someone's life.

In this case, they would let the head of the Praetorion know of the unavoidable death of the Supreme Consul of the Noktanian League.

The body convulsed one last time.

Then nothing.

The rods escaped Nym's tight grip and crashed against the floor, ringing and echoing in the surgery room.

Romos looked up at Pyrdos.

"I'm deeply sorry, Caput Major Pyordos. There's nothing else we can do. Supreme Consul Kahmaos Blongatos has passed away."

A pale Pyordos stared at Romos, then at Blongatos' body. Chest still open, heart exposed in the air for all to see, a pool of blood that soaked the toga and dripped down on the floor.

"That can't be, Physician. Just *can't* be. Do it again!"

Romos stepped down from the stool.

"Caput Major, there are things outside of the reach of Medicine."

He pushed the tray away but stayed three or four paces away from the shocked soldier.

"We can treat the living, yet unfortunately the Supreme Consul has been called by death for far too long. He's dead beyond any help you, or I, or the best doctor in the University Hospital could offer. My sincerest condolences."

Nym had seen all manner of reactions to devastating news. From attacks of hysteria to cold mutism, through to unbridled fury.

Lyontos Pyrdos appeared to be progressively slipping into the latter.

"I will now close him up and prepare the body for burial, if you wish."

Pyrdos unsheathed his sword and turned to the door.

"*Eysos, domon vosu exos! Arrantos!*" he shouted as he kicked the door. A rush of wind accompanied the movement of his leg. Romos upended the tray and covered behind it and Nym crouched beneath the operating table as a shower of splinters bore down on them.

"I'll kill the bitch myself!" Pyrdos growled as he left the room.

"Are you alright, lad?"

"I will be," Nym said numbly, looking for protruding bits of wood in his body. Unscathed, he crawled out from under the table.

Romos ran his fingers through his thinning hair.

"This is bad, Nymor. This is *very* bad. The Supreme Consul's assassination must be linked to the attack on the Senate."

Romos looked at his understudy. He walked over and put his hands on his shoulders, forcing Nym to look at him.

"Listen carefully. In the coming days things are going to get very difficult for anyone without citizenship in Noktanos."

Nym glanced at the cadaver on the table, already losing vivacity, turning stiff and grey. Several splinters had been driven into his skin. No blood was pouring.

"Do you understand what I'm saying?" Romos shook him. "You need to get your father and *leave*, Nymor. Put as many stadia between you and the Noktanian League."

A few days ago, he had been ready to leave. Rejected, doubting his worth, wanting to get away from the asphyxiating grip of duty, from the expectations of others rammed upon him.

A few days ago, he would have happily obliged.

A painful thought resonated in his mind.

Haleana.

His mouth opened, lips quivering on the verge of a response when Yevia ran into the room.

"Nym, come with me."

"What is it?" Nym asked.

"I was talking to the Senatorial Guards about the attack. The assassination... I think your father was involved, Nym. We must go *now*."

CHAPTER 18
✷ ✷ ✷
The Real Truth
Nymor Strethos. The Base. Rich Quarter. The Great City of Noktanos.

THE NIGHT WAS lit by the flames of a hundred fires.
 He could hear the wails of pain and despair, the clash of steel against steel and the shouted incantations, accompanied by the crashing sounds of boulders and the unnatural rushing of the wind.
 In the span of a bell, the entire city of Noktanos had descended into chaos.
 Yevia was already at the gates of the clinic walls. There, she held a hand up and used the slit to peer into the street.
 "What do you mean? How could my father be involved? What is happening, is he alright?"
 Nym's mind raced through the infinite possibilities of being harmed during an uprising of that calibre.
 "No. He isn't."
 Nym stood where he was, unable to move.
 "There is no time," she said heavily, voice laden with compassion.
 Numb, he followed her into the street.
 There was an altercation down in the closest bifurcation. Nym could see a mixed group of Quarter and City Watchmen in formation, spikes held high against an unseen foe.

A pillar of flames exploded toward the formation, its incantator hidden behind the houses.

One of the men in the front reacted quickly, covering his upper body with a round shield. He shouted an incantation and banged his spear against the metal plating of the shield, producing a wave of air that dissipated the flames. Though the watchman was unscathed, the flames reached the trees at the sides of the street.

"Let it burn! If we can't have it, they shouldn't either!" a scream came from the assailants.

Two people at the back of the formation, man and woman, stepped back from it and joined the tips of their spears. After a few seconds, a grey-black stream like a concentrated hurricane burst forth and quieted the screams of the rebels opposite.

Aided by the darkness of the night, a man with ragged clothing had snuck up on the watchwoman.

In one swift motion, his sword plunged deep into her back and out of her chest. With a soft whimper, the incantation broke and more swords bit into flesh.

The formation had been swarmed from behind.

"Shit. This way!" Yevia screamed, pulling Nym from his shirt.

She took him right, away from the fight and into a narrow alleyway between houses. They ran downhill. The next street over was Astis Way, Nym assumed they were heading in that direction.

"Yevia, please, tell me. Where is my father? I thought he was in the Slums...."

"He is not in the Slums, Nym."

He didn't have time for more questions. Yevia had brusquely stopped and he crashed against her back.

"What—"

He saw ahead. Astis Way was a battlefield.

Lampposts laid contorted and broken on the floor, trees and houses were on fire, mountains of debris, cobbles and boulders littered the avenue. There were many broken skirmishes along the width of the street, two or three uniformed soldiers battling disorganised rebels. Always outnumbered, they had the discipline and training. The rebels had unbriddled zeal.

Nym saw the colours of the City and the Quarter Watch, the Senatorial Guard and even the Nokturia. Expert incantators with black togas and barefoot, they were cutting through a big mass of armed rebels at the centre of the avenue.

At least two hundred rebels fought a large gathering of red-cloaked Senatorial Guards on the further side, their swords, lances and shields burdening the night with metal clangs. The closest side to them was dealing with the Nokturia, though there were only five of the warrior incantators.

A tall figure pushed its way out of the mass and faced the Nokturian. He was wearing the same sort of clothing as the rest of the rebels, but they looked cleaner, sharper on him. He brandished two swords and was using one to point to the closest of the Nokturia. Confident. Taunting. Nym knew that man very well.

Boss Kyrdos Engos.

"We need to get to the other side!" Yevia interrupted his thoughts.

"There!" Nym pointed up to a stone bridge, arched in the middle. It connected the two sides of the avenue a few buildings down.

Yevia nodded.

"Stay close!"

She retraced her steps into the alley and stopped halfway.

"*Eysos, domon vosu Exios! Hartos!*"

A wind current picked up under her and boosted her jump to overcome the wall, landing inside the estate. Nym repeated the same incantations and they were soon running across the garden. They were quick, running in a straight line, using momentum and Nokator to jump over to the next house over.

Once there, Yevia strolled across the small garden and banged on the door.

"Stay away! I am armed!" came a voice from inside. It was strained, and though it may have had carried truth, it sounded distant from the cry of a fierce warrior. It sounded exactly as it was. A Cyrosi with no knowlege of warfare and scared to the core.

"We are loyal to the Senate! We seek passage across your bridge, that's all!" Yevia shouted.

No response came back.

"We mean no harm, Cyrosi!"

Another long pause. Nym heard some whispers.

"…don't open it, Melimnos. We don't…"

Something clicked on the other side of the door, some rustling sounds, then it opened.

A naked blade greeted them. It was wavering, but a blade all the same.

"S-s-show me your hands!" the short man demanded, moving the sword from Yevia to Nym. They both put their hands up.

"K-k-keep them like that, I'm telling you!"

They nodded.

"W-w-what do you w-w-want from me?"

"We just need to use the communicating bridge, Cyrosi." Yevia repeated. The man Melimnos looked at her.

"That is *my* bridge between *my* house and *my* business. You will not steal from me, oh no, by Nok you won't!"

That is one dedicated *businessman. More preoccupied about his product being stolen than dying at the hands of potential revolutionary strangers.*

"We won't steal from you, Cyrosi. We need to get to the other side of Astis Way."

Melimnos regarded them one more time, then looked over their shoulders at the night tinged with shouting and fire.

"Alright. In. Quick. But keep those hands up! And don't touch anything!"

A woman that must be his wife opened the door fully and retreated inside, shooting disapproving glances to her husband, staying away from them.

"Those stairs there," Melimnos pointed to the left of the entrance hall. "Follow them all the way up, they'll take you to the bridge. There is a staircase that goes directly down when you get to the other side. Don't go into my business!"

"Thank you kindly, Cyrosi. We won't," Yevia promised, and they ran up the stairs.

The steps bypassed the family home, taking them into a spherical antechamber with the entrance to the bridge on the opposite side. The curved walls had concentric shelves displaying a wide assortment of vases, bowls, and other kinds of pottery of incredible craftmanship.

Yevia turned sharply toward the bridge entrance, unsheathing her sword.

They could hear voices.

"Never asked you, but I assume your years of Roaming have taught you some combat skills," she said, eyes locked on the darkness ahead.

"I know some things."

"Good. You might have to put them to use now."

Yevia walked into the bridge, Nym followed closely behind.

There were metal hooks with unlit oil lamps at regular intervals in an otherwise austere space, oval windows providing the only light in the penumbra. It was the faint orange light of the fires below, occasionally brighter by the intoning of incantations.

They advanced on a subtle slope upwards, the background cacophony of steel and death awakening a cold sort of worry in Nym. He had only felt this overpowering fear once before. The shuddering sensation of peering into his own demise over Death's Crossing. Startled by the many wavering shadows populating the bridge, they surpassed the equator and began to move downwards.

They managed a few steps before the silence was broken by two men and a woman entering the bridge from the other side. A long pause ensued, pregnant with tension. No one dared say a word.

Nym felt naked without a weapon. He squared his shoulders and anchored his feet, lowering his centre of gravity.

They were wearing ragged garments, had each stolen Senate-issued weaponry. A hoplos, the round shield with the Noktanian flag and the acronym SPQN, and a xyphos. A short, stout sword.

The woman stood closest to Nym and Yevia. She rose her xyphos and pointed it towards them. The double-edge blade was bathed red, blood dripped to the floor in fat droplets.

"Are you with the Revolution?"

"*Terros, domon vosu Exios!*" Yevia intoned the incantation as answer.

"*Panoplos!*" Yevia thrusted the hilt of her sword up. The ceiling above the group collapsed, opening the bridge to the night. The rebels shouted, raising their hoplos as stone rained on them.

Some of the debris broke off from the main boulders and flew toward Yevia, flattening into slabs that attached to her body to armour her.

Before the dust settled, the rebel woman screamed.

"*Prysos, domon vosu Exios! Phortos!*"

Nym was ready for a counter-incantation.

"*Eysos, domon vosu Exios!*"

He had started even before the rebel was finished. "*Eskodos!*"

The temperature in the bridge increased ten-fold when a pillar of flames burst forth from the woman's sword. Yevia didn't have a shield, she covered her face with her stone-clad forearm.

Wind roared from under Nym's feet and blew hard in front of them, turning into a protective wall of air upon which the flames struck. Nym didn't break concentration until the very last of the fire had been blown out into the night through the collapsed ceiling.

Yevia timed it well. She charged ahead as soon as the wind dissipated. Surprised, the woman barely had time to raise her sword to meet Yevia's. They exchanged several tentative blows, but Yevia was a trained swordswoman and soon gained terrain on the rebel.

"How... argh, Bashork damn you! Someone that fights this well is no Cyrosi!" the woman grunted, fending off Yevia's flurry of parries. "Join the Revolution! End the oppression!"

Nym was onto the other two men behind the fray.

One was face down on the floor near a pile of stones, his head a pulp of red, pink, and white.

The other one stood, hoplos raised. The bridge wasn't big enough for him to join his comrade, so he crouched and grabbed a broken slab of stone the size of his hand.

Nym was not about to let him throw it.

"*Eysos, domon vosu Exios! Hartos!*" Nym jumped and flew above Yevia and her rival, aided by the monstrous surge of wind.

He saw the battle down below momentarily as he soared, still raging on, before plunging back down into the bridge. His landing was rough, crashing to the man's left. He had put too much intention behind the incantation. Nevertheless, the cadaver with the split head cushioned his fall. He scrambled to his feet to face the other rebel.

He had wasted no time, already swinging his sword down on Nym.

"*Arrantos!*" Nym shrieked desperately, pushing his hands forth when the blade was mere inches from his face.

He felt the pull of Exios abandoning his body, fear altering his control.

In an instant, the air in front of his hands swirled savagely and a stream of grey roared forth. It struck true against the rebel, who soon found himself flying against the opposite wall. Both shield and sword left his hands and clattered against the walls flanking a window.

The man wasn't as lucky. He crashed against the window and fell down his death on the broken cobbles of Astis Way.

Nym shuddered.

I guess that's one way to do it.

He clambered to his feet, only to fall right back.

The landing had not been gentle on his right ankle. He couldn't weightbear, a wave of scalding pain climbing up his leg. Carefully, he touched the joint over the boot, eliciting more pain. He couldn't feel a bone sticking out, so he decided to leave it.

He stood again, this time using only his left leg. With one hand on the wall for support, he readied himself to help Yevia with the last remaining rebel.

They had somehow switched positions in the throes of their confrontation, Yevia's back to Nym.

That was when the world seemed to end.

Without any sort of warning, the windows and walls to his left exploded inward, ground shaking violently. He threw himself down and instinctively covered his head with his hands.

When he opened his eyes, there was no longer a bridge. A few paces ahead, where Yevia and the rebel had been fighting, the floor ended abruptly. There was only the black-orange night.

"Agh... Ah!" he heard to his right.

Next to her discarded sword, Yevia had escaped the collapse.

Or rather, half of Yevia.

Horrified, Nym saw she was missing her legs and hips. Blood was gushing out of her through her severed abdomen, strands of shredded viscera and brown fluid pooling around her.

Trying to avoid the abyss, he crawled toward her to assess the injury.

She must have jumped back toward Nym. The hurtling boulders likely smashing against her lower body with such force that the impact split her in half.

Knowing that was utterly pointless, though. There was *nothing* he could do to help her.

"Leave... it... Go... The... Tethimosi Maid...Go... see... your father..." she grunted with short, gurgly heaves, pushing him away.

"I'm so sorry, Yevia," he said, his throat constricted with sorrow. Yevia shook her head and looked at him. He saw the suffering in her eyes. A clear pleading for release from the terrible pain. Nym remembered the first tenet of the Hal'Gamac Oath.

First, you shall never do harm.

Nym knew what to do.

Gritting his teeth, he grabbed Yevia's sword.

"Good... lad..." she sputtered, closing her eyes, resting her head back. Exposing her neck.

Nym breathed in long and deep. Knowing the longest he waited, the hardest it would become, he swung the sword with all his might and in one continuous motion, the blade cut and struck the floor with a bloodcurdling twang.

Yevia had always kept her sword sharp.

He didn't hang around to take in the aftermath. Using the sword as a cane, he limped away from the bridge and down the stairs as best he could. There was no time for grief. Yevia had died for him, to get him to *The Tethimosi Maid.*

The stairs led away from Astis Way and into a quiet backstreet. Weary of more rebels, Nym kept close to the shadowed walls, watching ahead and over his shoulder every now and then as he limped.

He looked up and down the narrow passage, a jagged street with loading areas for the business that aligned the big diagonal avenue. He waited for several minutes and ventured across.

He reached the other side, limping close to the wall.

His mind raced as though precipitating down a corridor, catching brief glimpses of portraits on the wall. Yevia. His father. Romos. Haleana. Yevia again. And his father.

A gallery of madness.

How is this happening?

Several hours ago, he had been sorting through old archives. Now, the Supreme Consul was dead, Yevia decapitated by his own hand, and he was limping down a street whilst Noktanos plunged into chaos.

He picked a side-alley and staggered into it. It gave way to a narrow street winding down to the left, away from the Forbidden City.

He didn't recognise it at first, but upon closer inspection he realised the half-collapsed building in front of him was *The Tethimosi Maid*. Its remnants were littered with flaming planks, boulders and broken stone. The surrounding buildings weren't in much better condition, the big stone wedge that had been the brothel's ceiling had broken in multiple parts and protruded out of the skeletons of the other constructions.

He saw some movement out of the corner of his eye.

There, under a pile of debris.

His father.

"Dad!"

He ran down, paying no mind to the pain in his right foot. He hooked his hands under his father's armpits and used his bodyweight to pull him out of the rubble.

"Argh..." Tanor gruntled softly, a wet garble. He was limp, only his head moved slightly side to side. His face was white as an doctor's toga under the moonlights and his clothes were soaked with blood. Nym saw slashes all over his body and two big splinters protruding from his left thigh and his chest.

"Dad, I'm here. I'm here," he whispered, cradling Tanor's head on his lap.

"You will be alright, you will be just fine. You'll be fine. Just fine. Just fine," he repeated maniacally. Vision blurred by tears, he felt for his carotid pulse.

"It's not the strongest, but you will be fine. We just need some blood to infuse. I will take you back to the clinic and we will patch you right up, you'll see. You will be fine. Help! Somebody please help!" Nym cried in the lonely night.

"Son..." Tanor said softly, spitting blood.

"Yes, dad. I'm here."

"Son... son...look... at me... look at me!" he said, looking up. Tanor's eyes were void, darting left and right. Eyes that had stopped seeing.

"I am, dad," he sobbed, voice breaking.

"Always... remember..." Tanor's respiration was ragged and shallow. Despaired, Nym noticed how every breath took longer to come.

"Shhh, shh. It's alright, dad. Don't exert yourself, just hold on, hold on..."

"You... can.... be... *more*," Tanor said, expelling his last breath.

"Shhh. Shhhh."

Nym watched, terrified, as the next breath didn't come.

"No. Dad?! Dad! No. NO!"

He put his father's head down and knelt next to him.

"You are *not* leaving me again!"

He placed the heel of his hand on Tanor's breastbone, laced his fingers and squared his shoulders. He began compressing and releasing with steady rhythm.

"You. Can't. Die. You. Can't!" he growled as he counted to thirty, then gave Tanor mouth to mouth.

He kept at it until his arms felt like jam, then put his ear to his mouth, fingers feeling his neck and eyes watching his chest. Nym strained his senses for signs of life.

There weren't any.

"NO!"

He continued with the compressions.

I will carry on. Compressions until we can shock him. Then we infuse him, he will be fine.

His elbows buckled.

Compressions.

He was digging his nails on his hand. He heard the crack of his father's ribs, breaking under his strength.

Compressions... Compressions until... until...

He collapsed on his father's chest, sobbing.

"Why? Why?" he cried between heaves.

His father was dead. Just like Yevia was dead. And again, there was nothing he could do.

"Why…"

He realised the truth. The *real* truth.

For the longest time, he had been on his own, and he had managed just fine. Up until he made a crucial mistake.

He had let his father back into his life, succumbed to forgiveness. He had slowly allowed himself to rely on others. He had stupidly given into comfort, content to be living in what he knew, deep down, was a lie. A very attractive lie, where he had a happy family, and he could dream of a future as a Guild-certified doctor.

How very naive he had been. Those weren't things he could have.

Now I have what I deserve. What a bastard, whoring slave, scum of the earth really deserves.

He was, once again, alone.

CHAPTER 19
* * *
You Shall Never Do Harm
Damyra Pynarios. The Great City of Noktanos.

CONSCIOUSNES RETURNED TO Damyra in a shy trickle. At first, it was only the shadow of a thought, liberated of any corporeal burden. No consideration for its nature, but rather its *being*. Just like a dream, no beginning or end, no questioning of its reality.

Then that crispness, that unadulterated nature changed. It became sluggish with cognition.

She was Damyra Pynarios. She was still alive. That conclusion brought a world of pain.

"Mhhhh," she grumbled, guttural, pain consuming her.

Her head was on fire, like lava flowing within the trabeculations of her cranium. Her hips and elbows flared, she wished she had no leg, such was the pain of her knee.

"Mh.... mh!" she whimpered, straining to move.

She was shackled, so it seemed. Her wrists bound to the arms of a chair, so were her ankles to its legs.

She thought of an Exios-cheap incantation to free her limbs, but she realised her tongue was pushed down by a rough bundle of cloth shoved in her mouth.

Why am I gagged?

The events of the night before rushed into her battered brain.

Right. I killed the Supreme Consul of the Noktanian League.

The increasing waves of pain awakened her senses. She writhed against her bindings, every muscle aching. Next came her hearing. A faint hiss in her ears that gave way to a low grumble, slowly escalating. A crescendo of voices, many voices. Hundreds of them. Screaming, banging. Demanding.

"Order! Order in the Chamber!"

She peeled her eyes open.

Her chair was in a circular pedestal at the centre of an enormous room, tiny at the bottom of the cylindrical chamber. Gigantic columns bore the weight of a dome up ahead. It had a richly painted Noktanian flag, red and gold.

On the sides and arranged in ascending rows, throngs of Noktanian citizens shouted profanities from the galleries that would make a sailor blush. Hot, red fury spewing from them. All aimed at her.

In front of her, two elevated daises. The lowest had four men looking down on her, the highest above it six. Some angry, some bored, all powerful, men. She recognised one of the faces.

The cold, measured stare of Lord Uthos of House Astia.

"You bastard!" she shouted against her gag. All that came out was strangled incoherencies.

She saw Uthos' lips subtly curving into a self-satisfied smile, and she strained once again against her binds. She would send the Hal'Gamac Oath to Bashork's Hall and kill the bastard with her own hands.

The blinding pain made her stop.

Behind the men, a statue almost as high as the dome. The naked torso of a muscled man, the Prima Codex in his left hand and a raised sword that touched the apex of the dome, the centre of the Noktanian flag, with its tip. Tyrdos Moxos, Founder of the Noktanian League.

Her stomach sunk, nearly fainting with the realisation.

She was bound to a chair in front of the Tribunal of High Justices, in the Ulterior Court of the Noktanian League.

"Order!" repeated one of the Justices in the highest pedestal, banging a gavel.

Soldiers of the Senatorial Armies were interspersed in the multitude, keeping the fluctuating masses barely subdued with aggressive stances and scolding looks.

Another Justice, a withered man with a few strands of wispy hair raised a ledger. He fumbled with the long sleeves of his toga as he waited for the populace to quieten. No sooner than a complete silence was reached did he speak. A wavery, raspy voice that sounded like an old piece of paper rubbing on itself.

"Let the record show, we shall commence the extraordinary trial of Damyra Pynarios, former Head of the School of Medicine and Guild-certified Physician, accu—"

Damyra started laughing.

Former.

It was an ugly, croaking laughter, muffled by her gagging. Her shoulders convulsed, tears rolled down her cheeks.

The whole Tribunal stared down at her.

"I would think your circumstances far from amusing, Damyra Pynarios," the old Justice said as she continued with her bout of hysterical laughter.

Following the Justice's nod, a Senatorial Guard walked over from the edges of the Chamber and delivered a heavy blow to Damyra's face. A solid slap that made her vision go blurry and the pounding of her head increase manifold.

The laughing stopped.

"The trial of Damyra Pynarios" the Justice continued, "former Head of the School of Medicine and Guild-certified Physician, accused of High Treason, Sedition, Conspiracy against the Senate, Collusion with revolutionaries and Assassination of Supreme Consul Kahmaos Blongatos.'

"Death penalty! To the gallows! To the gallows!" people shouted from the stands.

"Order! Or you will be expulsed from the Chamber!" the Justice at the centre of the Tribunal banged the gavel again.

"Note the right for *Habeas Corpus* and a Jury of Peers has been suspended in these proceedings under Article 34 of the Foundation Charter. Furthermore, a Defence was appointed to the accused, but they lawfully refused under Article 66 of the Bill of Amendments. The Defence thus reverts to the defendant herself."

Damyra's head lolled forward. She was still recovering from the blow.

Defend... myself...

"Representing each of the Quartercyles of the sovereign Noktanian Senate," he proceeded, pointing down to the lower pedestal with a tremoring hand. "Their Excellencies Cyrosi Doriamor Pyklos, Lord Uthos of House Astia, Elder Xhamaros Lokmenos, and Cyrosi Drakos Damanos."

The youngest of the Justices, serious brow at the left end of the Tribunal opened the ledger in front of him and let the hefty leather cover plop down, sending ponderous echoes across the chamber.

"Due to the nature of the charges, the Tribunal overrides Prosecution and shall be conducting the proceedings directly. The Tribunal calls upon witness Caput Major Lyontos Pyrdos of the Praetoria."

Big doors on the left side of the Court were pushed asunder, the Praetorion that had lead Blongatos' guard entered the room.

He had an intensity to his walking. All the while he walked toward a stand in front of the lower pedestals, he did not take his eyes away from Damyra. Just as he hadn't during their stand-off the night before.

"Caput Major Pyrdos. Describe the events that befell late Supreme Consul Kahmaos Blongatos."

"I was in charge of Supreme Consul Blongatos' Guard during his nightly recreations. A half-bell past midnight two assassins, a man and a woman, used the attack on the Senate as a distraction to assault Supreme Consul Kahmaos. We gravely injured and repelled the man, but alas we were…"

Pyrdos trailed off, struggling to continue. With a visible snarl on his face, nostrils flaring, he stared down at Damyra. His knuckles were white, hands clutching the arm rests. Damyra thought she could hear the screech of wood under the duress.

"…unsuccessful in stopping the woman from stabbing Supreme Consul Kahmaos in the chest. We took him to the nearest Physician. He couldn't save his life."

"What is the fate of the man?" the young Justice asked.

"We are still looking for his body. We believe there was a third person involved, there are some witnesses that recount a boy arriving at the scene later on, presumably related to the man. We believe he took the body and fled."

"And who was the woman, Caput Major Pyrdos?"

His mouth contorted and spittle flew out as he lunged, thrusting an accusatory finger at Damyra.

"The woman on that pedestal, High Justice Kemyros!"

The Court erupted in chaos again. Screams calling for her incarceration, her burning, her death, her quartering, the death of her family and friends. Fists in the air, someone even threw a chair. It hit the floor next to her, breaking into a thousand pieces.

"That will be all, Caput Major Pyrdos," High Justice Kemyros said after the calls to order. Several people were escorted out, still shouting obscenities.

The Justice waving the gavel addressed Damyra directly.

"The defendant is now granted an opportunity to refute these claims."

The Guard that had brutally slapped her approached the pedestal again. He grabbed a fistful of her hair and pulled back. He yanked the ball of cloth from her mouth unceremoniously.

"Haaa!" she drew a sharp gasp and worked her jaw, burning by the gagging. She looked around her with despair.

Now that she could use incantation, she might be able to escape. Perhaps she could disintegrate the binding and rush for the doors?

And then what?

The Coalition probably had the Nokturia guarding the doors, or hidden in the stands, and the Armies had surely deployed the Silencer Corps.

No. She wasn't getting out of there.

Oh, if they want me to talk, I will *talk. Uthos fucking Astia and Senator Pamyros need to pay for this.*
When she opened her mouth, she couldn't say the words.
"Ga..." her voice caught in her throat, choking. She tried again, hard, yet the stronger the will the more her tongue stuck to her palate.
The Contract she had signed had been fulfilled, but the Secrecy Clause that Phanon hadn't removed still stood.
She shot a glance to Uthos. He stared at her knowingly as she kept trying, hoping against hope. She tried and tried until she vomited.
"Fine," she whimpered, tears welling in her eyes and head lolling onto her chest.
She was exhausted.
Exhausted of waking up in pain, of her bones grinding and bending her, of the cold indifference of her empty life. Tired of having a marriage only in name, a family only in imagination. Tortured and chased by her past. She had been feeling the grim, dark curtains of death descending for some time. Now they were setting on her faster.
I have lived. Now it ends.
She was not going to go peacefully, though. Oh, no. That wasn't her.
"Fine!" she shouted, acid burning her throat and mouth. Every tendon of her body taut.
"I killed Blongatos, I did! I fucking killed the depraved bastard! Is that what you stand for?" She looked to the stands above. "A Supreme Consul that roils in carnal filth, fiddles children, and fattens, and does *nothing* while the League collapses unto itself? Yes! I killed him! And I will say this in front of the Tribunal of High Shits. If I had him in front of me right now, I would kill him again!"
A powerful blow ceased her shouting.
Her vision blackened and she went limp for a couple of seconds. When she came to, she spat saliva, blood, and vomit onto the pristine marble floors.
"You will need to hit harder than that to finish the job, boy," she said with difficulty. Her jaw was probably broken. The Guard was nonplussed. He didn't deign look at her.
"Let the record show Damyra Pynarios' confession to Supreme Consul Kahmaos Blongatos assassination!" Justice Kemyros proclaimed as the Justice with the gavel called for order yet one more time.
"As for the other charges," Kemyros continued. "How does the defendant respond?"
"I killed Blongatos, but I have never been involved with the Revolution. I was just as surprised to see that man as Caput Major Pyrdos. Not guilty," she said with broken voice.
"I will ask again. Did you orchestrate the attack on the Senate as well as Supreme Consul Blongatos' assassination?"
"No."

"Were you involved in any way with the rebel leader Kyrdos Engos?" Kemyros queried, maintaining a calm baritone.

"No."

The High Justice conferred in whispers to the man to his right, and so did the rest of the members of the Tribunal.

A Justice that had remained silent until then spoke.

"Given the gravity of the situation, the existing confession has given the Tribunal reasonable doubt of the veracity of the defendant's declarations. The Ulterior Court has accepted the help of the Coalition of the Codex. We shall now begin Inquisitorial Proceedings."

The bloodthirsty audience cheered the Tribunal's decision, banging loudly against chairs and banisters.

She laughed.

"Torture? Really? Pain does *nothing* to me!" she shouted defiantly.

The gates opened with an ominous screech and the stands stilled instantly.

Loud steps by tall black boots reverberated in the Court as the Coalition Inquisitor entered. Tall, lithe walk, spotless red toga, gleaming black chains across the chest. He carried a big metallic case with intricately patterned filigrees.

He stopped in front of the pedestal.

It was Vysios.

Mutterings and gasps plagued the stands. Even some of the Justices exchanged words.

She stared at Uthos, who was openly smiling.

"You sick bast—"

The Guard slapped her quiet.

"Inquisitor..." Kemyros trailed off, waiting for Vysios to identify himself.

"Pynarios, High Justice Kemyros."

More gasps.

One of the Justices in the middle frowned, shuffling to address the Court. Kemyros rose a hand in front of him before he could say anything and said "Proceed, Inquisitor Pynarios."

Her husband obliged, scaling the few steps to the pedestal.

"Vysios."

He avoided her eyes. He opened the case and extended four rods, placing a metal tray on top. He then put smaller cases on the improvised table and placed a black codex he extracted from his toga next to them.

"Are you going to torture your *wife*, just like that?"

"Why did you do it, Damyra? Was this about the contract? Was this for Zar'Aldur?" he hissed, disgust boiling subtly on an otherwise immutable face.

"You don't have to do this, Vysios."

"You are wrong. I must."

He looked at her.

"But there would be no need for it if you confessed."

She looked up at her husband's eyes. Eyes lacking pigmentation, lacking emotion.

"Will you confess?" he said, projecting his voice across the chamber.

She spat on his face.

"To Bashork's Hall with you, you worthless shit! My only regret is not living long enough to see you die!"

He grimaced, using a red handkerchief to clean his face. He flipped the pages of the codex and read from it, eyes closed. The incantations were said so softly she couldn't understand a word.

A sharp pain arose in her right forearm. A straight line, as though she had been cut. Soon enough, her skin split, the edges of the perfect wound peeling apart from each other. She bit hard, decided not to emit a single sound.

Vysios continued muttering incantations.

Blood seeped out of the straight line, and as it flowed down her arm it burnt her, like molten rocks spilled on her skin.

"Grrrr," she struggled. She looked down, saw the edges of the wound separating, and even in that state of distilled pain, a recondite part of her brain hated Vysios viscerally for using Biothos to cause harm to her epidermal tissues, and not to cure. A terrible, grotesque travesty.

The skin adjacent to the red crevice bulged and squirmed, as though worms burrowed their way down her flesh.

She blacked out.

When the momentary blackness receded, she opened her eyes, saw Vysios inspecting her injured forearm.

"Will you confess?" he repeated, dropping her arm floppily.

"Fuck you."

Impassive as ever, he grabbed some vials, leather pouch and a mortar. He squeezed a paste out of the pouch and mixed it with some liquids.

"What are you doing?"

"This is something our physiologists have developed recently. A paste made from Tynita seeds. I'm mixing it with some Korphinium extract to keep you awake. We call it verathios," he said impersonally.

Damyra felt the taste of sour vomit in her mouth.

"Tynita seeds are hyperaesthetic and Korphinium extract a powerful stimulant. You are enhancing my pain, then making sure I'm awake to feel it, aren't you?"

"Precisely."

"You are a sick bastard."

"I merely serve. Now, open your mouth."

Damyra bit down hard.

Vysios looked at the guard. He approached Damyra and diligently pulled her head back, tugging her hair savagely.

"Ah!" she gasped. Vysios emptied the contents of the bowl in her mouth and pressed her jaw shut, clamping her nose.

She swallowed reflexively.

"Will you confess?"

"Fuck... you," she panted, tonguing her palate. The verathios had left a bitter taste in her mouth.

Vysios lowered his head to read from his codex.

A dull sensation settled in her little finger's nail, like a needle head pressing up from the inside. Slowly, steadily, strongly. The same feeling commenced in all of her fingers. The width of that needle head grew and grew, turning into a wedge driven out of each of her fingernails.

Pain.

She looked down at her hands, fingers trembling, and saw horrified how her nails were starting to come off.

Oh, so much pain.

"GRAAAH!" she shrieked. She couldn't hold it any longer. Her scream was feral, tearing her vocal cords.

Vysios was still muttering susurrous incantations, eyes closed, hands on the table with open palms to the ceiling.

An itch birthed behind both her eyes. It quickly grew in intensity, morphing, spreading all over her eyeballs. It was a maddening sensation, as though fiery ants crawled freely in her ocular globes, scratching the white surface with sharp chitin legs. Digging.

She wanted to gouge them out. She needed to scratch them, rip them. Her hands strained against the straps, burning the skin of her wrists.

"Oh Nok... Nok, make it stop! MAKE IT STOP! PLEASE! I don't know *anything* about the Revolution... I don't... I... wasn't... involved," Damyra croaked, tears falling down her cheeks.

The pain subsided.

"Tribunal, if I may. In her current state, it is my expert opinion that if keep pushing, she will perish. If she hasn't confessed after these Inquisitorial Proceedings, I highly doubt she was involved."

Uthos raised a hand.

"Lord Astia, permission to speak granted," the wispy-haired Justice conceded.

Uthos stood.

"Thank you, High Justice Dyrtos. I request permission to bring forth another witness."

"Permission granted. Inquisitor Pynarios, you may leave."

Vysios left without looking back.

"Pale bastard," she muttered, hating herself for having broken down, unable to battle against tears. That was her husband. Her *husband* who hadn't batted an eye as he had *tortured* her.

Uthos waved to a Guard. He opened the gates and let in a boy, no older than ten years of age.

He was escorted by a black-and-gold armoured guard, the emblem of House Astia prominent in the chestplate. He sat the boy down in the witness stand and stepped away.

"What is your name?" Uthos asked with authorative tone.

"Daesho."

"Daesho, the name of this woman is Damyra Pynarios. Do you recognise the name?"

The boy nodded.

"How do you know it?"

"A man came to see us. Da spoke to him, a lawyer or something. He mentioned her name. Da, the Boss and the others spoke to the lawyer when he told them about the Consul."

Murmurs spread in the Court.

"What about the Consul?"

"The man told them where he would be. Last night."

Murmurs turned into angry chatter.

"And what is the name of the Boss, Daesho?"

Daesho frowned. To his credit, the boy did not seem bothered at all.

"Boss Engos."

"To the gallows with the bitch!" someone shouted from the galleries.

Uthos nodded after gavel struck wood.

"That will be all. Thank you, Daesho."

His House Guard took the boy away.

The Tribunal whispered a handful of words among themselves to vigorous nods of consent before High Justice Kemyros leaned forward, addressing the Ulterior Court.

"The Tribunal does not require further deliberation. We hereby declare Damyra Pynarios guilty of all charges and sentence her to die."

"Surprise, surpr—"

The Senatorial Guard pulled her head back and stuffed the rancid ball of cloth back into her mouth.

But before he could do it, Damyra bit hard into his hand. The Guard screamed, retreating as Damyra spat the chunk of flesh she had bitten off and focused, looking up.

"*Exios, tryvon Dremos Karpos!*"

Those were words she had never uttered. She was *improvising* with her knowledge of Nokator, coming up with an impromptu incantation. Something that could have terrible consequences.

What could possibly go wrong? She was going to die anyway.

The statue's hand cracked at the wrist, small fractures crawling down the petrous arm.

By the time everyone reacted, the hand had fully detached from the body, sword swinging down like a lethal pendulum. It drew an arc that cut through the galleries, sending rubble and people alike flying down the Chamber, finally crashing tip-first into the marble floor. Its blade-side destroyed the Tribunal and the Senatorial Representatives pedestals.

To her disappointment, it did stop several inches short from Uthos' face, yet the sudden fear in his eyes was an excellent parting gift.

The Guard delivered a final blow, and as her consciousness became lax, flitting and flirting with obscurity, he stuffed the cloth back in her mouth.

Damyra was unsure when full awareness returned. It was hard to keep track of time when your senses were dulled by unrelenting pain, when you were abandoned in perpetual darkness, bound and gagged.

Her proprioception told her that her eyelids were up, but there was no difference in that suffocating shade of black when she blinked.

She felt no hunger, no urge to relief her bowels or bladder, so it couldn't have been more than a few bells since the trial.

Nothing had changed since she had regained consciousness in the darkness, her only companion the sound a lazy drop of water plinking every now and then in the corner of the dank room.

She heard a shuffle of steps after... minutes? hours? The clink of keys and wood rubbing on wood. Boots on stones. There on the wall of darkness appeared a rectangle of light, delineating a door.

She was seated with wrists bound to the arms of a chair, she could only shut her eyes tight before the torrent of light proceeded the door opening.

"Leave now. Return in a half-bell."

"Yes, my Lord."

Damyra's eyes took some time to accomodate to the weak light of the oil lamp through the blur of tears.

She was in some sort of cell. A wooden plank as a bed, a latrine, and a rickety table in front of her sturdy chair.

Lord Astia stood by the door, light painting a terrying portrait of his hairless head, making it look cadaveric, skeletal.

"You can plan, and plan. Plan obsessively until you're satisfied, and then everything unravels. Curiously, things worked out in a way."

Damyra stared at the table as he placed the lamp on it and sat in front of her.

"I happened on the boy by mistake when I searched the Slums last night. My surprise was monumental when he recounted how a lawyer, who if I'm not mistaken is Enkir Phanon Tamyros, told Boss Engos of the exact location of Kahmaos Blongatos."

He shook his head, scoffing.

"You see, the Revolution had been planning a coup for nearly a year, so it seems. They had every piece of the puzzle figured out except for a crucial step, and your old friend handed it to them on a silver platter."

Damyra would have never thought Phanon would betray her like that. Yet again, there was little anger she could feel in that moment. There was little *anything* she could feel.

He stapled his fingers and leaned onto the table.

"Yet there is something I'm missing, and I don't like missing things. Why would you go to Phanon? And why would the Coroner..." he trailed off, eyebrows raised.

"But of course. You tried to resuscitate him! Clever, very clever. That is something we didn't contemplate in the Contract. Once he was killed, the Agreement fulfilled, nothing was stopping you from trying to bring him back to life."

If it weren't for the gag, she would have asked him if that was admiration she sensed in his words.

"Alas, you were stopped and seized by the Praetoria. How tragic."

She felt her eyes drifting.

Bring on the fucking executioner. Bashork's Hall can't be worse than listening to this bald bastard patter.

"No matter. I'm glad I was able to find some use for you after the whole debacle. Your trial has worked wonders on the rabble. I am, however, a man of my word. Despite the questionable execution, Kahmaos Blongatos *is* dead, after all."

She refocused, bands tensing as she strained.

Alda.

"Zar'Aldur is dead. She is buried in an unmarked grave outside of Portos."

Her hands shook uncontrollably.

"I learned she didn't get very far in her exile from my Father's journals. He had her killed. It was better for everyone."

Dead. She's been dead this entire time.

Damyra had nothing left. No tears to shed, no clever retorts to shout.

Alda...

A knock came on the door.

"'Tis time, m'Lord."

Uthos dedicated her one last look.

"I just wonder what he'll say after this," he said cryptically before leaving.

Alda...

Several Guards entered the cell and released her from the chair. She didn't have enough strength to bear her own weight, let alone walking. Ignoring the last threads of dignity she retained, one of the Guards grabbed her waist and put her over his shoulder.

She was carried through corridors and up stairs to eventually exit the Senate building through one of its multiple side-doors into Central Square.

They followed the path around the circular structure, demarcated by a human fence of City Watchmen and Senatorial Guards, keeping a tide of bodies at bay.

Damyra's half-shut eyes were lost on the cobblestones as she swayed, and though she didn't see them, she could hear them.

People that had lost livelihoods, lost friends and family at the hands of the rebels. People that had fought for a government they believed in, and missed the untimely departure of their loved ones. She could hear the rage in their screams, the hurt hiding under vulgar profanity. She could smell the rotten food that hit her battered body, the spit from dozens of rabid mouths.

"I'm so sorry," she whispered, and she found it was true. Nevertheless, it came out as a cough dying in the bundle of cloth that gagged her.

She was taken to a series of gallows erected in front of the grand staircase of the Senate's main entrance. She was dropped in front of a tree stump on the far end of the platform, bearing the scars of many previous executions. She caught a glimpse of other bodies before she collapsed over the stump, their heads detached and strewn about.

The Guards positioned her so that she was kneeling, hands bound on her back and ankles tied together. Her head was then brusquely pulled back and her gag removed.

She was forced to watch the masses populating Central Square and the adjacent streets, as far as the eye could see. Calling for her head.

A Senatorial Envoy stood primly on a separate platform, waiting for the public to calm.

"Lastly, Damyra Pynarios!" he shouted, voice booming in the now quiet Square.

"You were charged with High Treason, Sedition, Conspiracy against the Noktanian Senate and Murder of former Supreme Consul Kahmaos Blongatos, by the Ulterior Court of the League. The punishment is death. Do you wish to say any last words?"

Damyra tried to ignore the executioner that stepped up next to her, a towering mountain of flesh that held a sharp axe like it was a fork. She looked at the sky, at the buildings of the city she had loved, and closed her eyes.

"First, you shall never do harm," she said weakly, tears welling in her eyes, before she was shoved down on the stump.

Her last thought was with Alda. A memory that remained. They were in bed, Damyra pressing her hand against her cheek, smiling tenderly. Exchanging soft words that meant nothing, charged looks that meant everything.

The axe descended swiftly, producing a whistling sound as it cut the air. Damyra heard it thudding against the wooden surface. The last thing she ever heard.

CHAPTER 20
✱ ✱ ✱
First Encounters
Lord Uthos Astia. Moxosi Badlands.

THE CARRIAGE HALTED so abruptly, Uthos was brought to his feet by the inertia. He collapsed back down awkwardly on the cushioned seat.

He banged his fist on the roof.

"Lamnos!"

"My sincerest apologies, m'Lord!" the driver shouted. "There's someone here on the road yonder."

Uthos stuck his head out of the carriage, grimacing at the scorching heat. A solitary figure stood ahead, cut against the infinite blackness of the sterile Moxosi Badlands.

That had to be him.

"Carry on. We are picking him up."

"Yes, m'Lord."

Lamnos reined the horses in as the carriage approached the static man, stopping a few paces away from him.

The man remained where he was, hands crossed on the small of his back, pitch-black robes that in the hazy starless night contributed to the illusion of a floating head. There was an out-of-place smile on his face that made Uthos uneasy.

He ground his teeth and exited, entering the hot Moxosi night. He wiped the beading sweat that formed instantly on his shaven head with a yellow-black handkerchief, the coat of arms of House Astia patterned intricately on it.

The man extended his arms to either side in a wide gesture of embrace.

After a year of correspondence, an image of the mysterious man had formed in his head, yet nothing would have prepared Uthos for the real one.

He looked like a cross of every ethnicity in Helados. A chimera of shocking contrast. His skin was patchy, white and brown and black, hair curly like a Parrah's but showing tufts of blonde and red. Out of all of his features, his eyes were by far the most unsettling.

One murky green, the other one clear blue. So clear it was almost white.

"Lord Uthos Astia. It is a divine pleasure to finally meet you in the flesh."

His voice was a low grumble that seemed to reverberate in the open space, strange as that was. As though there were two voices speaking at the same time. One coming from his lips, the other, deeper, speaking right *inside* his head.

"Joxel. Shall I take you to a more adequate location for our discussion in my carriage?" he turned toward the vehicle.

Joxel shook his head, the clicking of his tongue multiplied manifold.

"It's always business with you, Lord Astia. Cold and efficacious. No exchange of pleasantries, overlooking millennia of tradition."

"Consider it a mark of my haste in the matter. I must be back in Dytalis by sunrise, or I'll arise suspicion."

"Ah, now. That is reasonable, my good Lord. We shan't raise suspicion, no, no. Tradition or no, She awaits. And She is not fond of waiting."

Joxel turned sharply, long cloak flapping about. He began walking away with uncharacteristic lithe for the uneven terrain.

"*She?*" Uthos raised his voice. "It was my understanding that we would meet alone!"

"See, my Lord, that's where you have it all wrong. I am but an intermediary. Ha! How exciting. I've been waiting for this moment for a long time. So long, in fact, that if I told exactly how much it would make your mind *reel*."

Joxel plunged ahead with wide strides.

Uthos set his jaw.

"Lamnos, stay with the carriage," he said, grabbing his scabbard from under the seat and securing it on his hip.

"As you command, m'Lord."

With the familiar weight of Concordance on his left hip he rushed after Joxel, accusing the asphyxiating heat.

The Great Noktanian Road led to Moxos through a cleared pass in the system of active volcanoes, yet Joxel was heading west in a straight line. To a place where inhuman heat, corrosive smoke and rivers of flowing lava made for an inhospitable environment.

"I must enquire as to our destination, Joxel," Uthos panted, the tarry black ground turning into increasingly steeper hills. After a short trot, his undershirt was soaked through with sweat and stuck uncomfortably to his skin.

"Steady onwards, Lord Astia."

They climbed up and down, mountains with orange-tinged tips coming ever closer. Uthos licked his cracked lips and dabbed his bald head with a sodden handkerchief.

Soon, the hills grew so tall they became cliffs, and he battled on in the deep recesses, barely able to see whether Joxel had disappeared left or right.

He started noticing a low rumble, a subtle roar that ricocheted in the depths of the gorge-like trail.

He nearly bumped into Joxel.

"Virthos is astounding, I'll give Her that."

The strange man moved to the right, revealing what laid ahead.

The jagged wall of the volcano, grey and black in the distance, broken by descending rivulets of dark red, orange and yellow that confluenced in a breath-taking lava cascade.

Uthos was too drained to react. The heat was unbearable.

Joxel looked at him, clearly expecting a bigger reaction. He threw a hand in the air.

"How stupid of me! I must apologise, Lord Astia. I tend to forget how pervious to the elements your kind can be."

He browsed the insides of his flowing robe and handed Uthos a metal-cast canteen.

It was freezing cold to the touch.

Uthos took a long, burning sip and used the remnants to splash his face. Momentarily refreshed, he observed the surroundings.

The lava cascade crashing a few hundred paces away was the source of the rumble. It formed a river of sorts that flowed westwardly through a break in the clearing.

Uthos frowned at Joxel, who gave him yet another mysterious smile. The ravine they were in was the only pathway out of the rock enclosure.

"I beg your pardon, my Lord."

Joxel stepped forth and set his feet on the ground. Solid, shoulder-length, and clenched his fists to either side.

The Broken Oath

He took a big breath, chest swelling, then he lunged, fist pointing to the cascade.

Uthos noted no incantation was uttered.

There was a soft clicking in his ears preceding a quake under his feet. There in the distance, the cascade began splitting in two at the tip, as though Joxel had drawn them like curtains.

"How d—"

Joxel was again on the move. Lord Astia hurried along, steeling his mind for the skin-blistering heat. Joxel waited for him at the right edge of the split cascade, where the lava was reduced to a trickle.

"I recommend you stay close to me for this next part."

Joxel entered the mouth of the big tunnel he had uncovered. Uthos pressed on by his side. To his surprise, the closer he was to him, the colder he felt.

They walked on in the obscure tunnel, Uthos directly behind Joxel under the umbrella of the cooling halo that accompanied them.

Right, left, right and left again. The obscurity morphed into penumbra, then finally into blurry orange as they approached an exit.

Uthos' breathing hitched when they entered an open cavern, several times larger than Dytalis' own Grand Hall. Long stalactites populating the shaded top, like a thousand gaping maws. A few paces from where they stood, the edge of a bubbling lava lake.

"What is this place, Joxel? Why are we here?"

Joxel clapped.

"Ha! Because She's always had a flair for the dramatic."

Uthos frowned reflexively.

He had no time to ask further questions.

A light vibration crawled up his legs, followed by a booming sound from the depths of the cavern. Slowly, steadily, the vibration increased until it made his footing unstable. He retreated toward the tunnel, but Joxel, unaffected by the shaking ground, stopped him from leaving.

"Move! What is the meaning of this!?"

No response. Only a cryptic smile and a green-white stare.

Another boom and the quake brought Uthos to the ground. He shuffled, back against the wall. He covered his head against the precipitating debris falling from the ceiling.

A last deafening boom was followed by concentric ripples originating from the centre of the lake. They grew in size, ripples gave way to waves as an enormous mass erupted from it.

Bigger than some of the minor castles in the Forbidden Citadel, two membranous wings connected to a lizard-like body. Black with bright red cracks that seeped lava. A haunting head, reptilian eyes with eliptical pupils, redder than fire, maws sharper than swords.

Uthos had read enough pre-Kahmirian mythology to recognise what the creature was.

A dragon. One made of *magma*.

"Nok Almighty."

"Not exactly, no. Ha!"

The dragon roared, a blue plume of fire projected up into the cave. It instantly crystallised some of the stalactites.

It came down, gigantic claws crashing down a few paces away from Uthos. Its head lowered. It was *looking* at them.

Joxel stepped forth and knelt, bowing his head low.

"Helad. I am forever humbled by your presence."

The dragon grumbled, speaking with an ominous voice that came from everywhere. Echoes from the lava, the rocks, the air.

"Rise, Joxel. It has been long since you've had to bow to anyone."

Uthos teeth clattered with the sonic intensity.

"I know. I simply like to remind you where my loyalties lie."

"Spare me. Your loyalties are as predictable as the death of stars."

He conceded, bowing his head yet again. He turned to look at Uthos.

"As promised, I've brought you Lord Uthos of House Astia."

Uthos dared look up.

"Helad," he murmured. Helad, Goddess Creator.

Uthos had never believed in Nok or any of the gods in the Kahmirian Pantheon, not truly. He had never uttered a single incantation, fearing the tampering of reality using the Titillation would bring instability. And there he was, looking at *Helad*. The Defeated, the Enemy of Nok. A dragon, staring down at him.

"Uthos Astia. Rise."

He stood, dusting off his ruined garments. He didn't look as stately as it was normal, but he would take in stride the unexpected circumstances, outlandish as they were. He was Lord Uthos of House Astia.

"It is unfortunate," Uthos crossed his hands on his back, a practised gesture of confidence. "Our enterprise has not borne any fruits. The sovereignty of the Senate remains."

Helad looked at Joxel.

"You were right. He learns quickly."

Joxel bowed his head with a curlicue of his hand.

Uthos glanced down.

"I have failed you, Goddess Creator. The assassination was carried, yet the events that unfolded later made the seizing of power impossible."

Another teeth-clattering grumble. She was laughing.

"The Brames have their way. Fated things cannot be changed."

Helad shifted in the lake, waves of molten rock flowing dangerously close to him.

Her head was feets away from him now. Enormous nostrils flaring, the smell of sulphur clawing at him. Double-lidded reptilian eyes bearing down.

"Uthos of House Astia. You are a key player in a Game that far outreaches the confines of this world. And the Game has already started."

THE END OF THE BROKEN OATH

EPILOGUE

"WHERE IS HE?"

The weathered sailor had survived a dozen wars, hunger, torrential rain, uncountable storms in the high seas and one particularly murderous woman. Yet, somehow, the person in front of him was the most terrifying thing he had ever faced in his life. It had much to do with the fact that members of the Senatorial Intelligence Corps acted with impunity in the eyes of Noktanian Law.

They weren't in Noktanos, though.

"I dunno what yer talkin' 'bout, but even if I did, I'on have to tell ye shite."

The SCI agent looked down at the table with a contorted smile. She bit her lower lip and shook her head ponderously, stapling her fingers in front of her. She was very pretty, but he wouldn't fall for that. The seas were equal parts beautiful as they were cruel. He knew better.

"Captain Menthias, let's drop the pretence. I'll be frank with you. Our intel is solid and points to you harbouring a fugitive of the law involved in Supreme Consul Blongatos' assassination. I am asking a simple question, with a very easy answer and potentially grave consequences if you fail to comply. Where is the boy?"

"I don't owe Blongatos *shite*, woman. Or ye for that matter. We're in the Free City of Fuertos and ye hav' no power here."

The woman took a prolonged breath, all the while staring down at the captain with vicious intensity. He tried to appear calm as the sea on a windless day, reclining on his seat and resting his hands on his barrelled abdomen.

"Fuertos is a Free City only in name, sailor. It is every bit a Noktanian Protectorate as Tyvos or Kymanos. City governance doesn't wipe a single arse without permission from the Senatorial representative first. Besides, do you really think Governor Umaros will give half a shit if they find your bloated corpse by the docks?"

Menthias swallowed.

"No, he wouldn't. But I told ye, I'on know no boy."

The SCI agent clasped a Smaragdos on her neck.

"Aight, aight. I says I know no boy, but I might know someone who do."

The woman stared expectantly.

"Y'know, sailors speak 'n' all, ha!"

"My patience grows thin, Captain."

"Sure, sure. Yer a busy lass. I overheard Yellow Rathios down by The Distant Shore talkin' drunken with a maid. Summat 'bout a runaway lad paying handsome for a cabin, if ye ask me sounds just like yer lad. I'd have a gander yonder and see Rathios out, he knows summat' the rotten bastard, I'm sure."

"Captain Menthias, I'll have you know part of our training involves a lengthy attachment to the Coalition Inquisition. If I find this information to be false, I will hunt you down and fashion a coat with your skin, making sure you feel every shade of pain known to man."

The woman pushed the chair back with a stomach-curling screech.

"Farewell."

Captain Menthias waited a prudent few minutes before bursting into roaring laughter.

"Feisty one, ain't she, lad? Ha, ha! I reckon a rough tumble is what she needs, nothin' more. Ha!"

A hidden trapdoor beneath the table clicked open and a young boy, wearing a bloodied cloak, emerged into the room.

"Thank you, Menthias. I owe you my life."

The boy was covered in filth. Dried blood caked his hair and face, a clear trail of tears had wiped some of it down his cheeks. He collapsed on the empty chair, head lolling backwards.

"Forget 'bout et. Shame 'bout your old man. Least I could do."

"Truly. I am painfully aware of the position I've put you in. No one wants to be on the SCI's bad books."

"Everyone is in some book or other. Bastards ar' everywhere."

The seaman pushed his weight back from the table and hobbled to the window. He casted an expert eye to the night skies, reading the swirling clouds that reflected the lights from the ships and docks of the Free City of Fuertos.

"What happens when she finds out that Yellow Rathios knows nothing?"

Menthias slapped his gut soundly.

"No matter, he is a right cunt. He likes his rum though he does, the bitch'll have to visit every rat-infested tavern and there are those aplenty in Fuertos, ha! Anyway, I ain't sticking 'round to find out. Hope you have a stomach for rough seas, lad. There's a storm abrewin' and we set sail 'afore dawn."

APPENDIX

Complete Compendium of Virthan Terms, History and Mythos, by the Archivist

Of all the wonderful creations in the Brames, I must admit Virthos holds a special place in my heart. It is a fascinating planet born out of spite, of utter contempt for the Hexad and their beloved System. It is uncertain whether the inauspicious Foretellings are right, but the Fall was a declaration of open rebellion against the Hexad, under the eyes of our Bramelord Ygdral. Foretellings notwithstanding, I can't ignore the signs. I must warn you, darling Merhia. Virthos will be a central piece in what is to come. Before long, you will be tasked to come here, so I've compiled this book help you understand a most interesting peoples and culture.
Always yours,
Esio.

A
Athospos: a highly energetic concoction that allows those who drink it the usage of high amounts of Exios without suffering Exios-exhaustion.

B
Baby Curse: common name given to Eklos syndrome.
Bashork: It is said that Nok the Savior is cursed with a terrible duality. One in which he is his own enemy. Nok and Bashork, good and evil, two sides of the same coin.
Bashork's Eye: a maelstrom in the southwest of Helados, south of the Pyrinosi chain.
Bashork's Leaf: plant endemic of the Tynar forest with psychoactive effects.
Bashork's Touch: common name given to schizophrenia and/or general "madness".
Biothotic Codex: compendium of incantations using the Biothos dialect.

C
City Patron: Portos has a political system entirely reliant on economical prowess, where City Patrons, the wealthiest elite, have a Council with executive power.
Codex, normal Codex or Nokator Codex: compendium of incantations that includes all dialects that tap into the Titillation except for Biothos and Nokmollos.

Cruk'Ix, The Crossroads City: located where the old Kahmirian Road trifurcates in the heart of Helados. Many also give it the title of New Kahmir, as it is the only standing city founded during the existence of the Kahmirian Empire.

Cyrosi: an official title meaningHigh Citizen.

Cyrosox: Citizen's Duty. There are no norms on sexuality across the Noktanian League, yet when a person reaches a certain age, they must fulfil their Citizen's Duty. They must find a mate of the opposite sex and produce offspring to further the Noktanosi lines. Whilst the Cyrosox is sporadically followed in the lower classes, it is *always* respected in the higher classes.

D

Death Crossing: a perilous passage northwest of the Vast Peninsula, claiming more than half of the foolish travellers that venture to go across it.

Dorok: a half-drakma.

Drakma: the main currency in the Noktanian League.

Durmos: the lowest coin denomination in the Noktanian League. One drakma is equivalent to 50 durmos.

E

Eklos syndrome: raised blood pressure of unknown origin during pregnancy. It can threaten the development of the foetus and may be potentially lethal to the mother.

Elder Council: the oldest form of government in Helados, formed by very elderly members of the populations in Tunedos, the island that gives the name to the Tunedosi Bay and archipelago.

Elder plant extract: concentrated and purified substance from Elder plants, white blossoming flowers autochthonous of the Pyrinosi chain that helps lowering the blood pressure. Its use is discouraged in pregnant women as it can lead to congenital malformations.

Ei'Tulahi: pertaining to Ei'Tulah, the most populous city in Helados. It is located in the Vast Peninsula and capital city of the Ei'Tulahi Empire.

Engos faction: the Slums is divided in territories controlled by organised crime bands. One of them is the Engos faction.

Exios: the Nokator word for energy, a nebulous term that represents the physical manifestation of the Titillation.

F

Fibrillation: an abnormal electrical pattern in the heart.

Forbidden Citadel: the old seat of government in the Fist of Nok prior to the Great Exodus, an *en masse* migration of refugees from the Kahmirian Empire after its demise. It is located in the tallest and broadest hill in the island of Katadia, walled, and containing seven fortresses pertaining to the most ancient families in the peninsula. Nowadays, it forms part of the Great City of Noktanos.

G

Ghart'Avur Dystany: last royal family that reigned the Kahmirian Empire before its Fall.

Gigos architecture: a style of architecture where the inclusion of Titillation permits the use of enormous blocks and inorganic shapes that results in gigantic constructions of often geometrical outlook. The Guild of Builders combines Gigos architecture with Heladian mythology to showcase outlandish buildings.

Guild's Way: elevated pathway that connects Katadia and the rest of the landmass of the Fist of Nok, offering fast passage from Noktanos and its satellite towns to the rest of the peninsula.

H

Hal'Gamac Oath: Hal'Gamac is considered the Father of Medicine, his postulates of the Four Pillars of Medicine have rippled through history and define modern medicine. The most known is the First Pillar; *First, you shall never do harm.*

Hemispherectomy: surgical procedure that consists in the excision of one of the brain hemispheres.

Hetarinas: a substance that thins the blood.

Hexad: a typical grouping of days in Virthos consisting of six days. There are six hexads in a mexas, six mexas in a year.

Horvos device: an apparatus invented by the famous physician Koshos Horvos used to measure blood pressure.

Horod's Leaf: plant which sap emits powerful hallucinogenic fumes.

Hoplos: round shield issued by the Senate for the Legions.

Houses of Nok: churches throughout the Noktanian League pertaining to the Coalition of the Codex.

K

Katadia: island in the centre of the Eye of Nok, the second largest inland sea in Helados after the Salinos. The Great City of Noktanos and several minor satellite towns comprise most of its surface area.

Kahmirian: related to the old Empire established by the city of Kahmir. The Fall of the Kahmirian Empire occurred 1050 years ago.

Kausanosi powder: white powder obtained from a plant autochthonous of the island of Kausanos. It has tremendous stimulant and addictive properties.

Kontivos Doxos: a duel where two affronted parties summon a construct and battle to settle a dispute.

Kytoshi plant: a type of vegetation from the Westernlands whose fibres are very elastic and malleable. It is widely use in the crafting of medical equipment.

M

Molosbark: Molos is a tree that grows in the Sylvari coast of Salinos whose bark has sedative properties.

N

Neokahmirian: most languages in the south of Helados derive from proto-Kahmirian, the language spoken in Ancient Kahmir. Neokahmirian is the derivation spoken in the Fist of Nok and the eastern islands of the Krossosi and Tunedosi archipelagos.

Nokmollos: Nokator dialect used by the Guild of Lawyers in their trade.

Nokmo'mathar: Nokmollos word that translates to Nokmollosi Influence, an oft overlooked effect due to its macabre nature that results from contravening a Binding Agreement. Going against the clauses creates an illness that can only be resolved by doing what the contract states.

Nok's Might: alternative way to refer to the Titillation with strong religious undertones.

Noktanos: the capital city of the Noktanian League, a political union of 5 cities located in the Fist of Nok. It is the second most populous city in the continent of Helados, only second to Ei'Tulah in the southwest. Its foundation dates back 453 years when the old noble families of the Old Regime, the Coalition of the Codex and the Guild Association signed the Foundation Charter.

Noktanosi: from or related to Noktanos.

Nokturia: a military branch of the Coalition of the Codex that acts as the armed forces of Nok. It is formed by four Nokturian legions (previously five but the Fifth Legion was outlawed by the Noktanian Senate).

P

Pavaras, Goddess of Stability: not much is taught about Kahmirian religion in the increasingly secularised Noktanian League, other than it was polytheistic.

Profunda femoris: deep branch of the femoral artery, it supplies the back of the thighs.

Pylmos root powder: a preparation of the Pylmos tree from the Sylvari jungle which provides heightened concentration and stimulation for six to eight hours.

Pyrinosi warriors: skilled swordsmen and women, famous for their use of iron-clad capes, that both protect and rule the small settlements in the Pyrinos mountains.

Q
Quarter Watch: different from the Senatorial Guard and the City Watch, it is a policing force solely for the Rich Quarter and maintained largely by pooled resources of residents and the treasuries of the different wealthy families and noble houses.

R
Roaming: activity done by Roamers, experts on gathering incantations all over Helados. They travel the land, trade with their knowledge of Nokator and rarely stay in one place more than a month.

S
Scothos: ceremonial shields used by the Praetorion.

Sphygmos disease: essential (idiopathic) hypertension.

SPQN: acronym that stands for Senate of the People, Quorum of Noktania.

Syldenaphil root: a potent vasodilator agent that increases perfusion in penile tissues, promoting erection.

T
Tunedosi Protectorate: Noktanian foothold in the Tunedosi archipelago. Though the League has officially no lands in the Tunedosi Bay, the cities of Tymos and Kymanos have a strong allegiance and allow free trading in exchange for protection against the belligerent Krossosi.

Tobos' Leaf/herb: addictive substance smoked commonplace throughout Helados.

U
Underground Arena: a popular illegal league of Codex Games, taking place in the Slums.

V
Vylar elixir: potion made from the Vylar tree with the same effect of Elder plant extract, except it has far fewer side effects and can be used safely in pregnancy. It is however rarer and harder to obtain.

X
Xyphos: stout sword issued by the Senate for the Legions.

Z

Zereri Tribes: nomadic horse lords that dominate he hills and grasslands of the eastern coast of The Fist of Nok.

Pablo Suarez was born in February of 1997 in Valsequillo, a minuscule village in Gran Canaria, one of the main islands of the idyllic Canarian archipelago. Despite the beauty of the holiday destination for most, ever since he was a child, he felt confined by the mountains of the valley he grew up in. Through the foresight of his parents, he dedicated a great part of his upbringing to learning languages, primarily English.

He moved to the United Kingdom when he was 18 years old to pursue a career in medicine, all the while nurturing his ever-growing love for storytelling, world-building, and all things fantasy.

Nowadays, Pablo spends most of his time balancing studying his fourth year of medical school, making videos for his YouTube channel, writing blog posts for his website, and compulsively adding words to his interminable list of works in progress.

Printed in Great Britain
by Amazon